P9-DVX-640

COMICS SQUAD

RECESS!

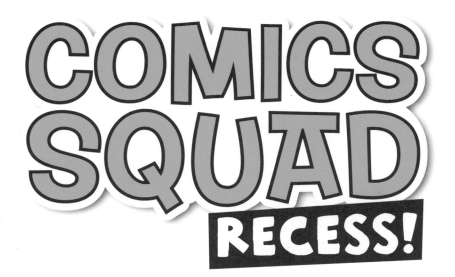

☆ **COMICS BY** ☆

JENNIFER L. HOLM & MATTHEW HOLM

JARRETT J. KROSOCZKA

DAV PILKEY

DAN SANTAT

RAINA TELGEMEIER & DAVE ROMAN

URSULA VERNON

ERIC WIGHT

GENE LUEN YANG

COMICS SQUAD
RECESS!

· EDITED BY ·

JENNIFER L. HOLM, MATTHEW HOLM &
JARRETT J. KROSOCZKA

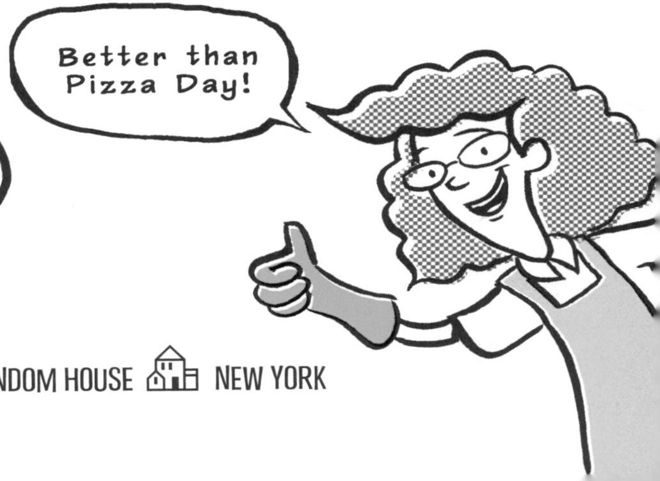
Better than
Pizza Day!

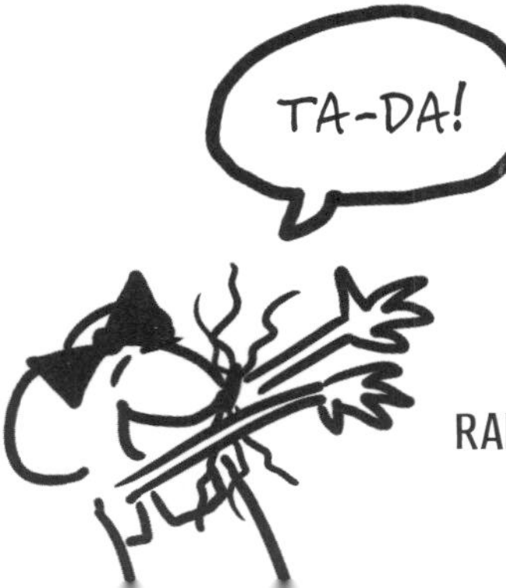
TA-DA!

RANDOM HOUSE NEW YORK

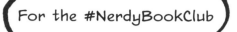

For the #NerdyBookClub

THEY ROCK!

Visit us on the Web! randomhousekids.com

Educators and librarians, for a variety of teaching tools, visit us at RHTeachersLibrarians.com

Library of Congress Cataloging-in-Publication Data
Comics Squad : recess! / comics by Jarrett J. Krosoczka, Gene Yang, Eric Wight, Jennifer L. Holm and Matthew Holm, Ursula Vernon, Dan Santat, Raina Telgemeier and Dave Roman, Dav Pilkey ; edited by Jennifer L. Holm, Matthew Holm, and Jarrett J. Krosoczka. — First edition.
p. cm.
Summary: "A collection of comics about every kid's favorite school subject: recess" —Provided by publisher
ISBN 978-0-385-37003-5 (trade) — ISBN 978-0-385-37004-2 (lib. bdg.) — ISBN 978-0-385-37005-9 (ebook)
1. School recess breaks—Juvenile fiction. 2. Schools—Juvenile fiction. 3. Humorous stories, American. 4. Children's stories, American. 5. Graphic novels. [1. Graphic novels. 2. Recess—Fiction. 3. Schools—Fiction. 4. Humorous stories. 5. Short stories.] I. Krosoczka, Jarrett. II. Yang, Gene Luen. III. Wight, Eric, 1974– IV. Holm, Jennifer L. V. Holm, Matthew. VI. Vernon, Ursula. VII. Santat, Dan. VIII. Telgemeier, Raina. IX. Roman, Dave. X. Pilkey, Dav, 1966– XI. Title: Recess!
PZ7.7.C658 2014 [Fic]—dc23 2013035223

MANUFACTURED IN CHINA
10 9 8 7 6 5 4
First Edition

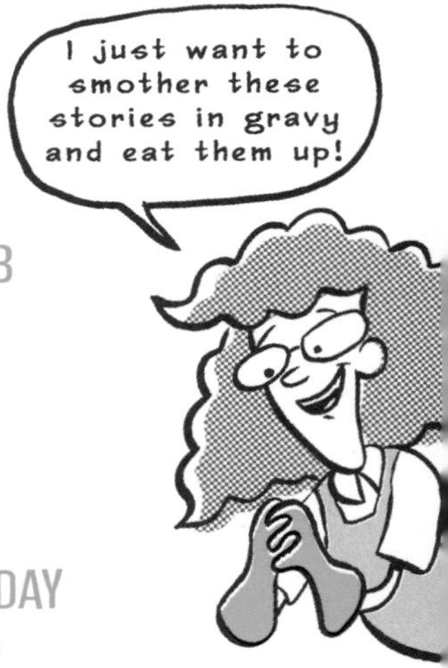
I just want to smother these stories in gravy and eat them up!

★ CONTENTS ★

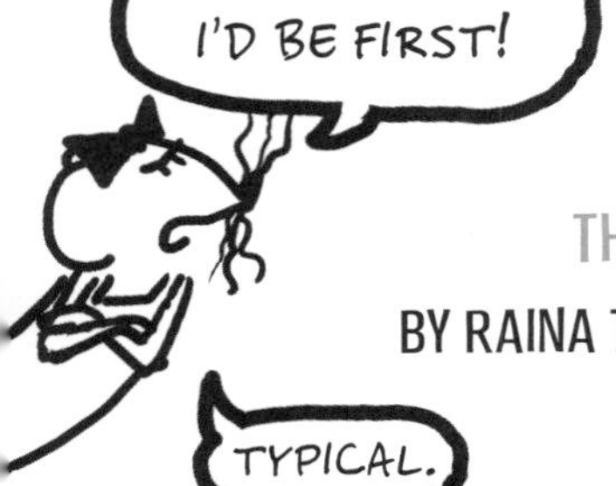
THEY TOLD ME I'D BE FIRST!
TYPICAL.

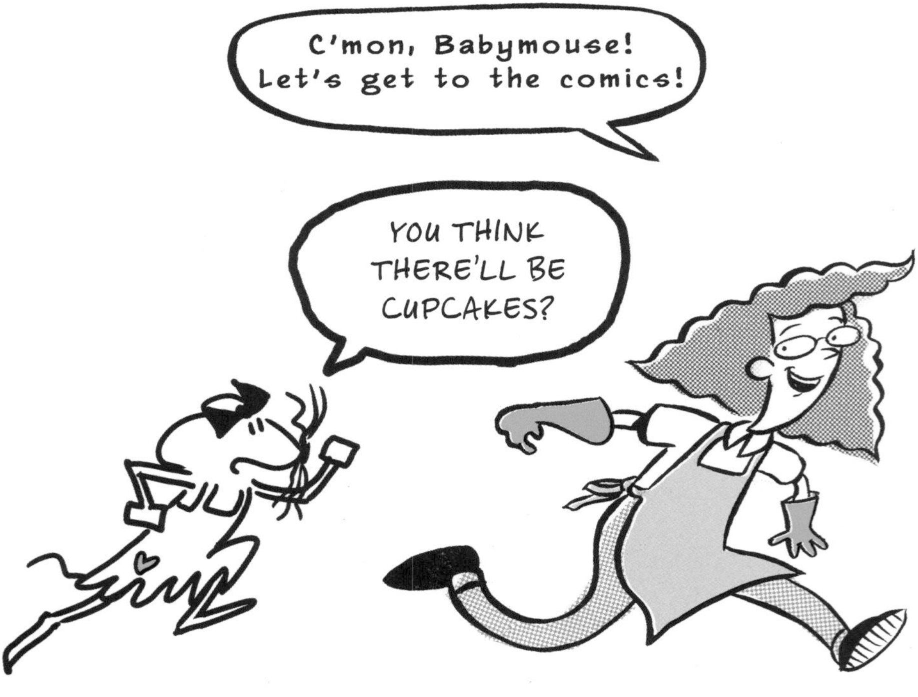
C'mon, Babymouse!
Let's get to the comics!
YOU THINK
THERE'LL BE
CUPCAKES?

THE SUPER-SECRET NINJA CLUB

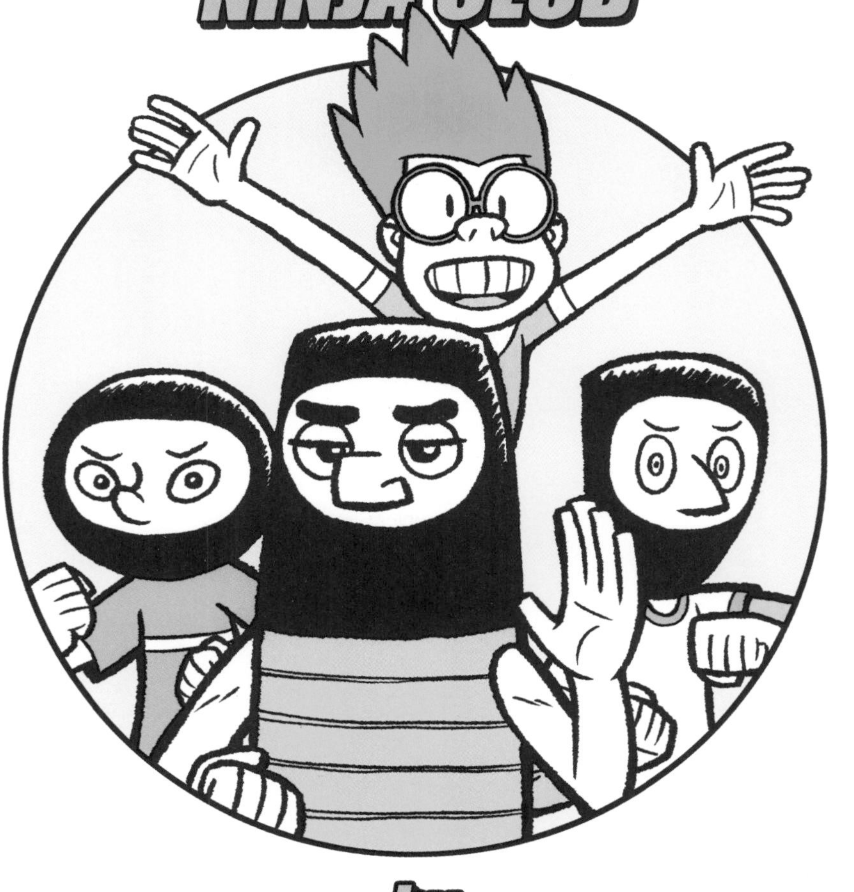

by
Gene Luen Yang

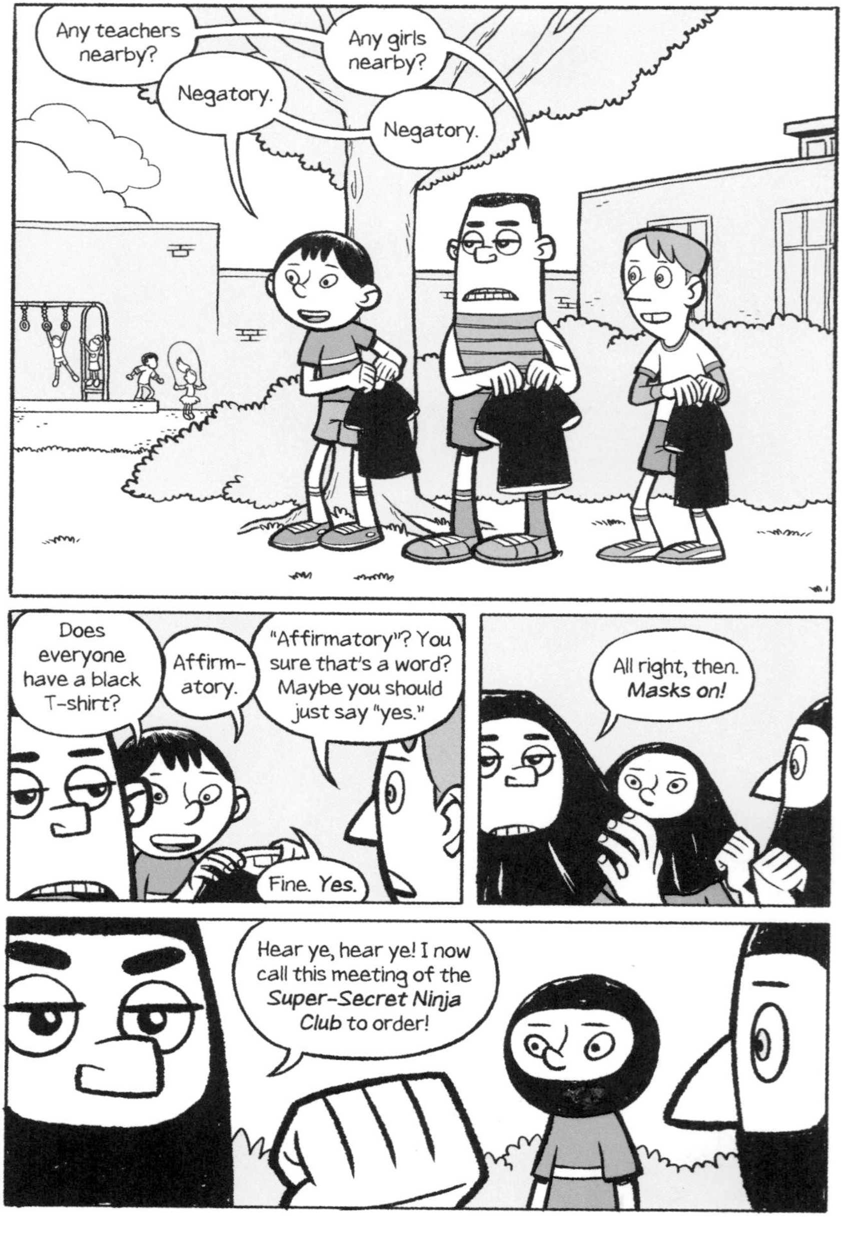

Any teachers nearby?
Any girls nearby?
Negatory.
Negatory.
Does everyone have a black T-shirt?
Affirm-atory.
"Affirmatory"? You sure that's a word? Maybe you should just say "yes."
Fine. *Yes.*
All right, then. *Masks on!*
Hear ye, hear ye! I now call this meeting of the *Super-Secret Ninja Club* to order!

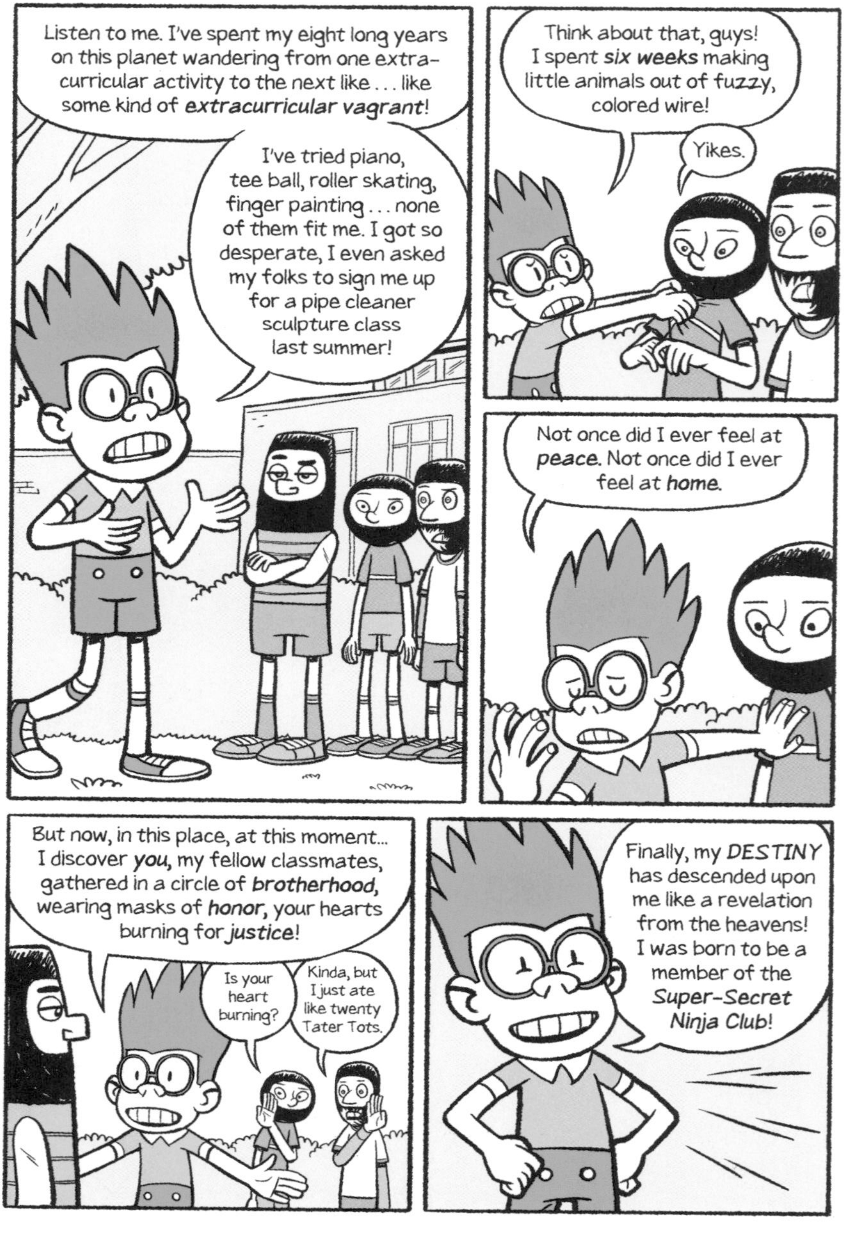
Listen to me. I've spent my eight long years on this planet wandering from one extra-curricular activity to the next like . . . like some kind of extracurricular vagrant!
I've tried piano, tee ball, roller skating, finger painting . . . none of them fit me. I got so desperate, I even asked my folks to sign me up for a pipe cleaner sculpture class last summer!
Think about that, guys! I spent six weeks making little animals out of fuzzy, colored wire!
Yikes.
Not once did I ever feel at peace. Not once did I ever feel at home.
But now, in this place, at this moment... I discover you, my fellow classmates, gathered in a circle of brotherhood, wearing masks of honor, your hearts burning for justice!
Is your heart burning?
Kinda, but I just ate like twenty Tater Tots.
Finally, my DESTINY has descended upon me like a revelation from the heavens! I was born to be a member of the Super-Secret Ninja Club!

BRiiNG!

Aw, man! Lunch is over and we wasted our entire meeting listening to Daryl make a stupid speech! And he's not even a *ninja*!

You mean, not a ninja *yet*!

No, we mean not a ninja *ever*!

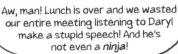

What?! You guys can't do this to me! You can't deny a person his *destiny*!

Oh, just watch me! I'm about to deny you right in the forehead!

Stop, *stop*! You guys go to class! I'll handle this!

Go!

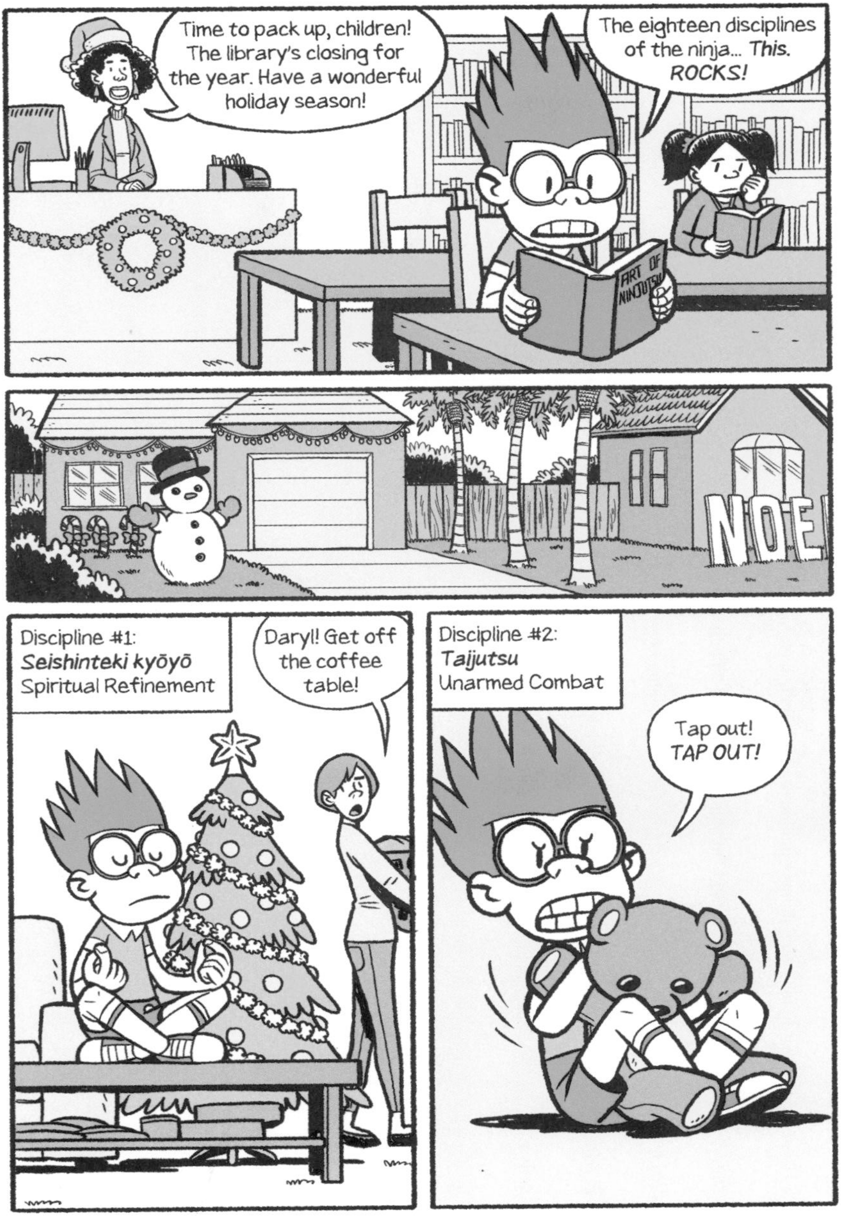
Time to pack up, children! The library's closing for the year. Have a wonderful holiday season!
The eighteen disciplines of the ninja... *This.* *ROCKS!*
ART OF NINJUTSU
NOEL
Discipline #1: *Seishinteki kyōyō* Spiritual Refinement
Daryl! Get off the coffee table!
Discipline #2: *Taijutsu* Unarmed Combat
Tap out! *TAP OUT!*

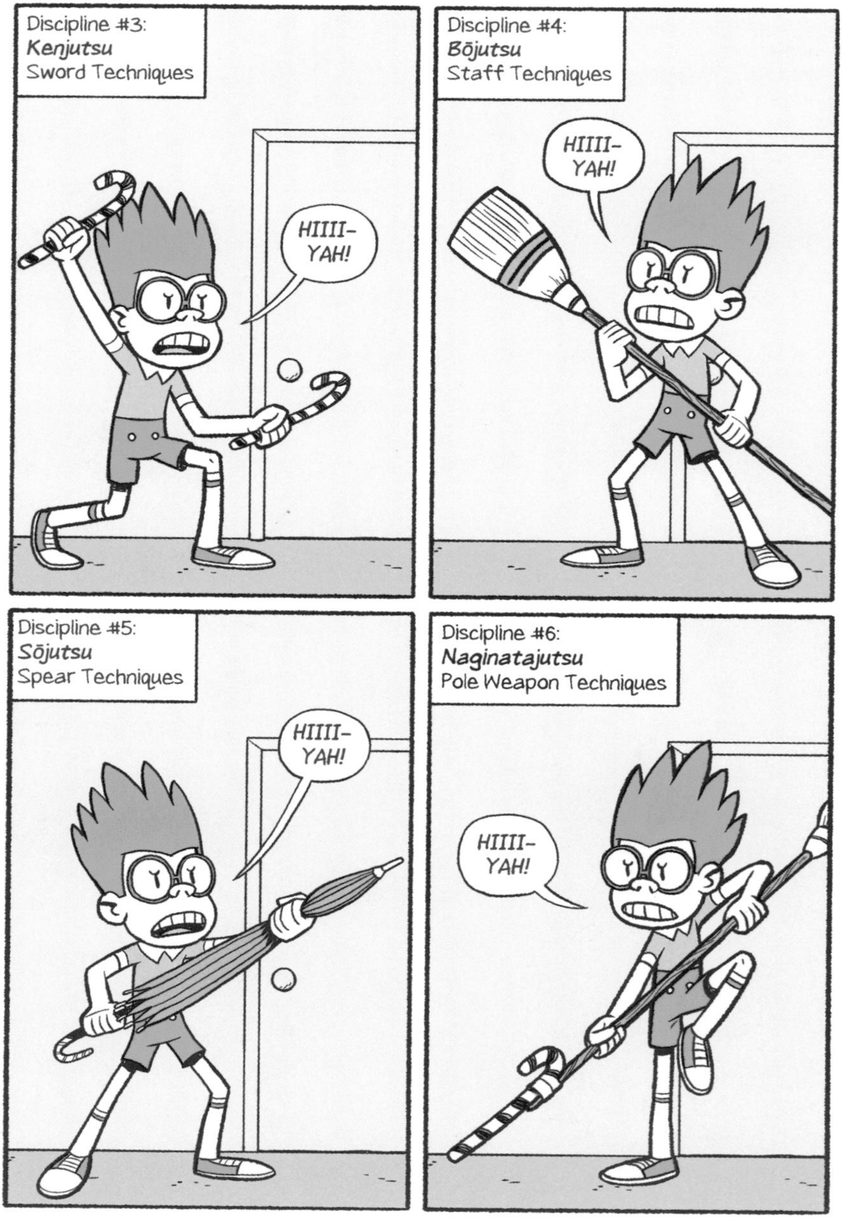
Discipline #3:
Kenjutsu
Sword Techniques
HIIII-YAH!
Discipline #4:
Bōjutsu
Staff Techniques
HIIII-YAH!
Discipline #5:
Sōjutsu
Spear Techniques
HIIII-YAH!
Discipline #6:
Naginatajutsu
Pole Weapon Techniques
HIIII-YAH!

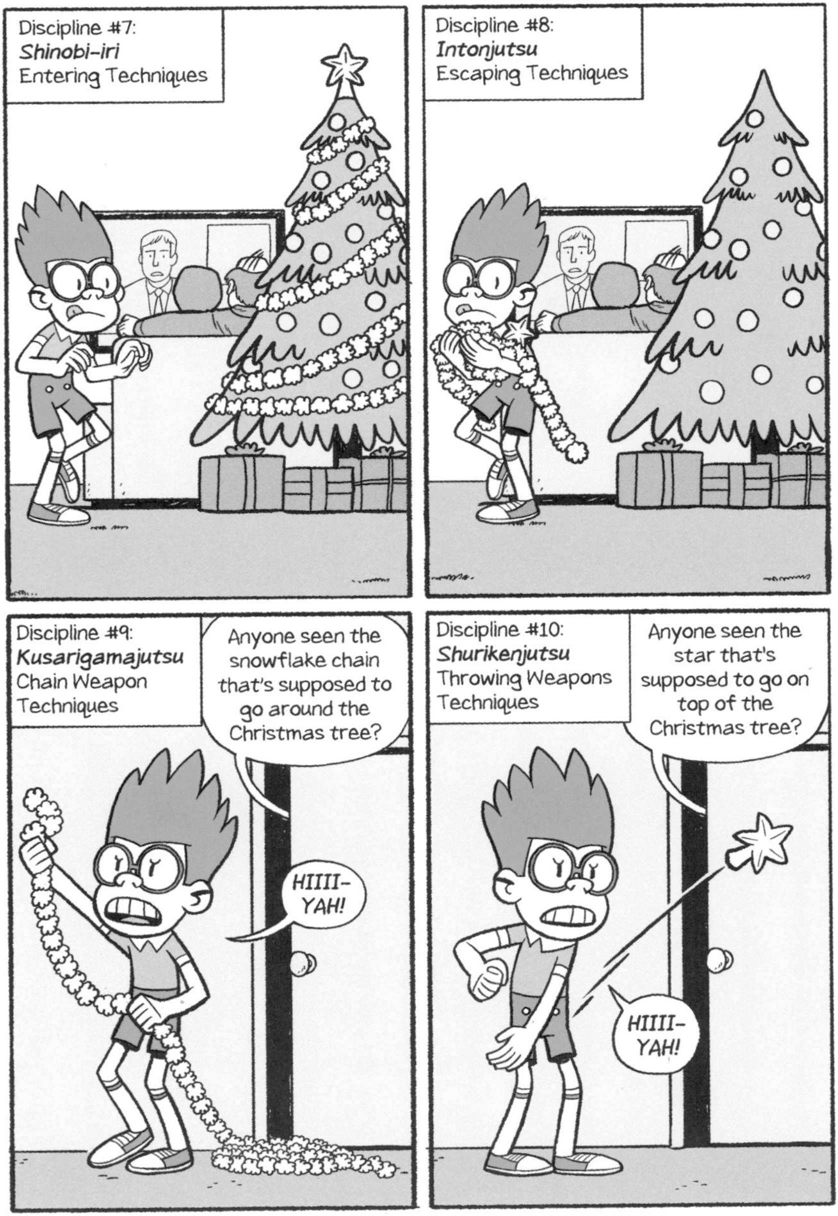
Discipline #7:
Shinobi-iri
Entering Techniques
Discipline #8:
Intonjutsu
Escaping Techniques
Discipline #9:
Kusarigamajutsu
Chain Weapon Techniques
Anyone seen the snowflake chain that's supposed to go around the Christmas tree?
HIIII-YAH!
Discipline #10:
Shurikenjutsu
Throwing Weapons Techniques
Anyone seen the star that's supposed to go on top of the Christmas tree?
HIIII-YAH!

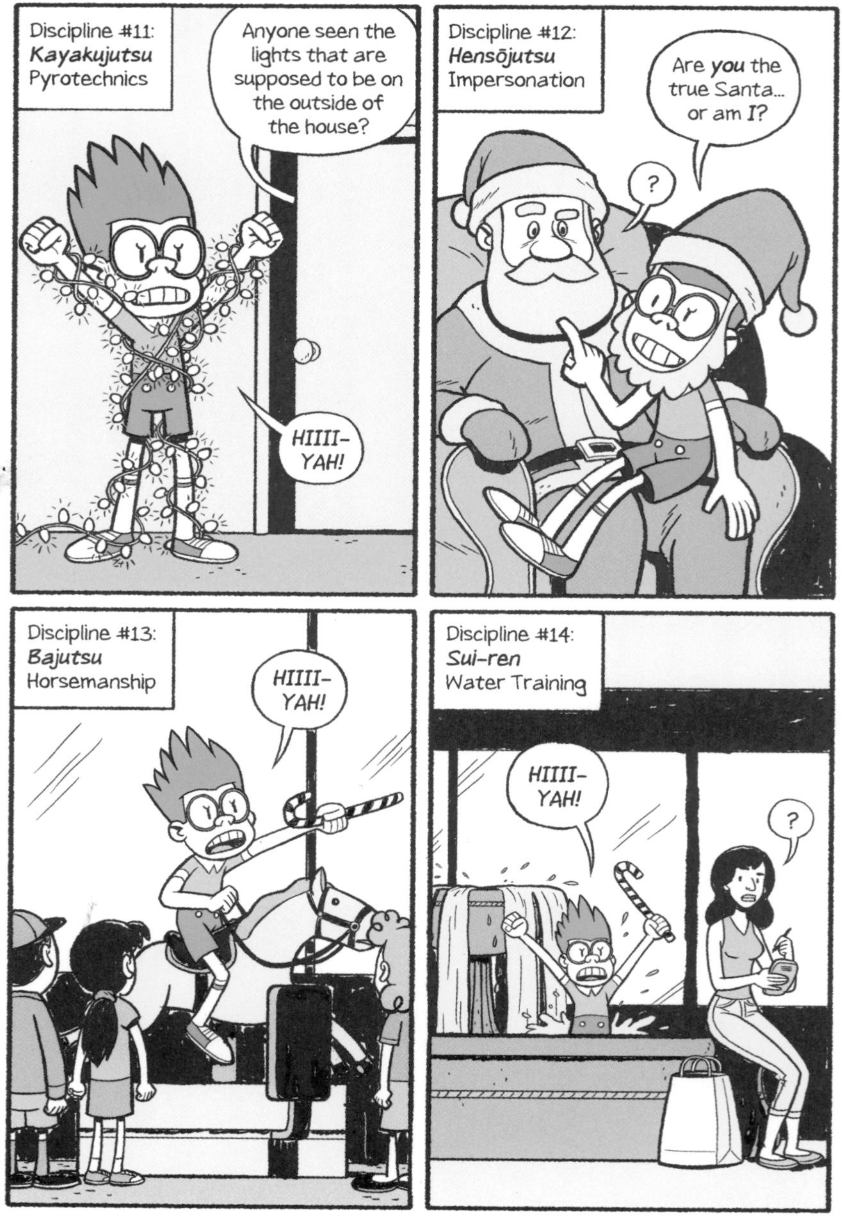

Discipline #11:
Kayakujutsu
Pyrotechnics
Anyone seen the lights that are supposed to be on the outside of the house?
HIIII-YAH!
Discipline #12:
Hensōjutsu
Impersonation
Are you the true Santa... or am I?
?
Discipline #13:
Bajutsu
Horsemanship
HIIII-YAH!
Discipline #14:
Sui-ren
Water Training
HIIII-YAH!
?

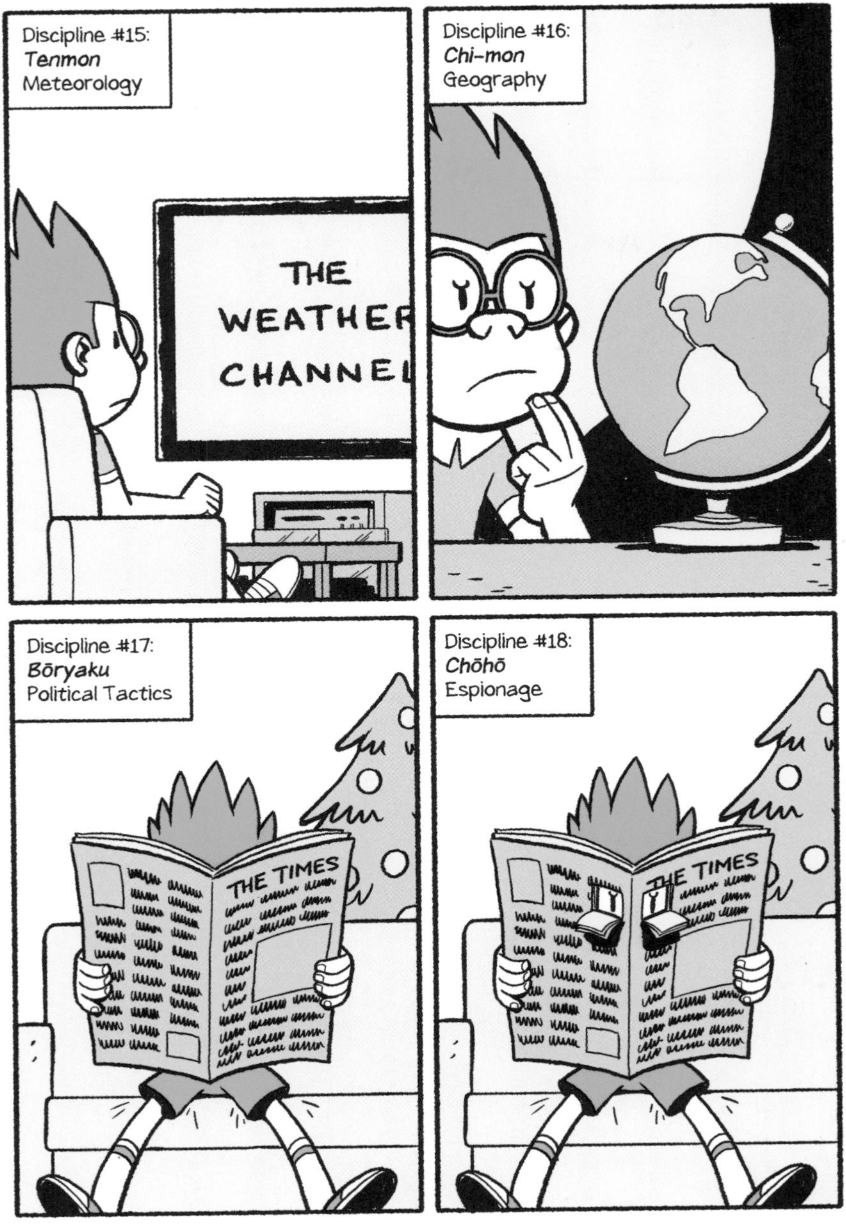
Discipline #15:
Tenmon
Meteorology
THE WEATHER CHANNEL
Discipline #16:
Chi-mon
Geography
Discipline #17:
Bōryaku
Political Tactics
THE TIMES
Discipline #18:
Chōhō
Espionage
THE TIMES

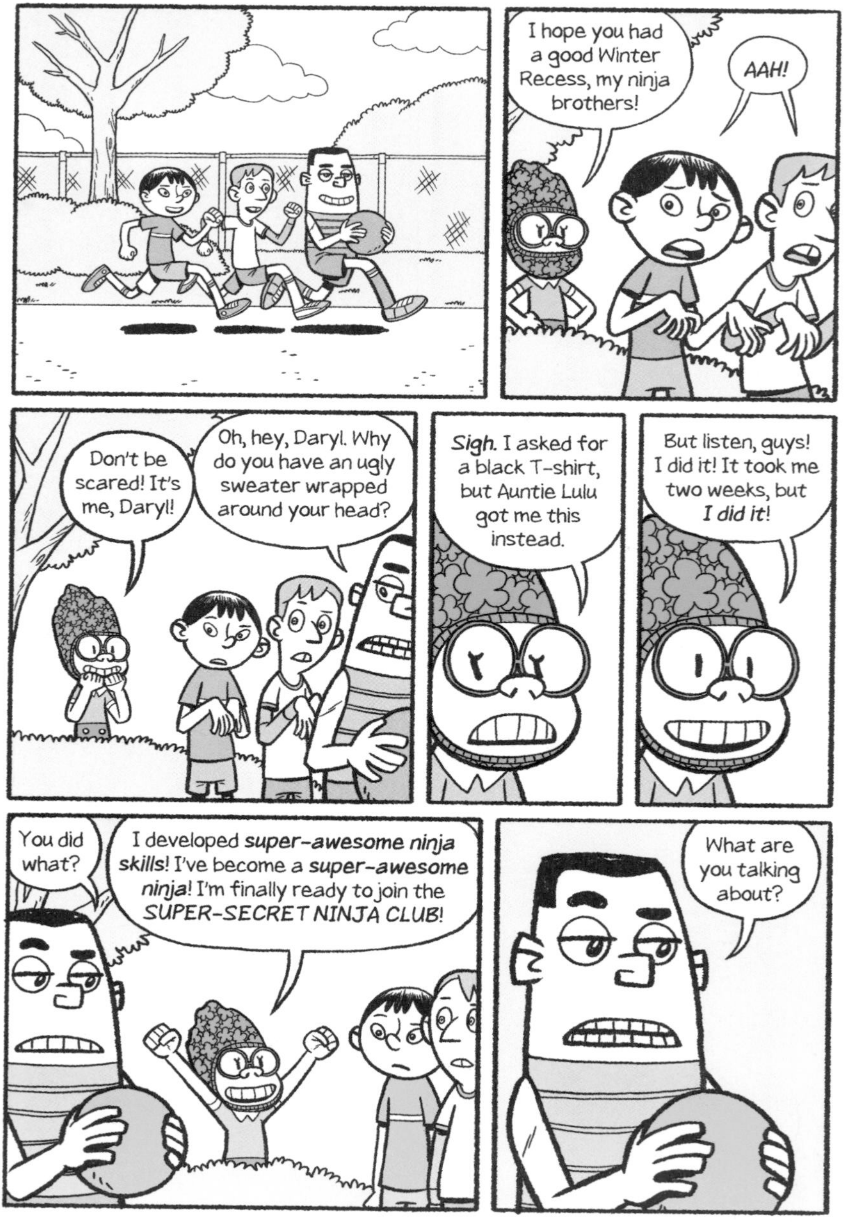

I hope you had a good Winter Recess, my ninja brothers!
AAH!
Don't be scared! It's me, Daryl!
Oh, hey, Daryl. Why do you have an ugly sweater wrapped around your head?
Sigh. I asked for a black T-shirt, but Auntie Lulu got me this instead.
But listen, guys! I did it! It took me two weeks, but *I did it*!
You did what?
I developed *super-awesome ninja skills*! I've become a *super-awesome ninja*! I'm finally ready to join the *SUPER-SECRET NINJA CLUB*!
What are you talking about?

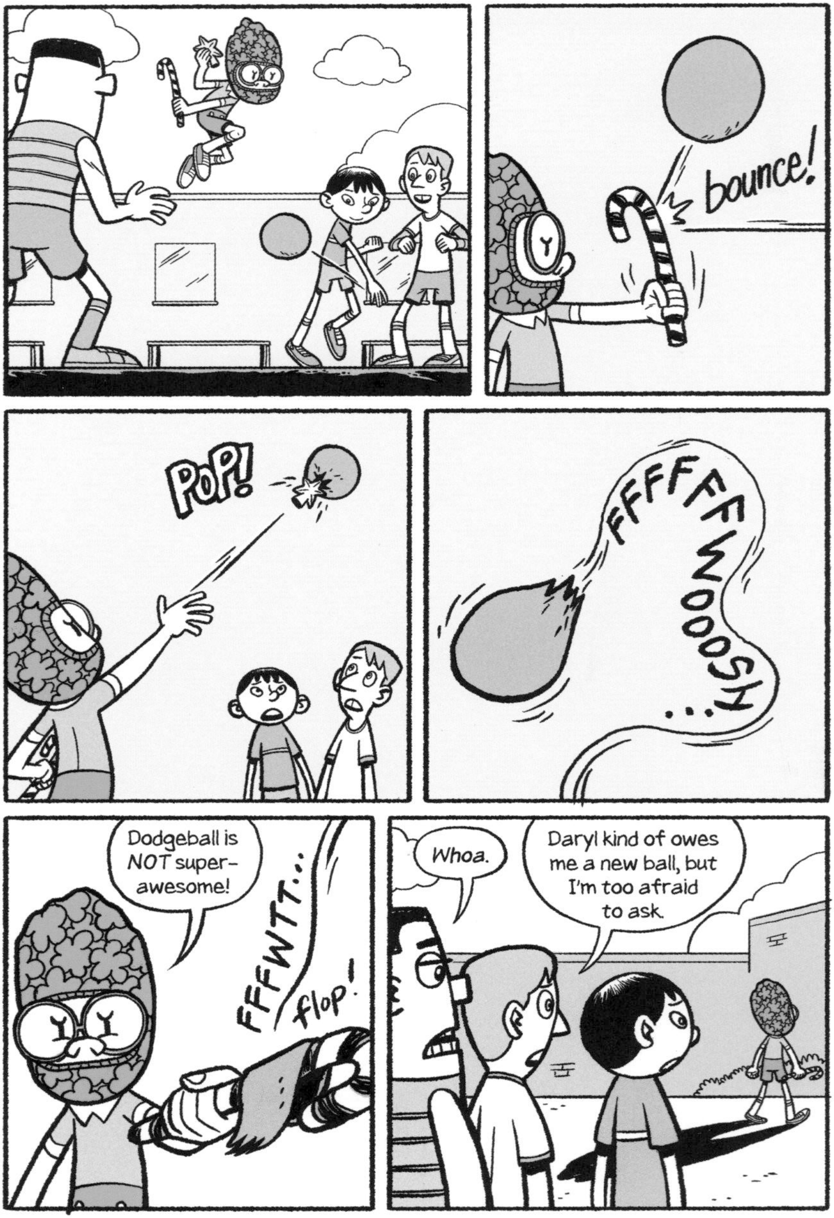
bounce!
POP!
FFFFFFWOOOSH...
Dodgeball is NOT super-awesome!
FFFWTT...
flop!
Whoa.
Daryl kind of owes me a new ball, but I'm too afraid to ask.

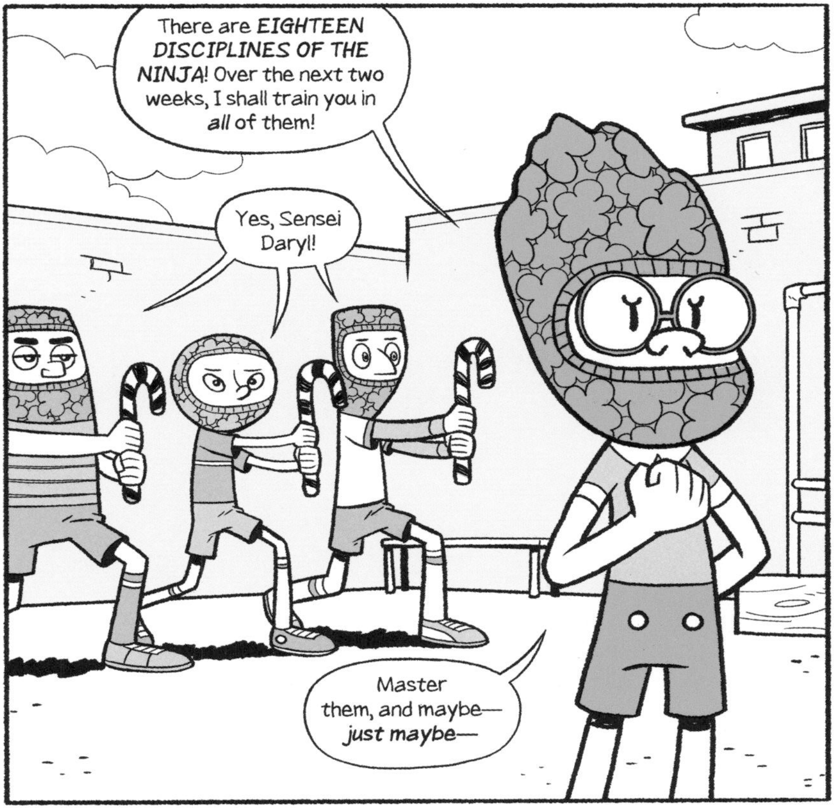
There are EIGHTEEN DISCIPLINES OF THE NINJA! Over the next two weeks, I shall train you in all of them!
Yes, Sensei Daryl!
Master them, and maybe— just maybe—
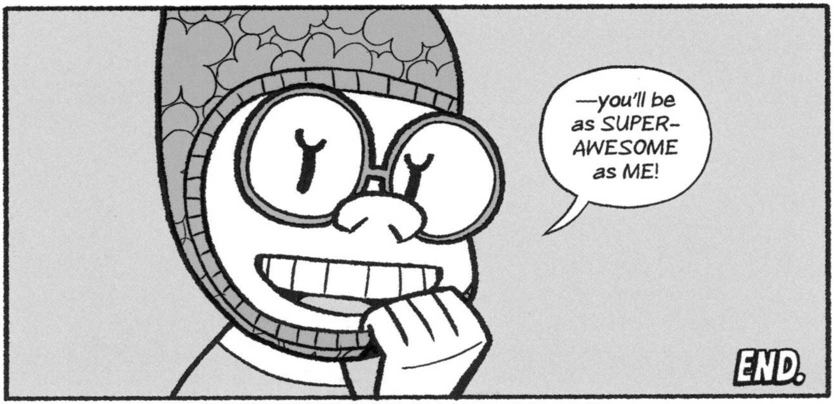
—you'll be as SUPER-AWESOME as ME!
END.

MASH-UP MADNESS!

BABYMOUSE   LUNCH LADY   LUNCH MOUSE

BETTY   SQUISH   SQUISHETTY

LOCKER   FLIPPY BUNNY   FLIPPY LOCKER

NOW GO TRY DRAWING YOUR OWN MASH-UPS!

16

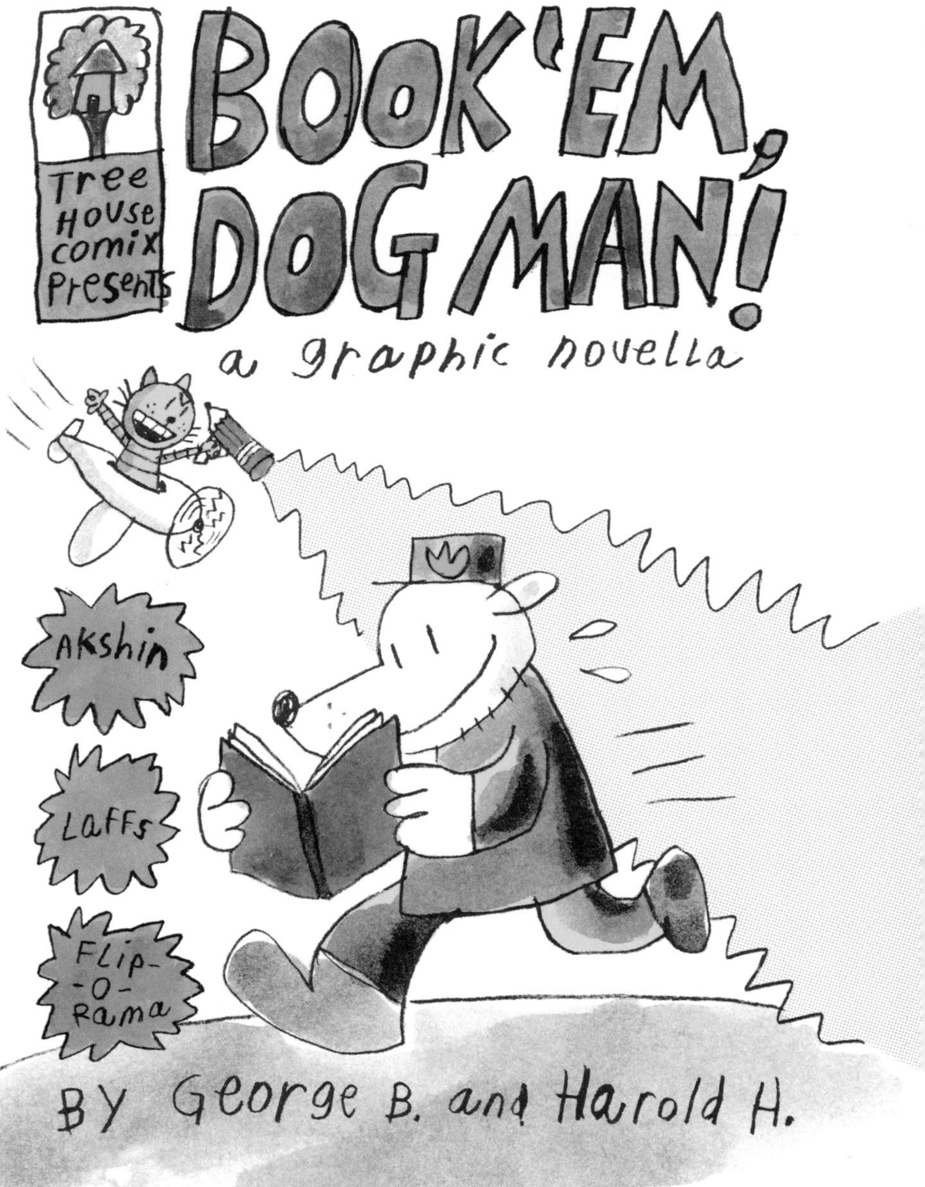
Tree House comix Presents
BOOK'EM, DOG MAN!
a graphic novella
Akshin
Laffs
Flip-O-Rama
BY George B. and Harold H.

Jerome Horwitz Elementary School

We put the "ow" in Knowledge

Dear Mr. and Mrs. Beard,

Once again I am writing to inform you of your son's disruptive activity in my classroom.

The assignment was to create a WRITTEN public service message to promote reading. Your son and his friend Harold Hutchins (I am sending a nearly identical letter to Harold's mother) were specifically told NOT to make a comic book for this assignment.

As usual, they did exactly what they were told *not* to do (see attached comic book). When I confronted George about his disobedience, he claimed that this was not a comic book, but a "graphic novella." I am getting fed up with George's impudence.

I have told both boys on numerous occasions that the classroom is no place for creativity, yet they continue to make these obnoxious and offensive "comix." As you will see, this comic book contains multiple scenes of stealing, violence, and unlawfulness . . . and don't get me started on the spelling and grammar!

George's silly, disruptive behavior, as well as these increasingly disturbing comic books, are turning my classroom into a zoo. I have spoken to Principal Krupp about *Dog Man* on numerous occasions. We both believe that you should consider psychological counseling for your son, or at the very least some kind of behavior modification drug to cure him of his "creative streak."

Regretfully,

Ms. Construde

Ms. Construde
Grade 1 Teacher

BOOK 'EM, DOG MAN

Tree House Comix

BY George B. and Harold H.

One day Petey sat in his Jail cell feeling sad.

News
DOG man wins again

Rats! Every time I have a evil Plan, DOG man always OUT-smarts me!

How come Hes so Darn smart???

So Petey Decidid to Find Out!

19

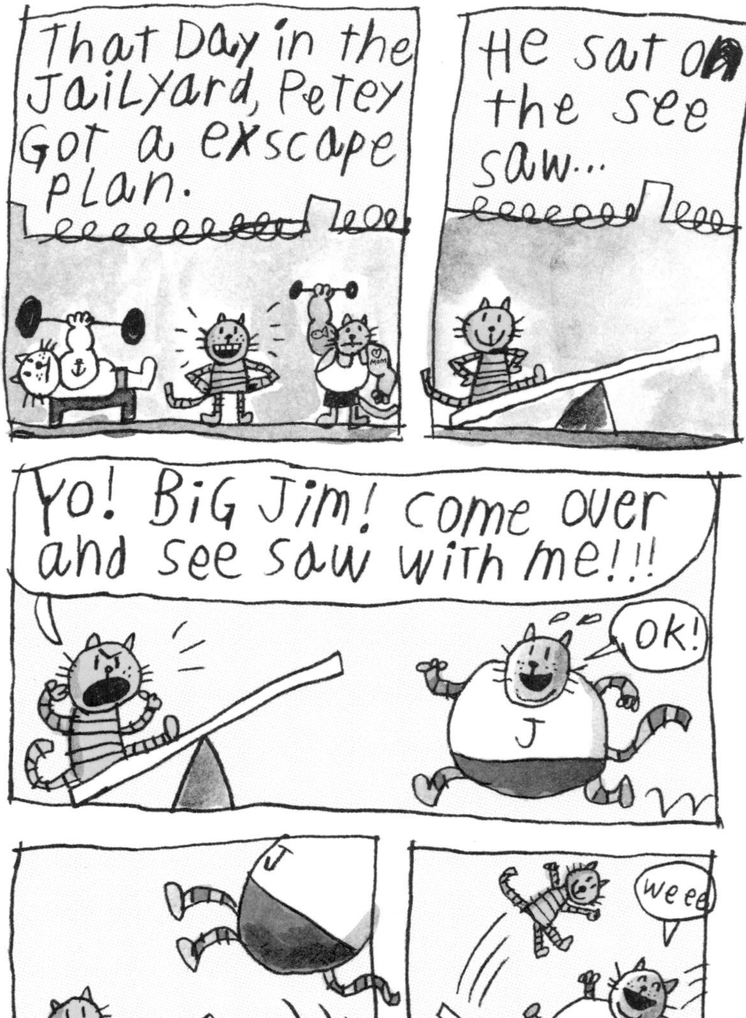
That Day in the JaiLyard, Petey Got a exscape plan.
MOM
HE sat O the see saw...
Yo! BiG Jim! come over and see saw with me!!!
OK!
weee
BONK

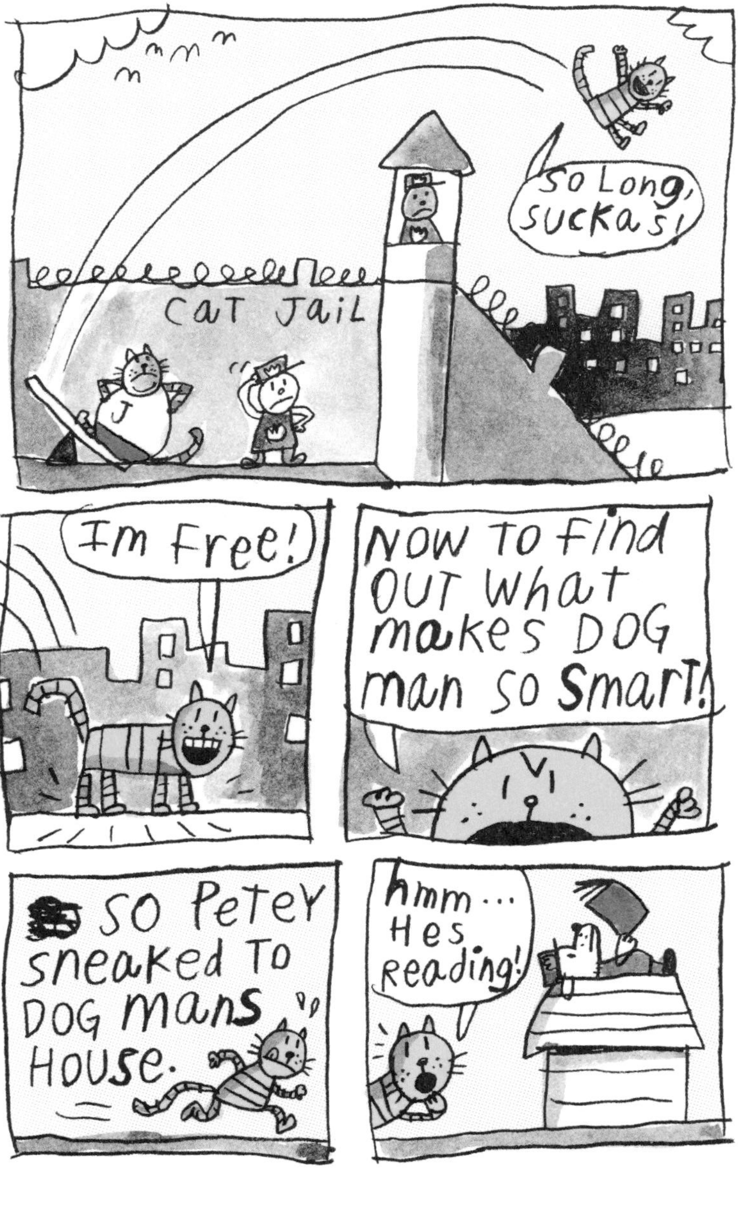
So Long, suckas!
CAT JAIL
Im Free!
NOW TO Find OUT What makes DOG man so Smart!
[redacted] SO Peter sneaked TO DOG mans HOUSE.
hmm... Hes reading!

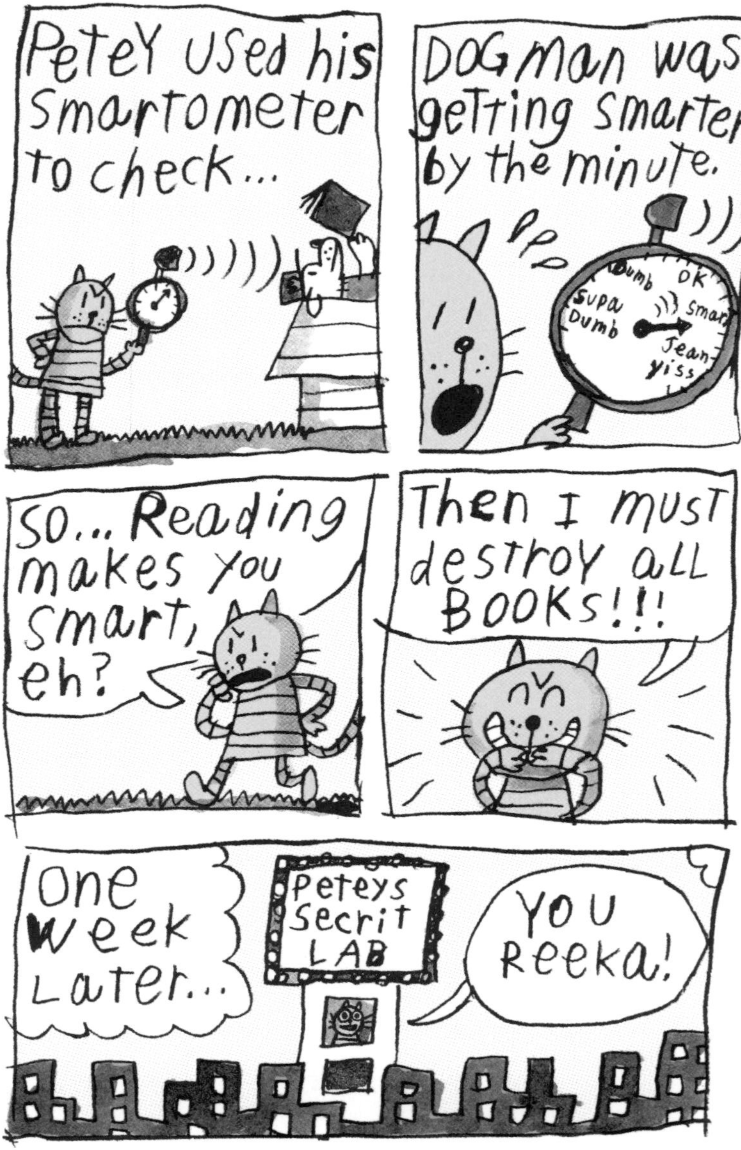
PeteY used his Smartometer to check...
DOG man was getting Smarter by the minute.
Dumb
OK
Supa Dumb
Smart
Jean-yiss
So... Reading makes you smart, eh?
Then I must destroy all BOOKS!!!
One Week Later...
Peteys Secrit LAB
You Reeka!

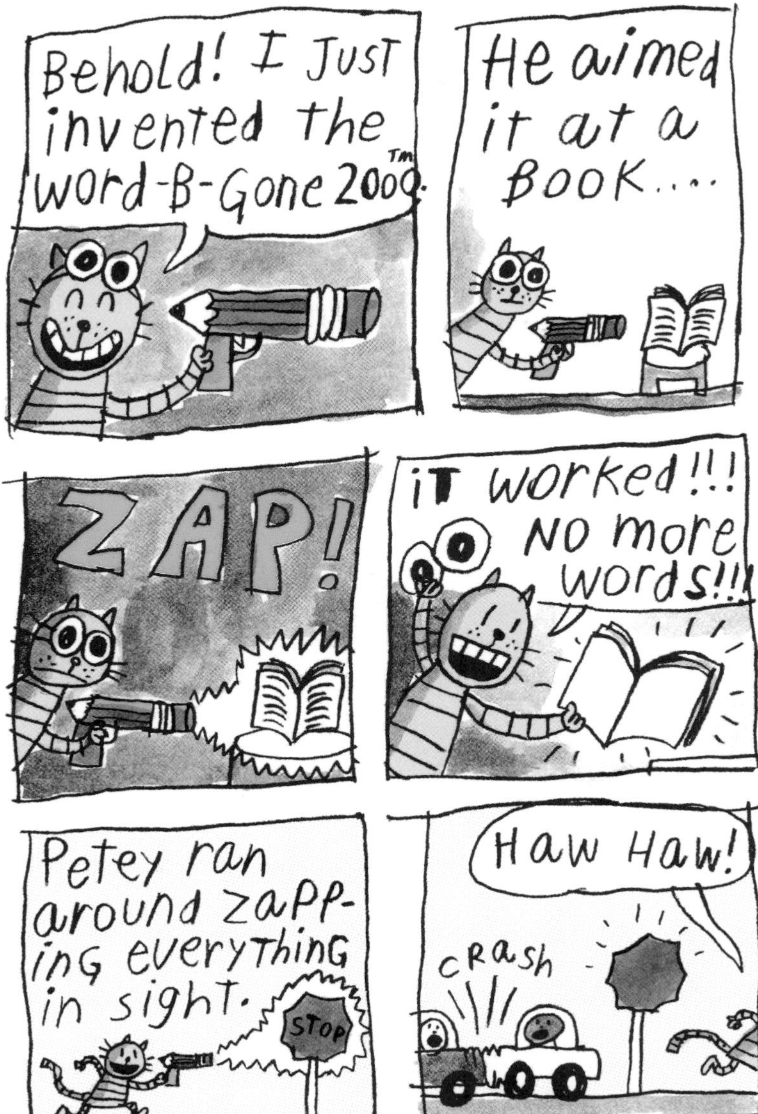
Behold! I JUST invented the word-B-Gone 2000™.
He aimed it at a BOOK....
ZAP!
iT worked!!! NO more words!!!
Petey ran around zapp-ing everyThing in sight.
STOP
Haw Haw!
cRash

The world is supa dumb!!!

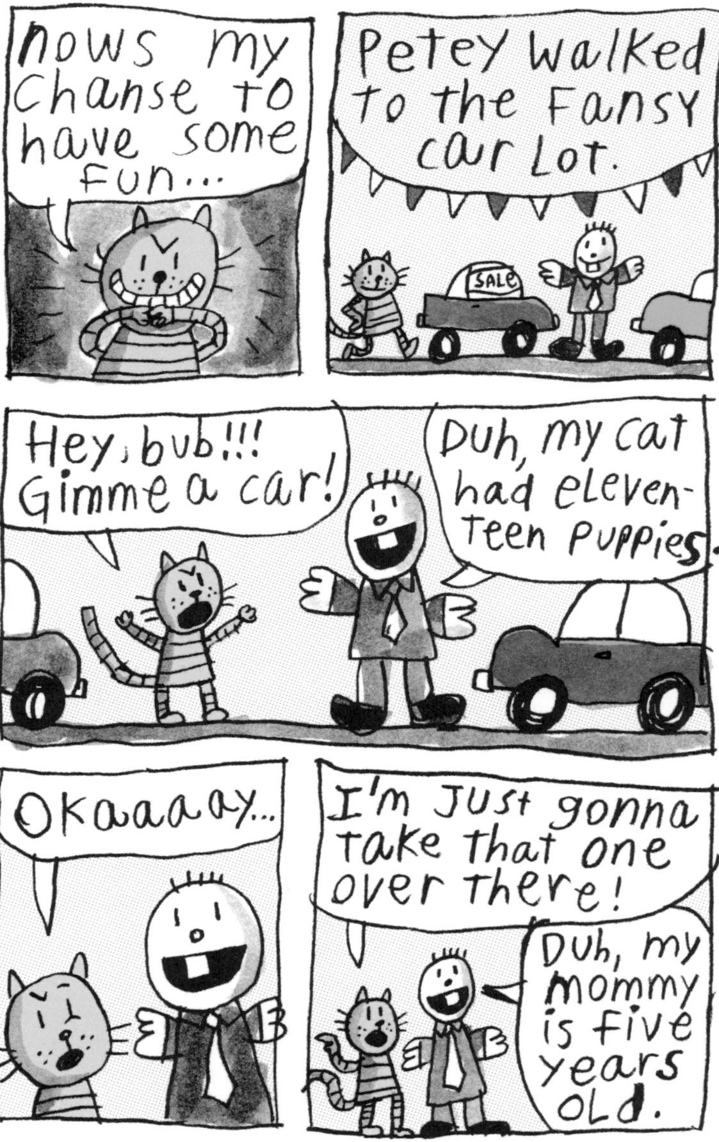
nows my Chanse to have some fun...
Petey walked to the Fansy car Lot.
SALE
Hey, bub!!! Gimme a car!
Duh, my cat had eleven-teen puppies.
Okaaaay...
I'm Just gonna take that one over there!
Duh, my mommy is five years old.

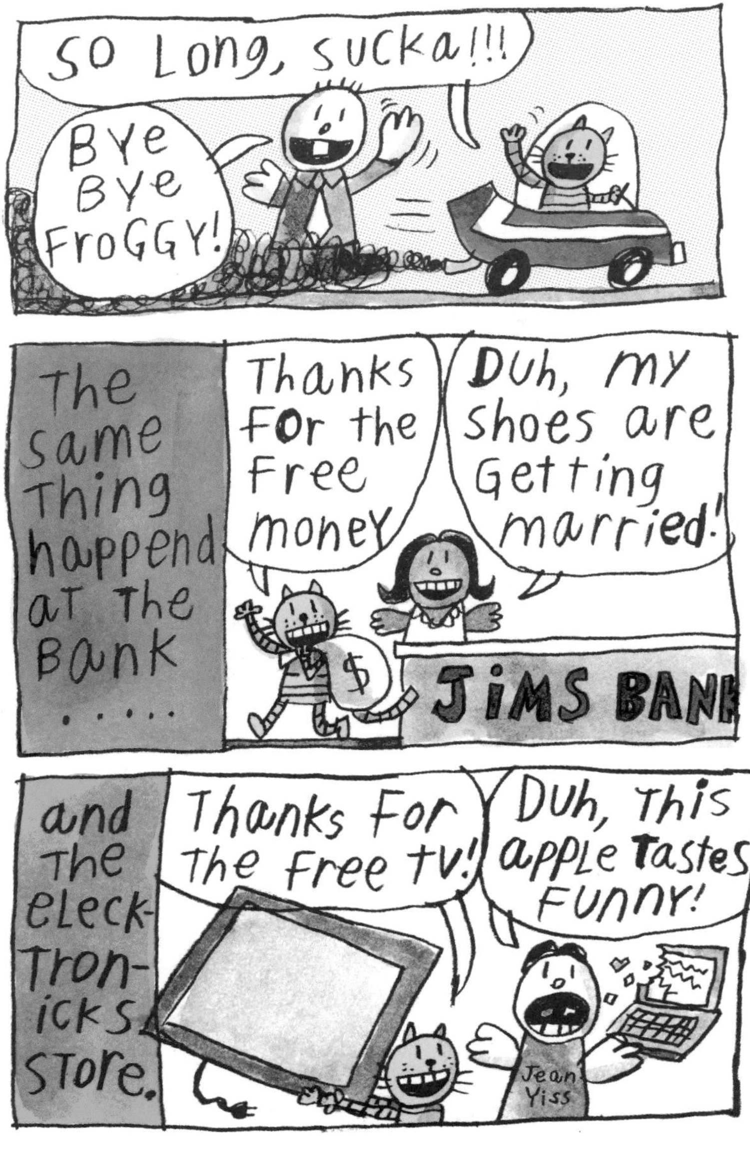

SO LONG, SUCKA!!!
BYE BYE FROGGY!
The same Thing happend at The Bank ....
Thanks FOr the Free money
DUh, my shoes are Getting married!
JiMS BANK
and The eleck-Tron-icks Store.
Thanks For The Free TV!
DUh, This apple Tastes FUNNY!
Jean Yiss

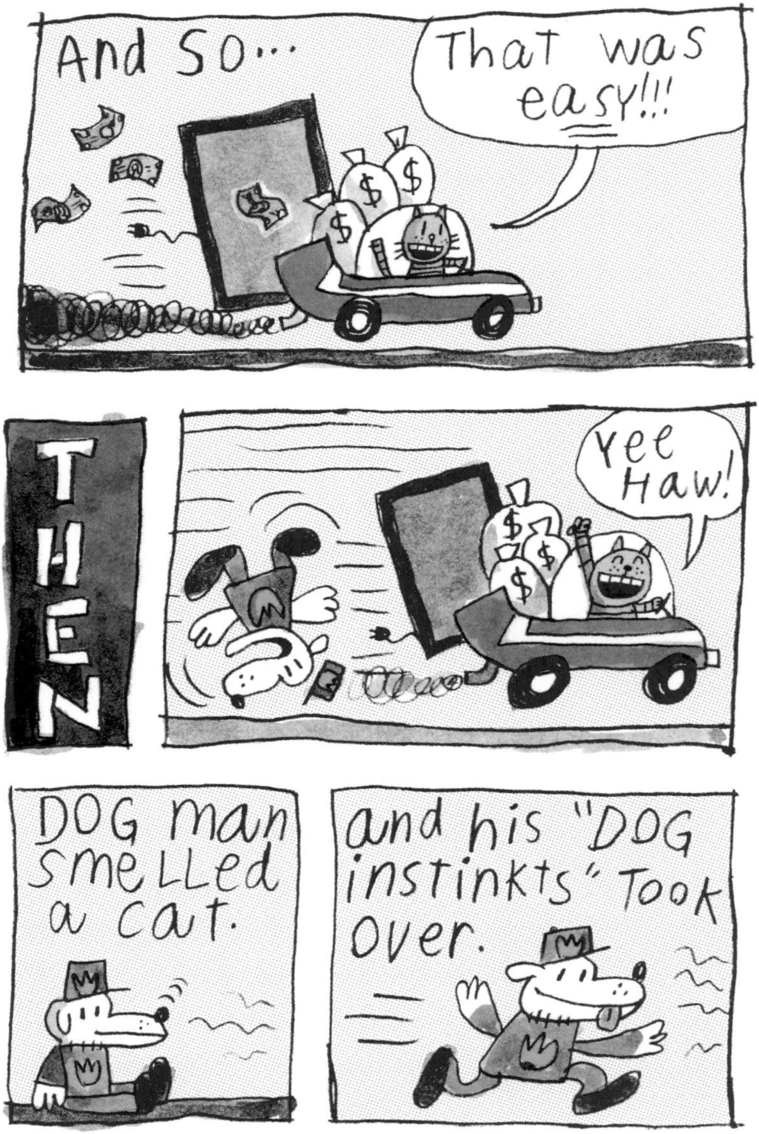
And so...
That was easy!!!
THEN
Yee Haw!
DOG man smelled a cat.
and his "DOG instinkts" Took over.

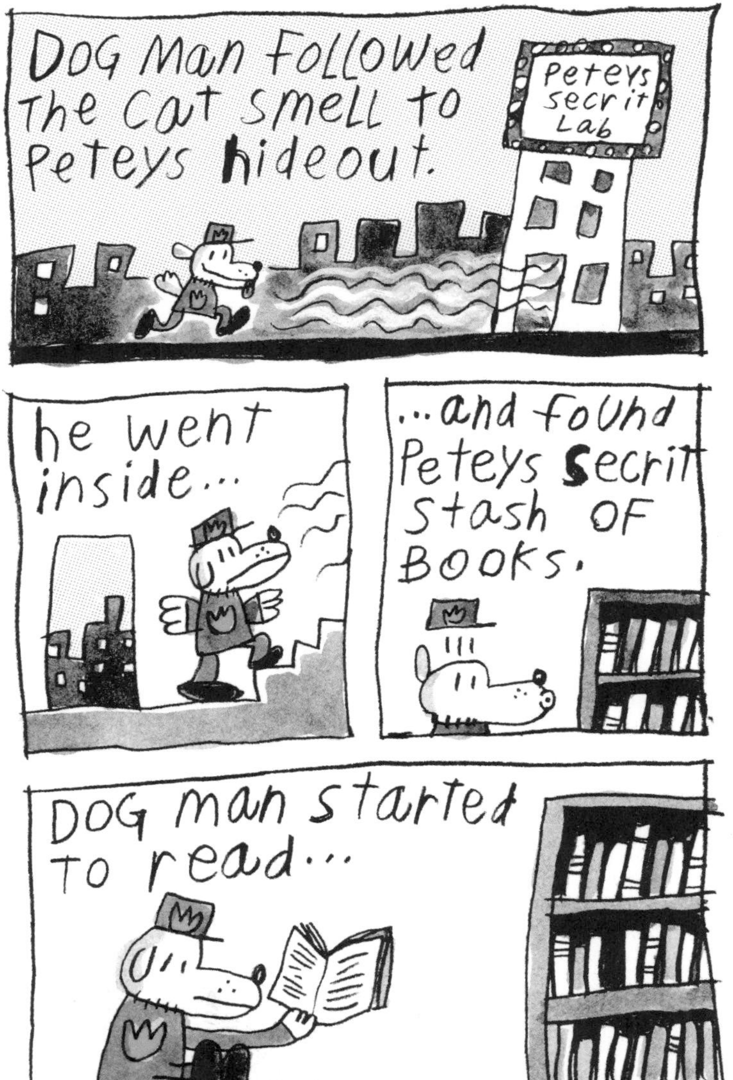
DOG Man FOLLOWed The Cat SmeLL to Peteys hideout.
Peteys secrit Lab
he went inside...
...and found Peteys Secrit Stash OF BOOKS.
DOG man started TO read...

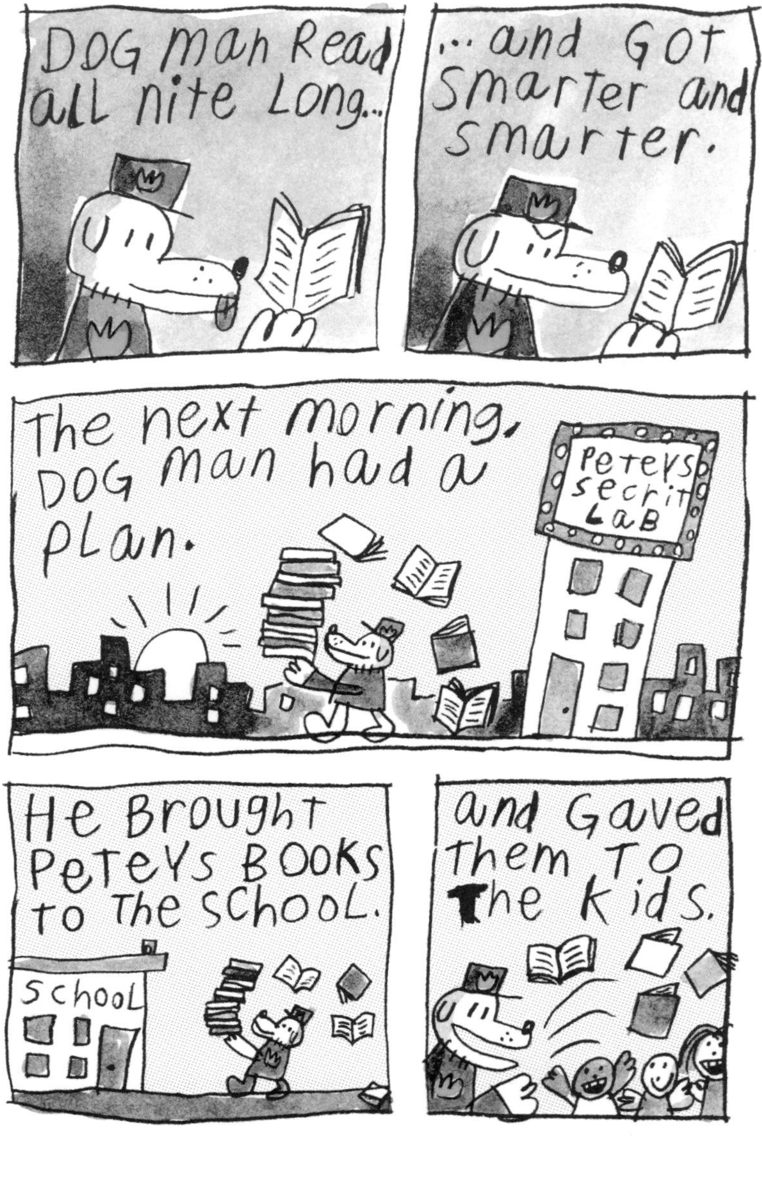
DOG man Read all nite Long...
...and GOT Smarter and smarter.
The next morning, DOG man had a plan.
Peters secrit LaB
He Brought Peters BOOKS to The school.
school
and Gaved them TO The Kids.

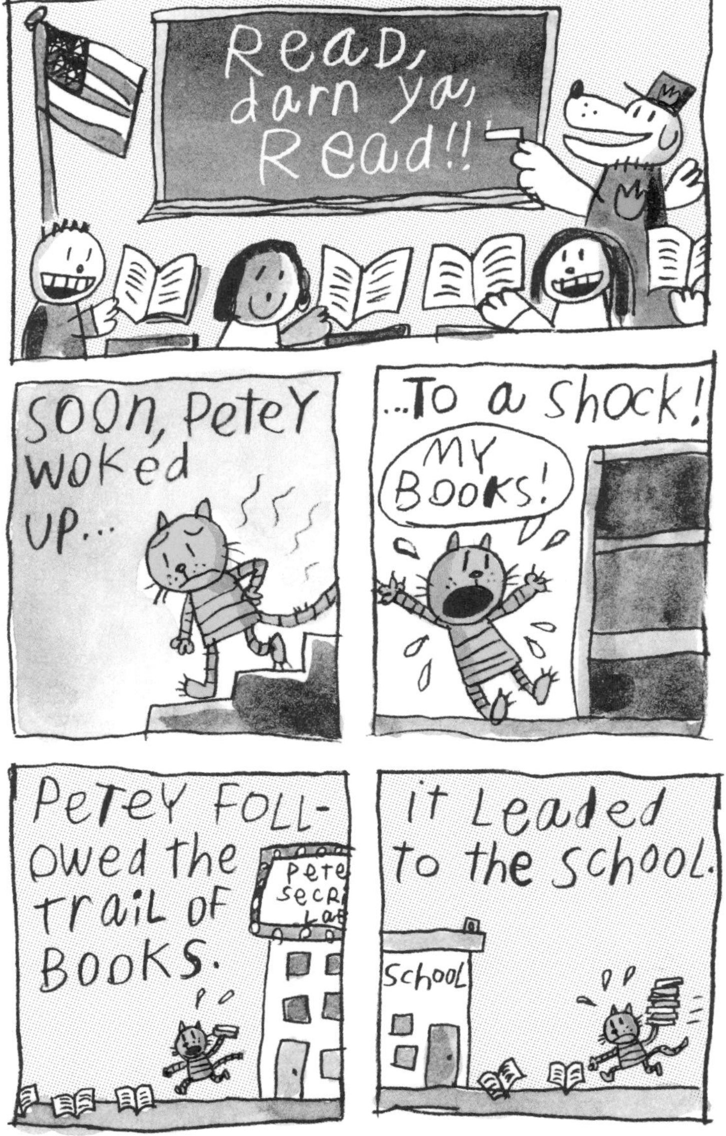
Read, darn ya, Read!!
SOON, PeteY woked UP...
...To a Shock!
MY BOOKS!
PeTeY FOLL-owed the Trail of BOOKS.
it Leaded to the School.
SchooL

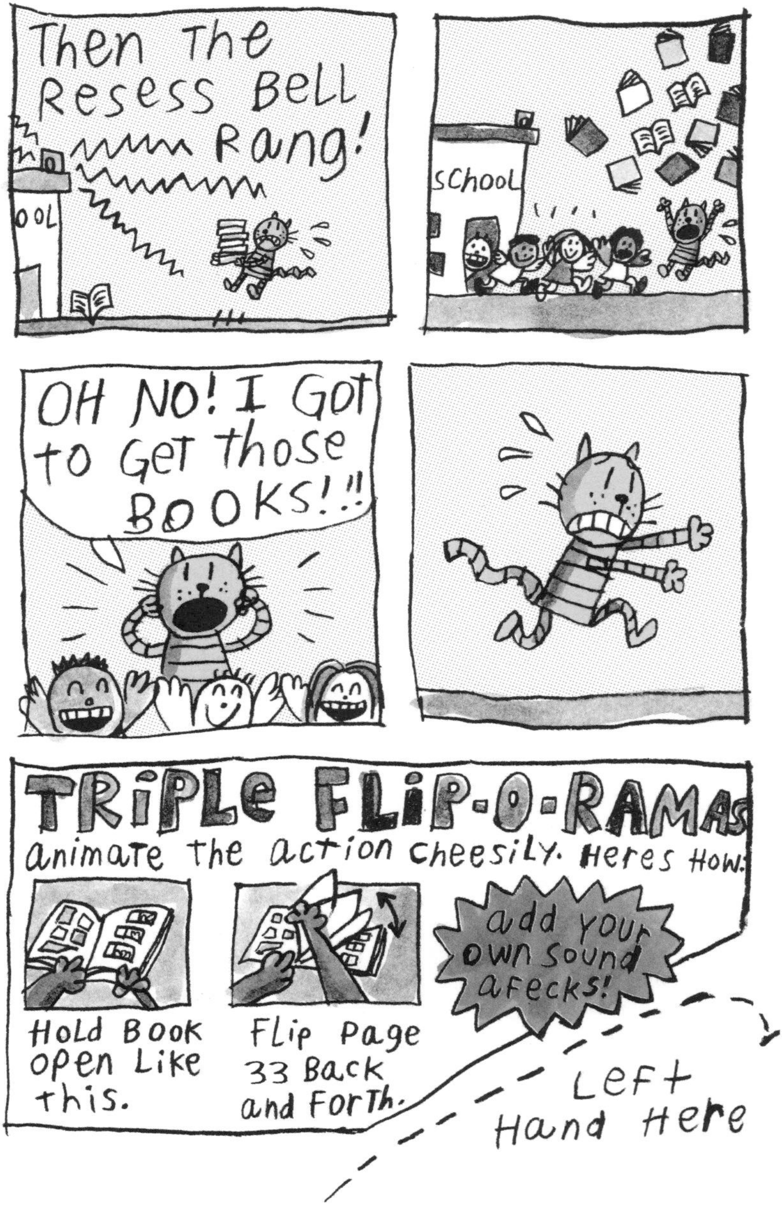

Then The Resess Bell Rang!
SCHOOL
OH NO! I Got to Get those BOOKS!!!
TRiPLe FLiP-O-RAMAS
animate the action cheesiLY. Heres How:
Hold Book open Like this.
Flip Page 33 Back and ForTh.
add your own sound afecks!
Left Hand Here

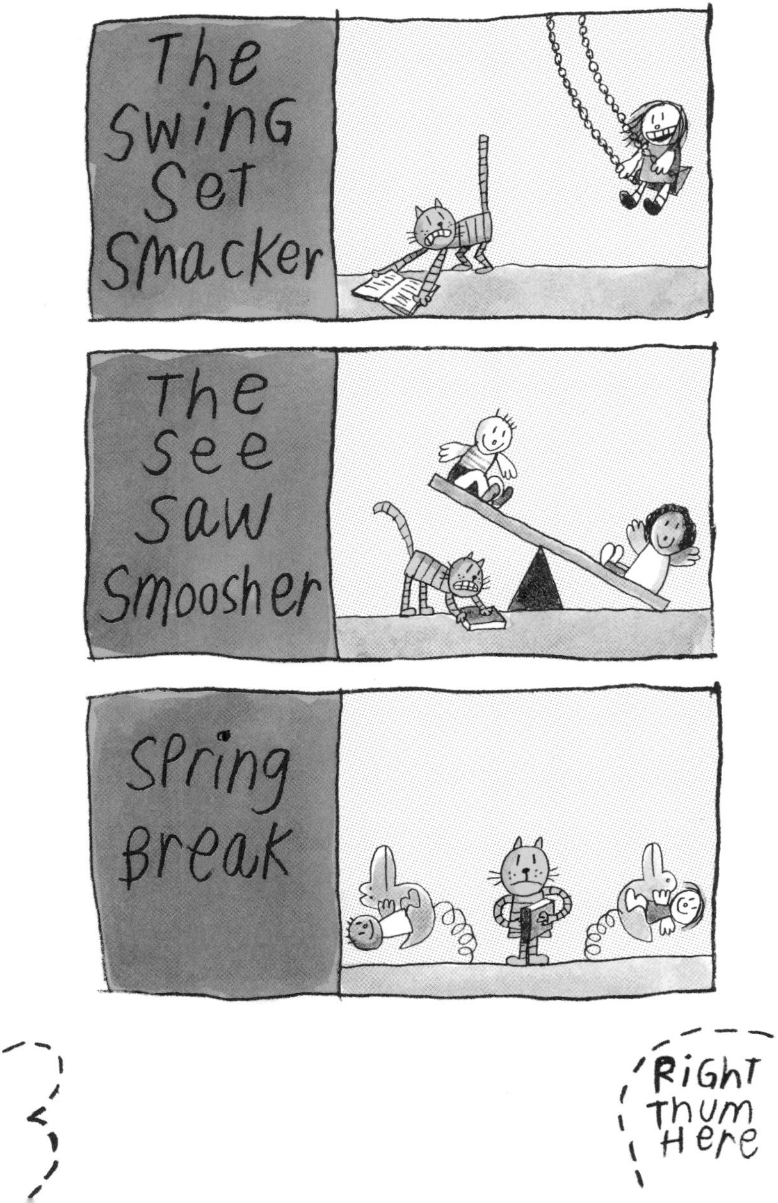
The Swing Set Smacker
The See Saw Smoosher
Spring Break
Right Thum Here

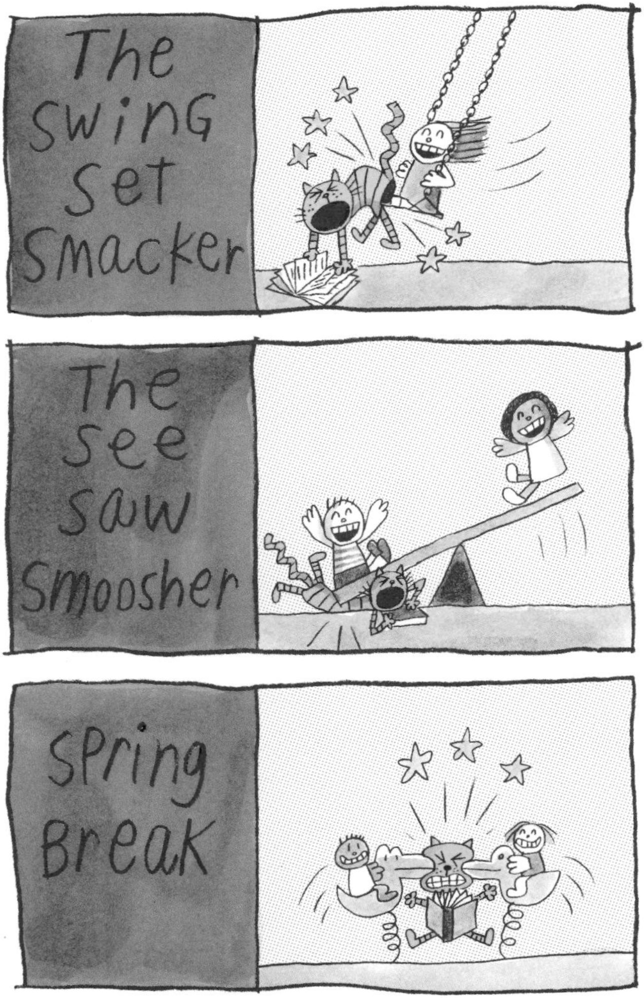
The Swing Set Smacker
The See Saw Smoosher
Spring Break

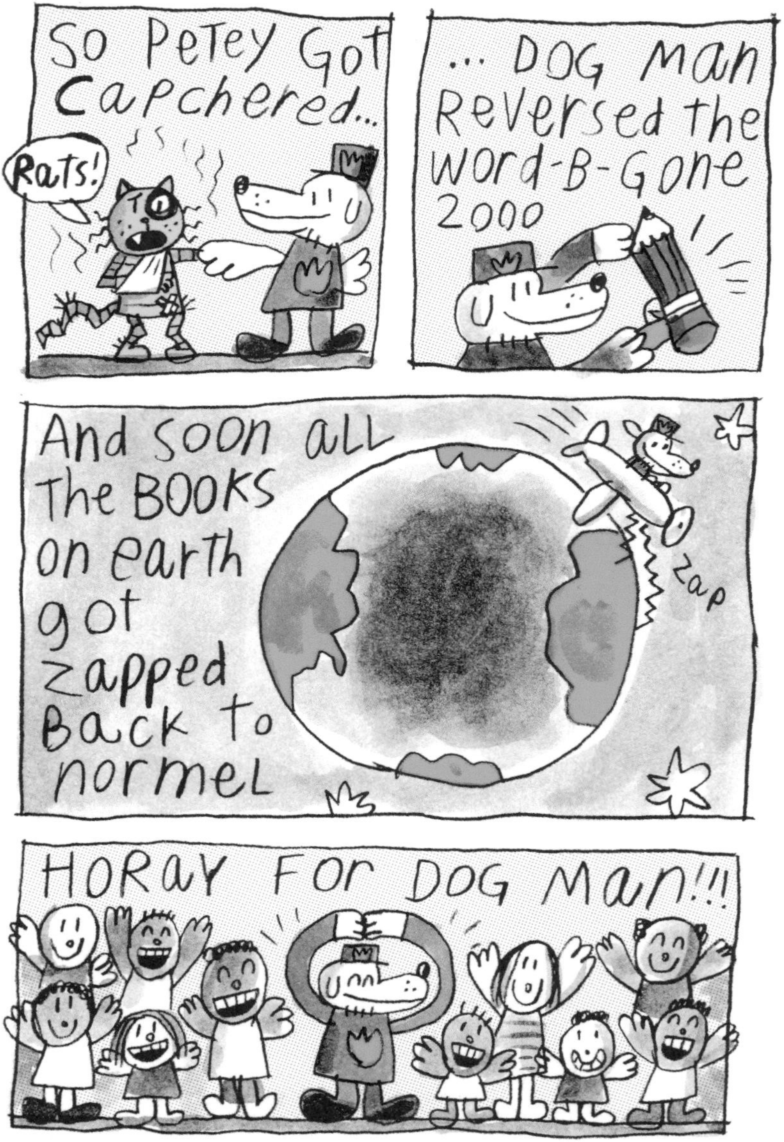

So Petey Got Capchered...
Rats!
... DOG Man Reversed the word-B-Gone 2000
And soon all the BOOKS on earth got zapped Back to normel
Zap
HORAY For DOG Man!!!

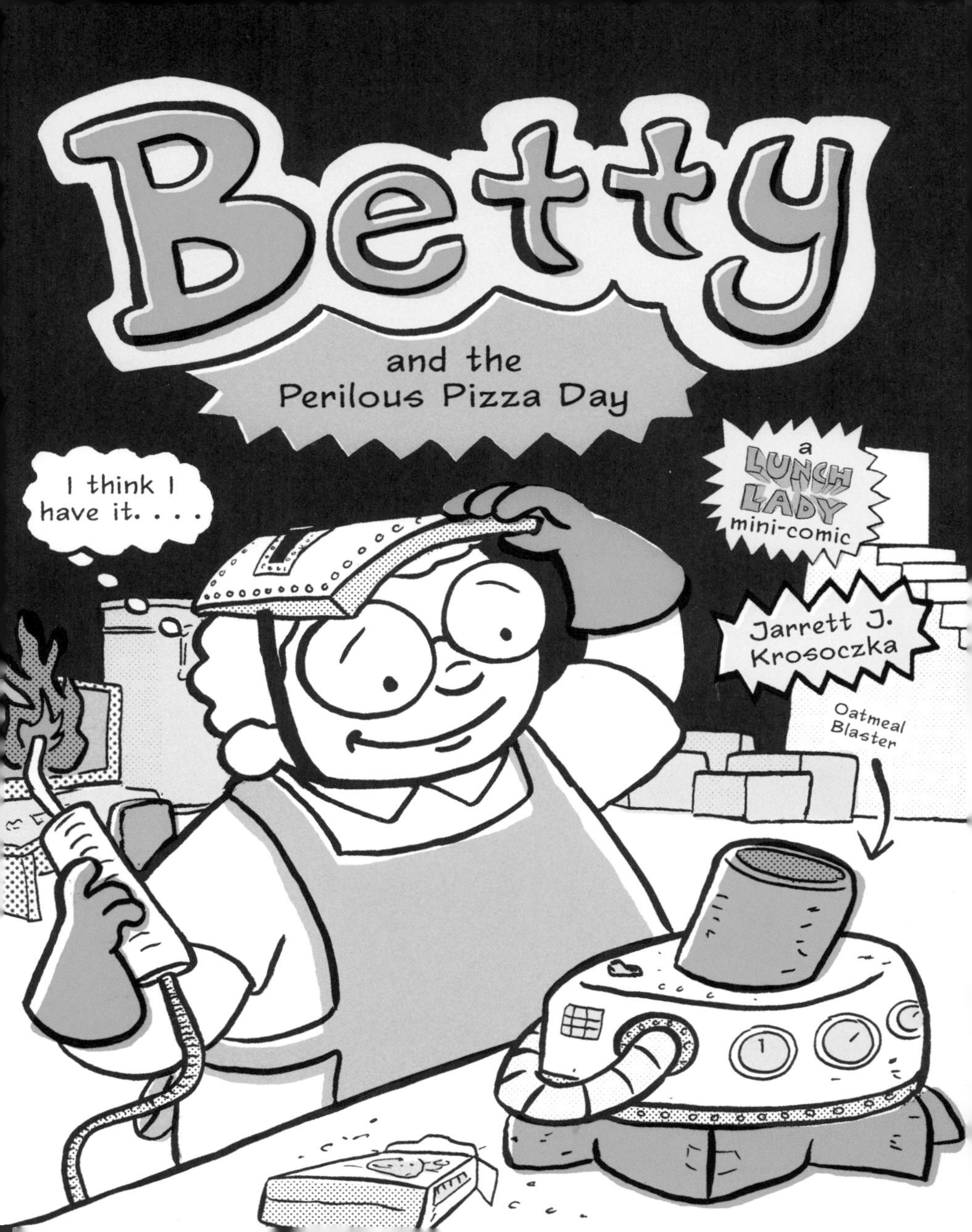
Betty
and the
Perilous Pizza Day
I think I
have it. . . .
a
LUNCH
LADY
mini-comic
Jarrett J.
Krosoczka
Oatmeal
Blaster

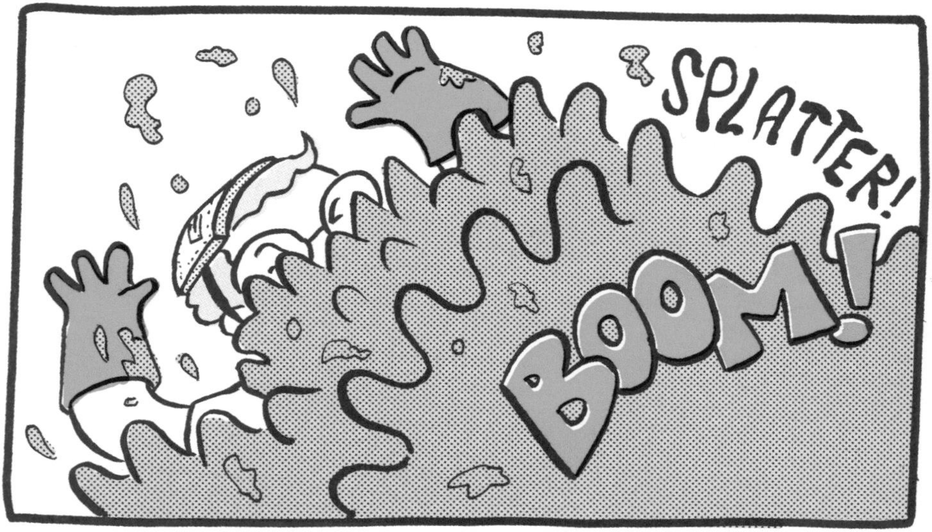
SPLATTER!
BOOM!

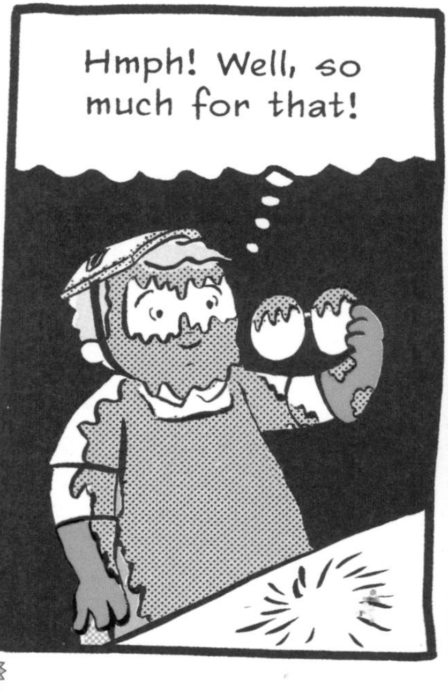
Hmph! Well, so much for that!

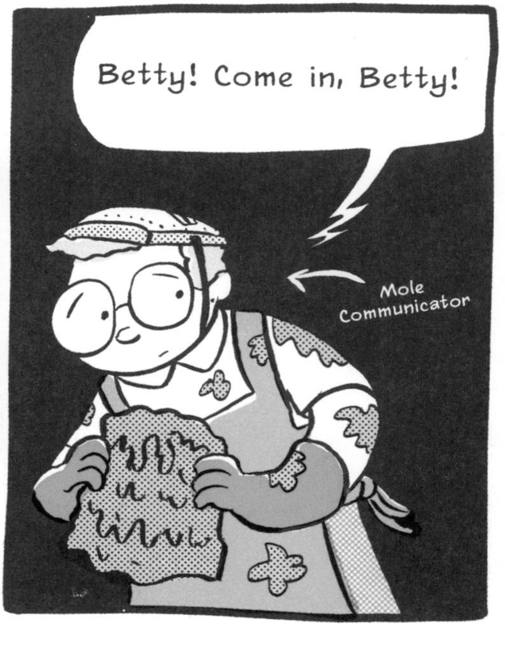
Betty! Come in, Betty!
Mole Communicator

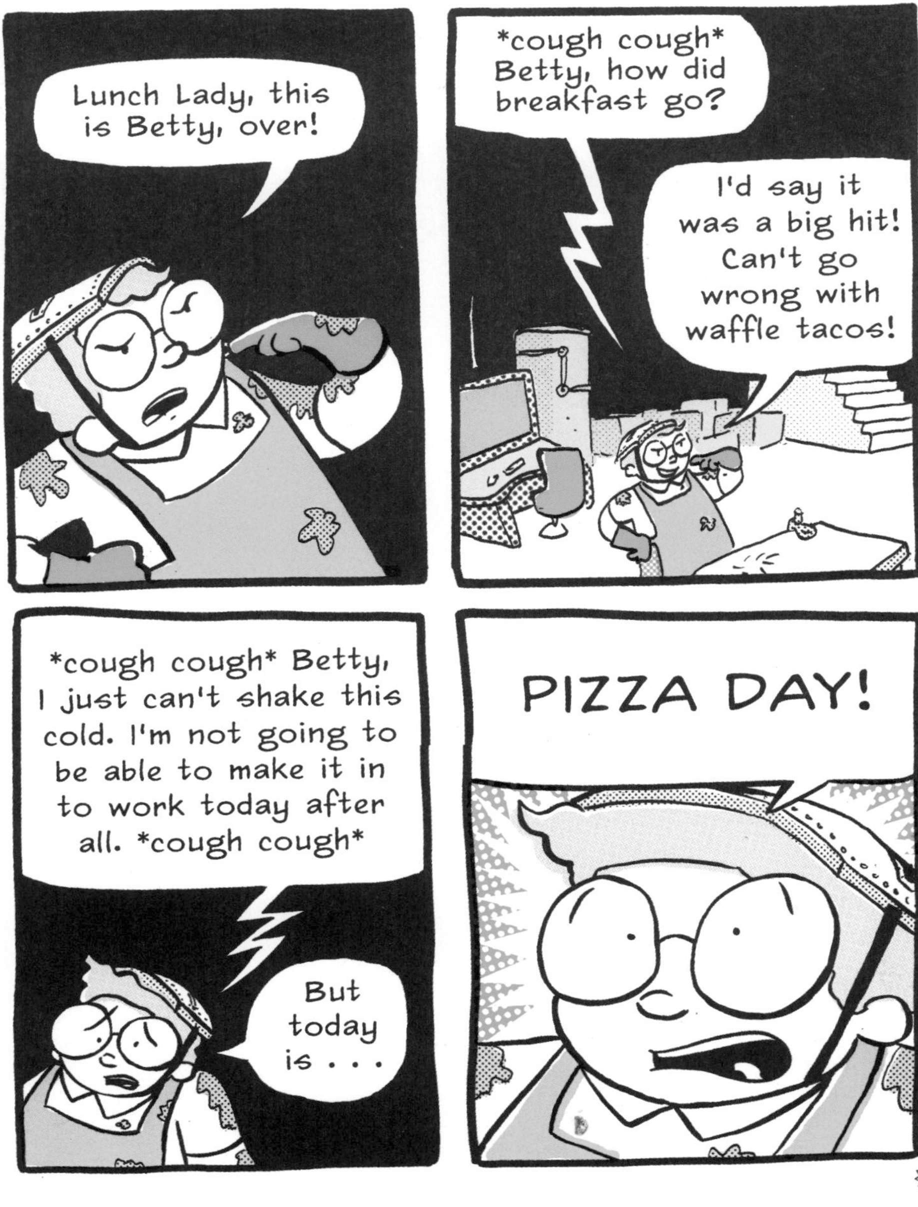
Lunch Lady, this is Betty, over!
cough cough Betty, how did breakfast go?
I'd say it was a big hit! Can't go wrong with waffle tacos!
cough cough Betty, I just can't shake this cold. I'm not going to be able to make it in to work today after all. *cough cough*
But today is . . .
PIZZA DAY!

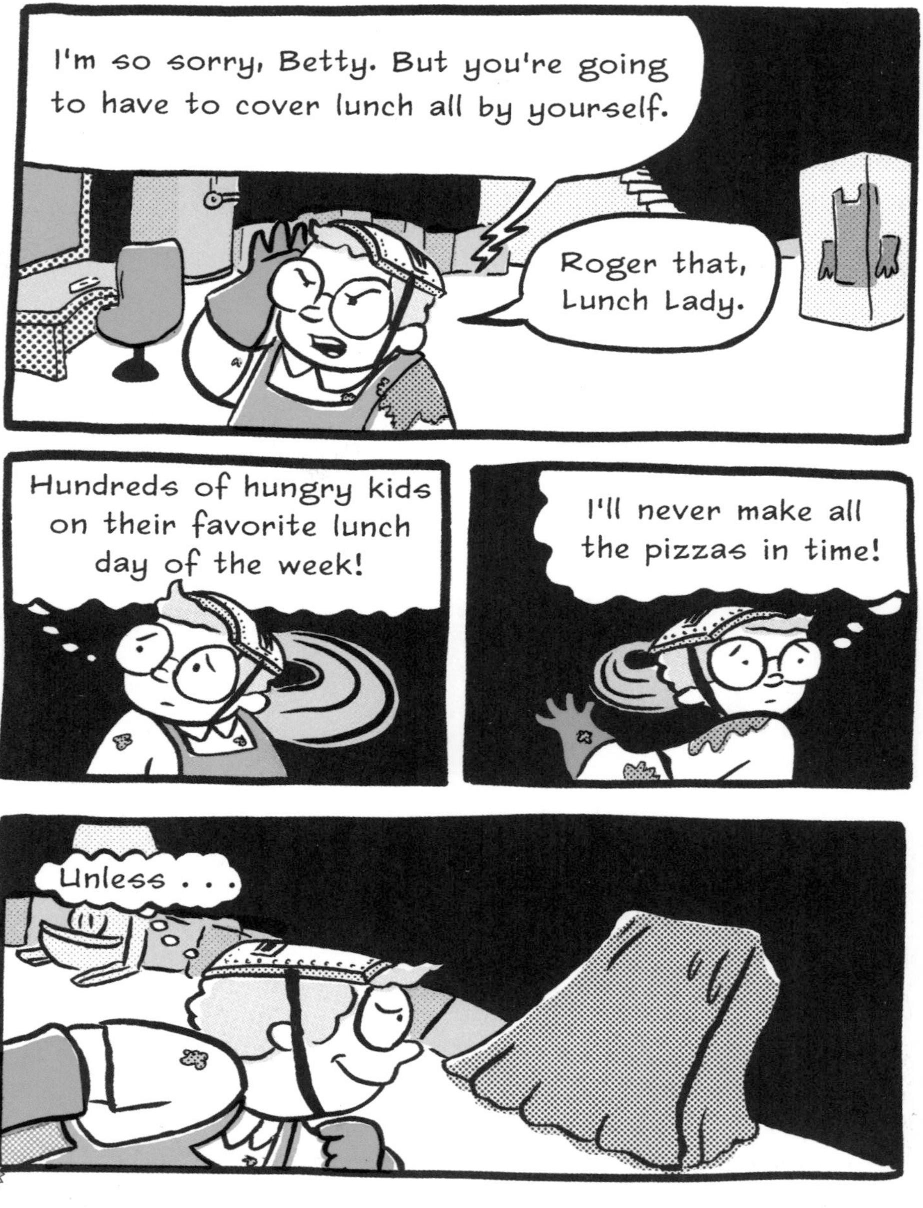
I'm so sorry, Betty. But you're going to have to cover lunch all by yourself.
Roger that, Lunch Lady.
Hundreds of hungry kids on their favorite lunch day of the week!
I'll never make all the pizzas in time!
Unless . . .

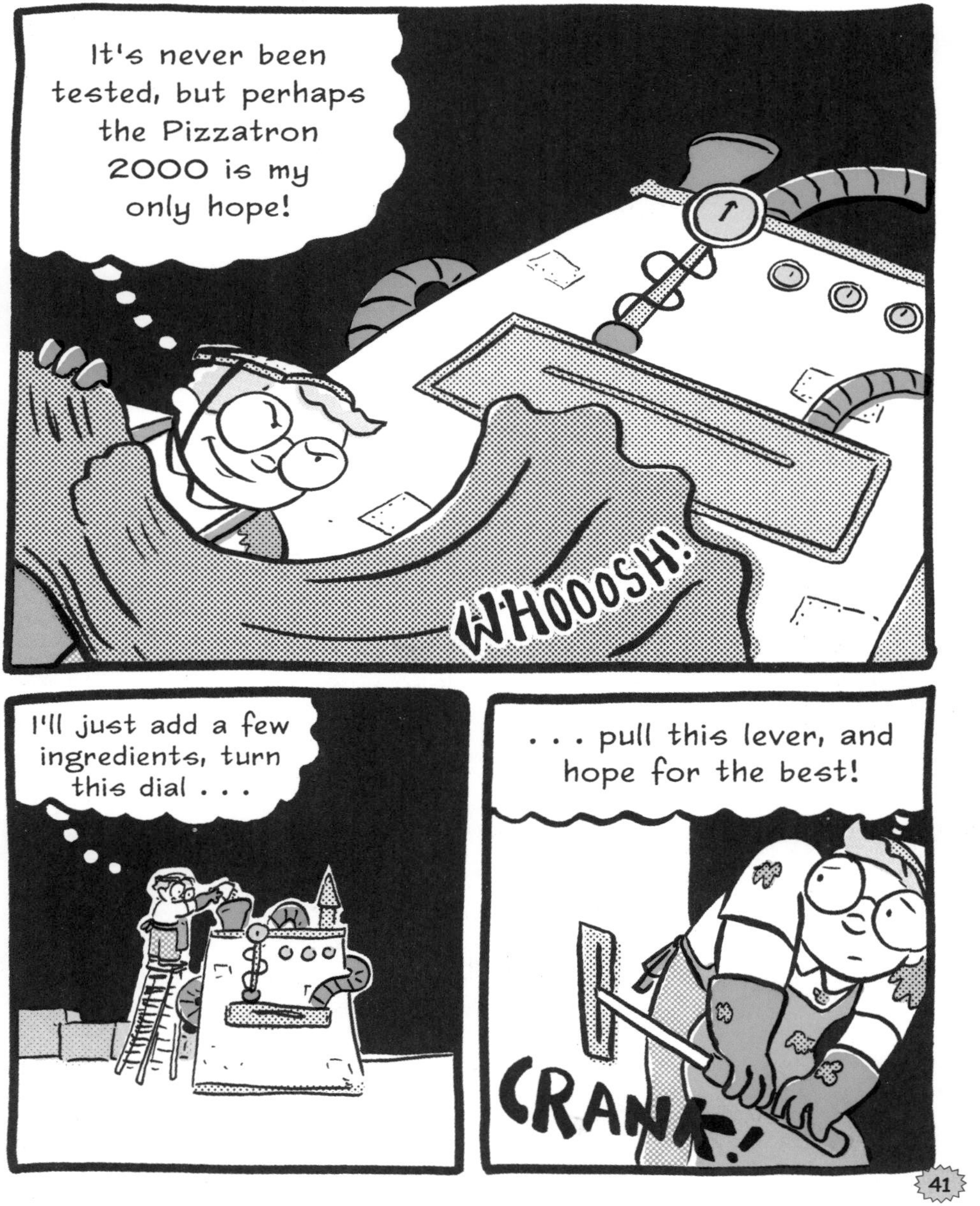
It's never been tested, but perhaps the Pizzatron 2000 is my only hope!
WHOOOSH!
I'll just add a few ingredients, turn this dial . . .
. . . pull this lever, and hope for the best!
CRANK!

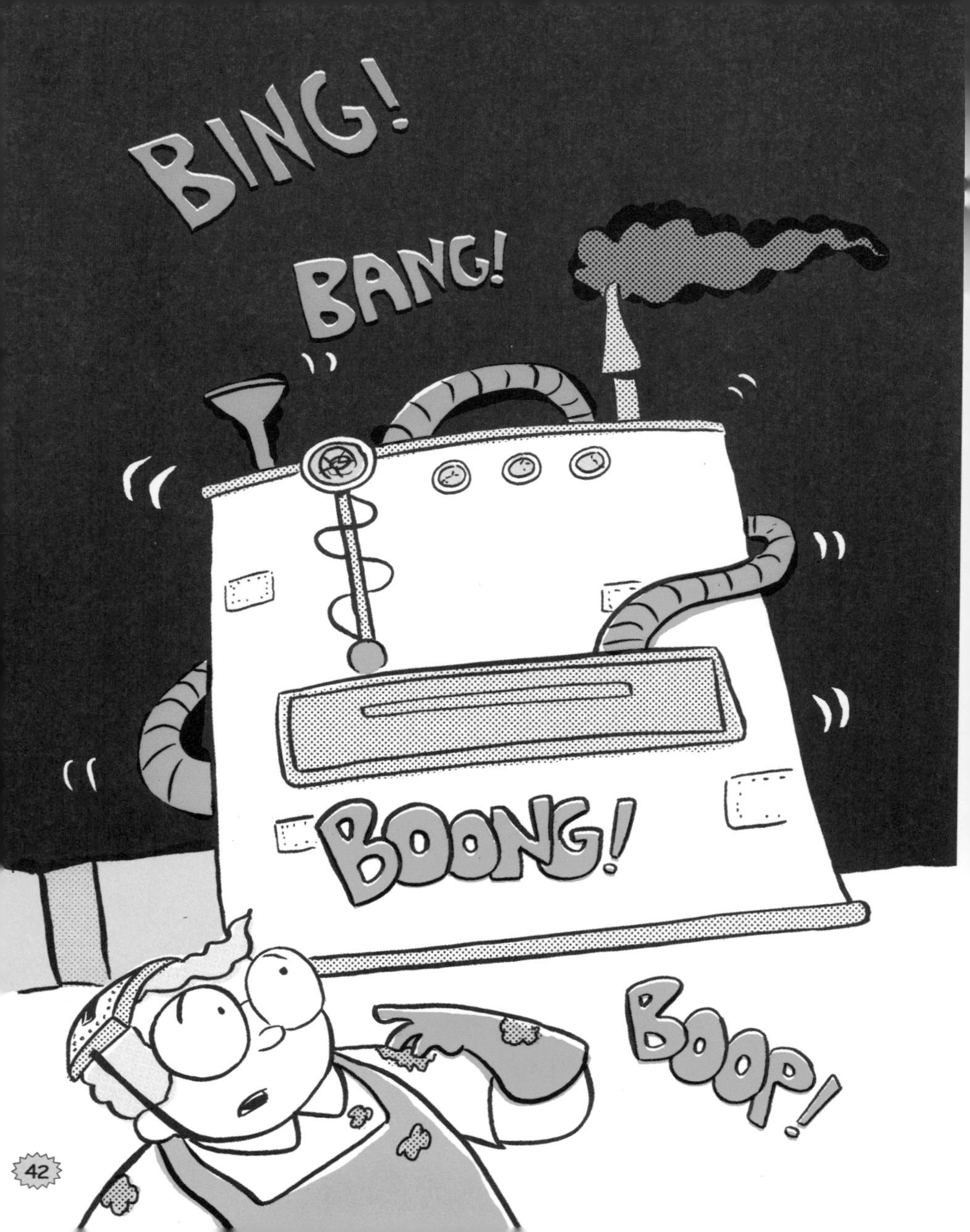
BING!
BANG!
BOONG!
BOOP!

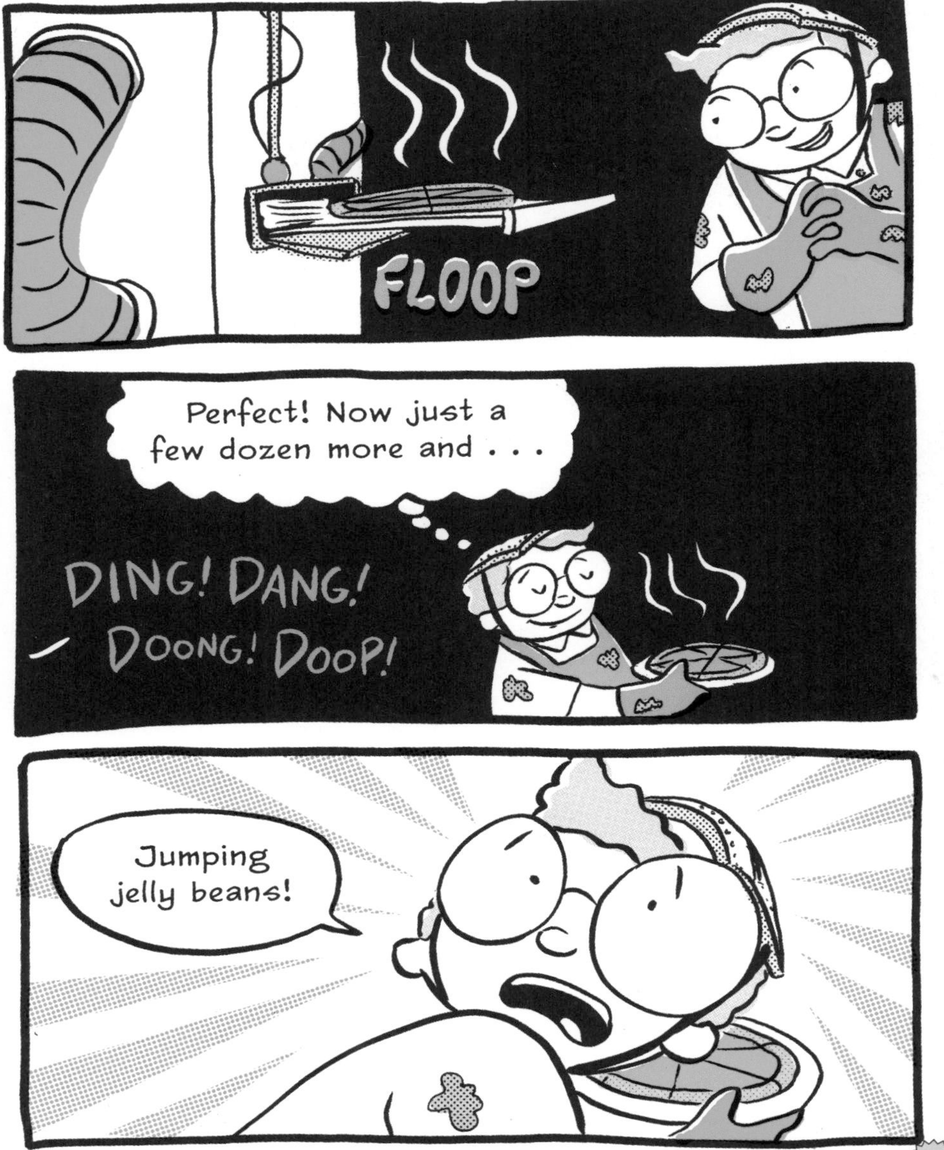
FLOOP
Perfect! Now just a few dozen more and . . .
DING! DANG! DOONG! DOOP!
Jumping jelly beans!

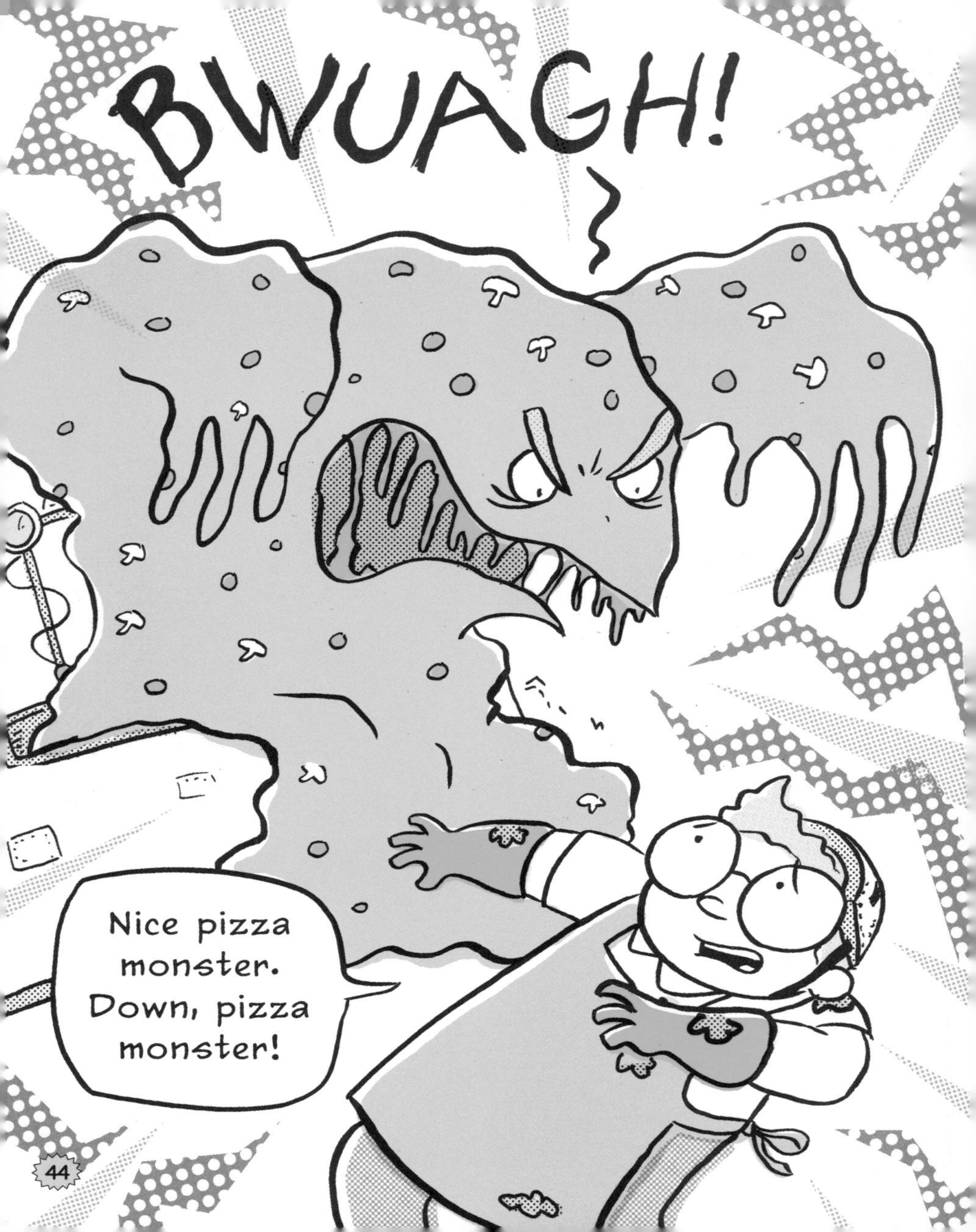
BWUAGH!
Nice pizza monster. Down, pizza monster!

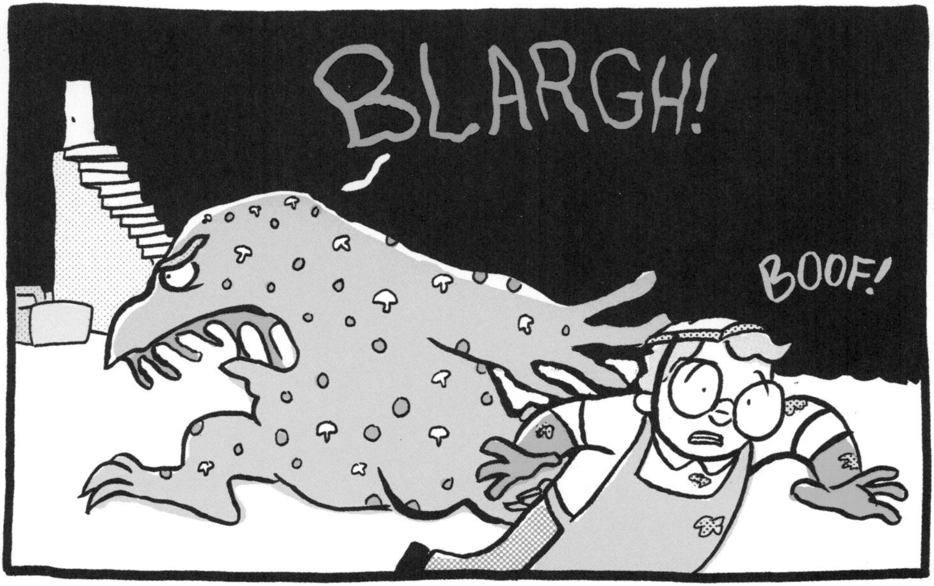
BLARGH!
BOOF!

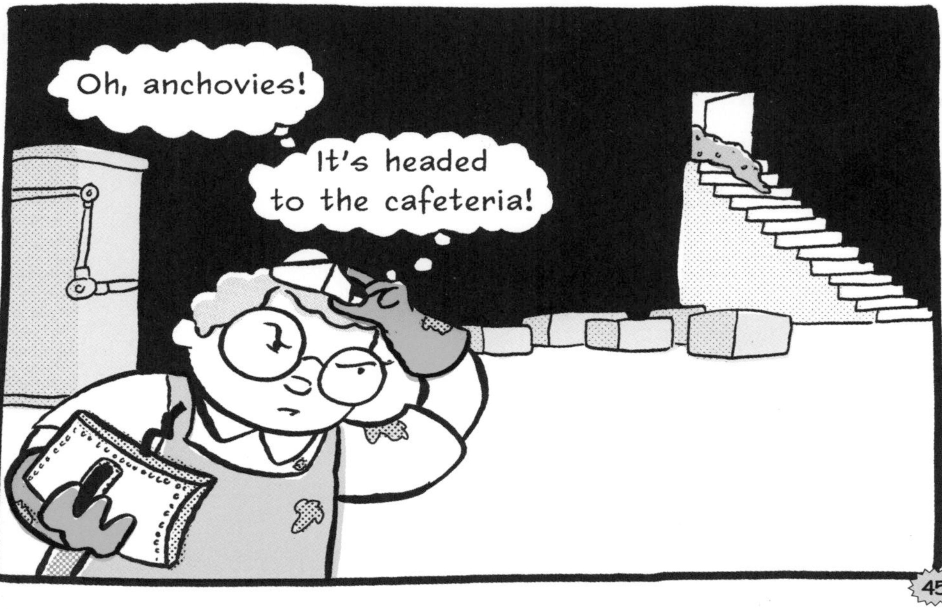
Oh, anchovies!
It's headed to the cafeteria!

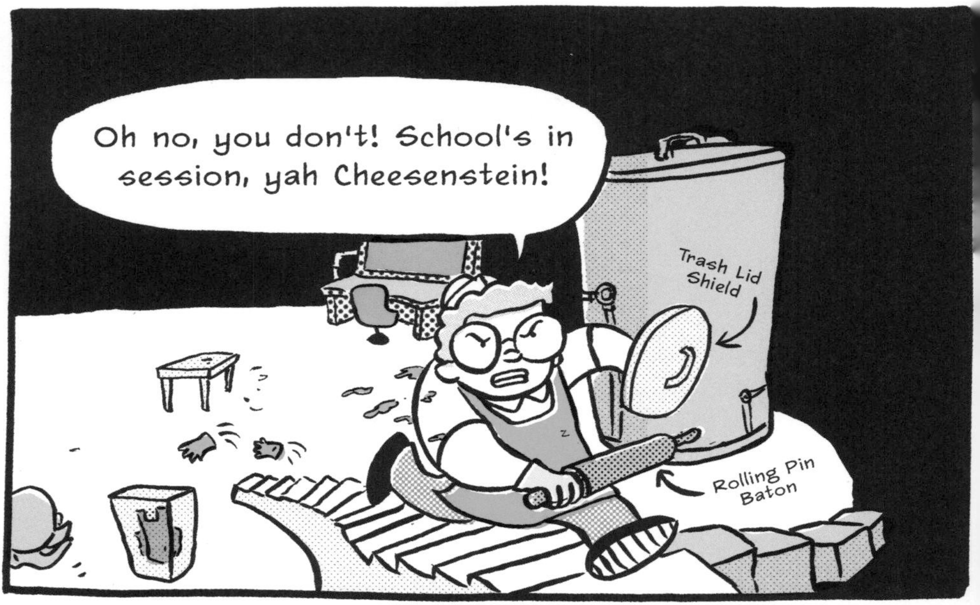
Oh no, you don't! School's in session, yah Cheesenstein!
Trash Lid Shield
Rolling Pin Baton

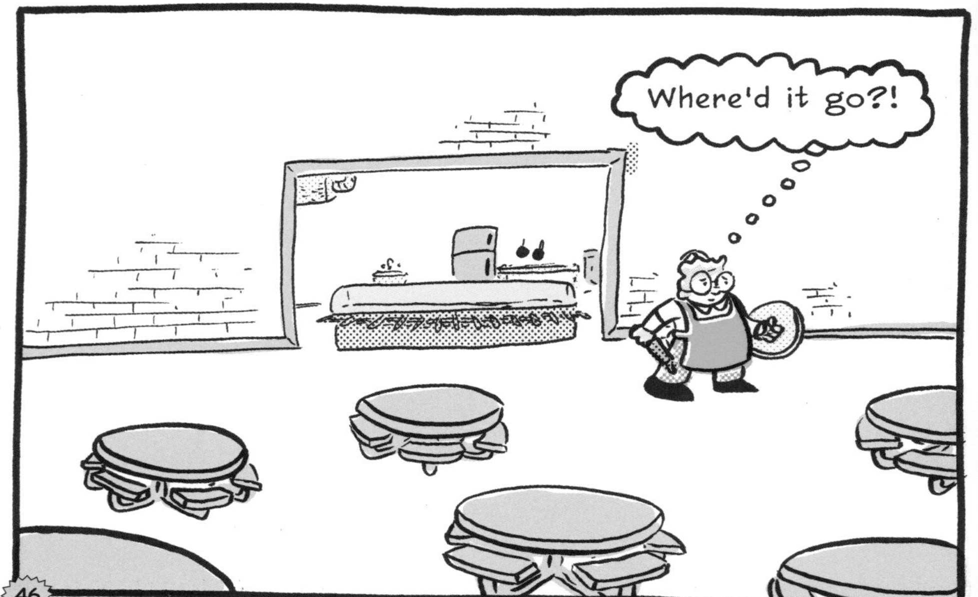
Where'd it go?!

47

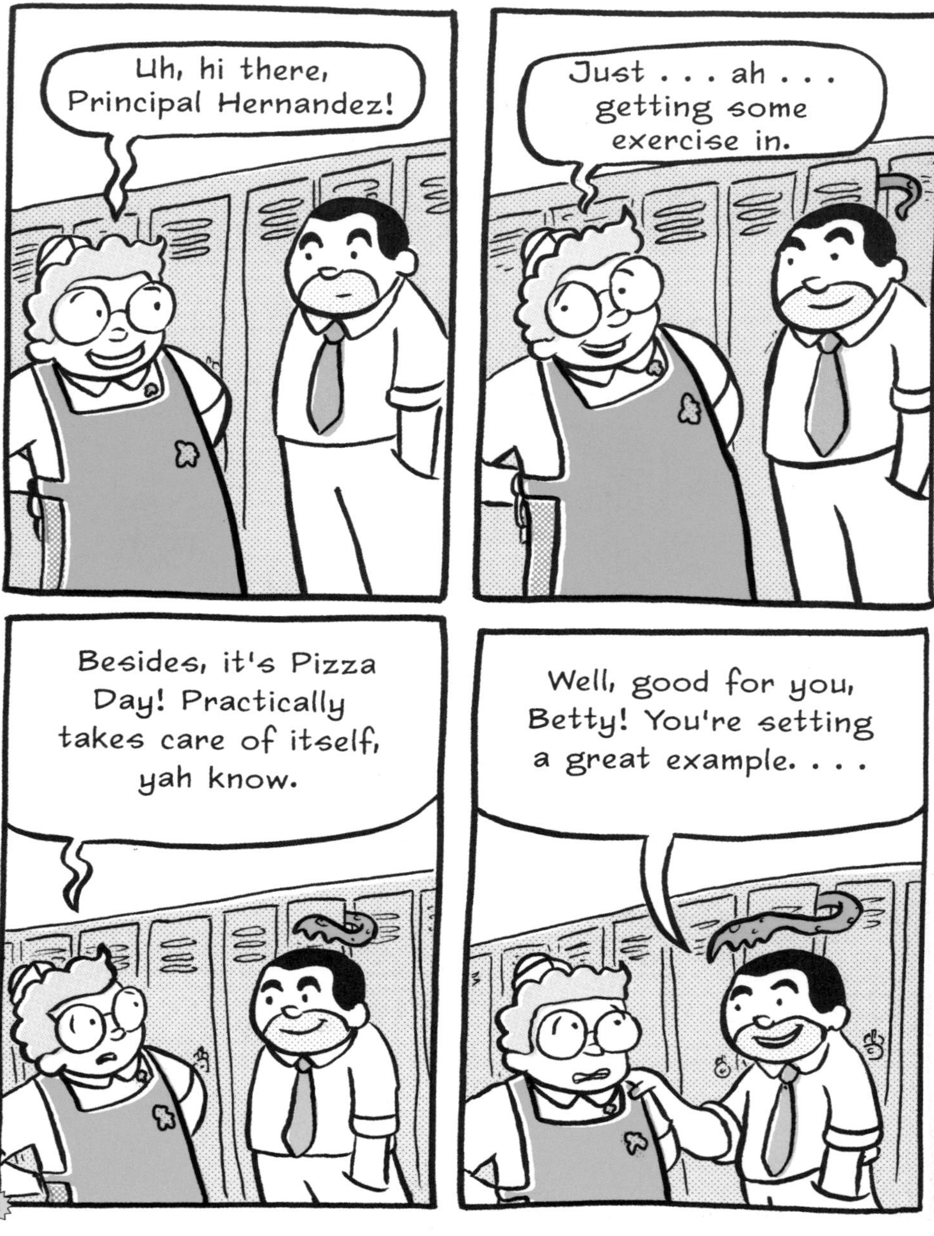
Uh, hi there, Principal Hernandez!
Just . . . ah . . . getting some exercise in.
Besides, it's Pizza Day! Practically takes care of itself, yah know.
Well, good for you, Betty! You're setting a great example. . . .

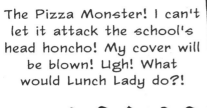
The Pizza Monster! I can't let it attack the school's head honcho! My cover will be blown! Ugh! What would Lunch Lady do?!

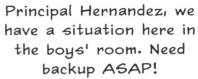
Principal Hernandez, we have a situation here in the boys' room. Need backup ASAP!

Please don't tell me it's Milmoe again. I'll be right there!

Come on out and play, buddy!

CLANK!

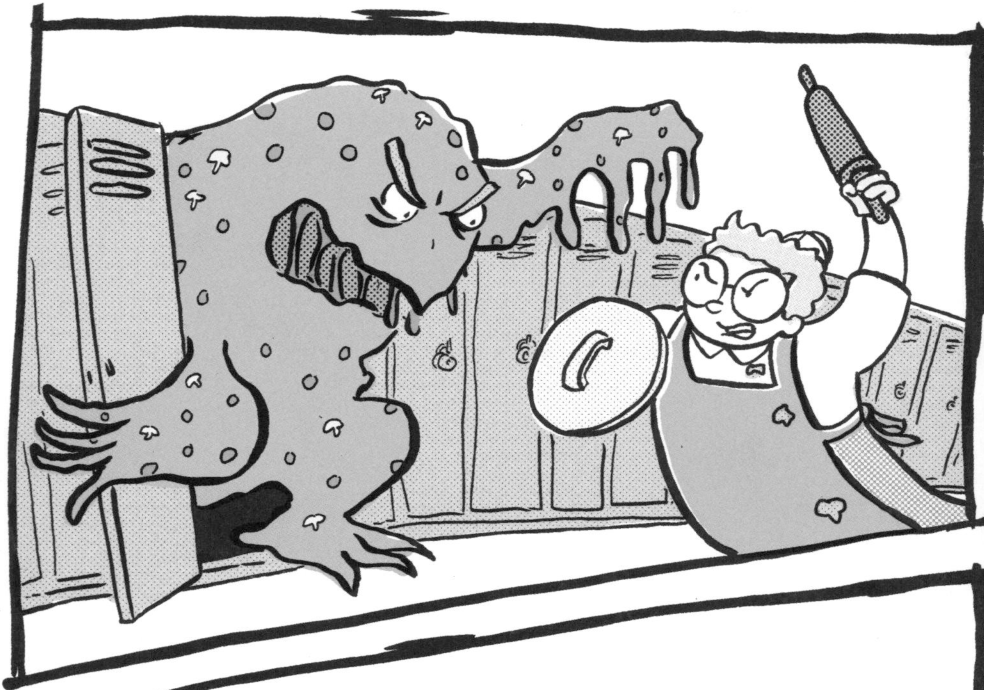

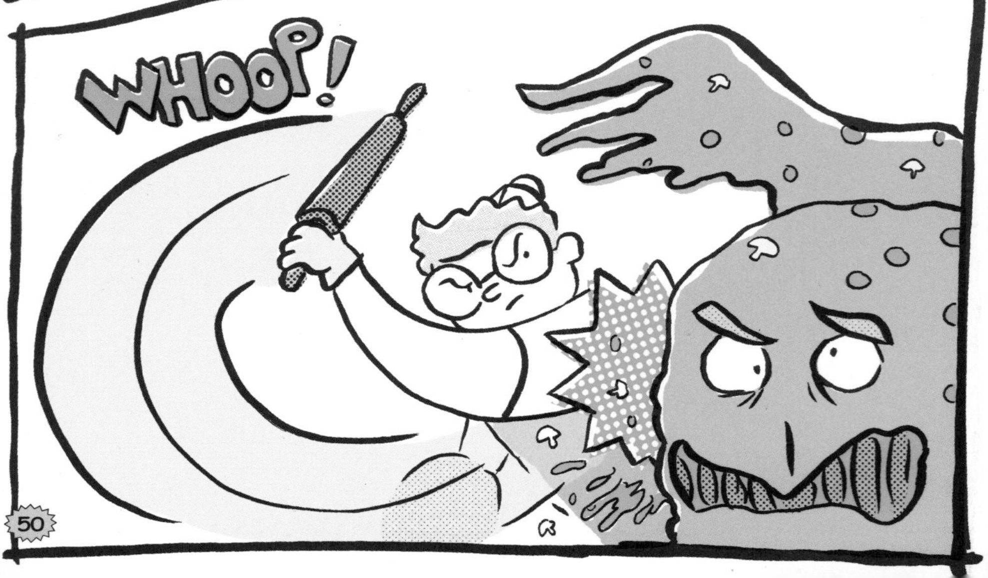
WHOOP!

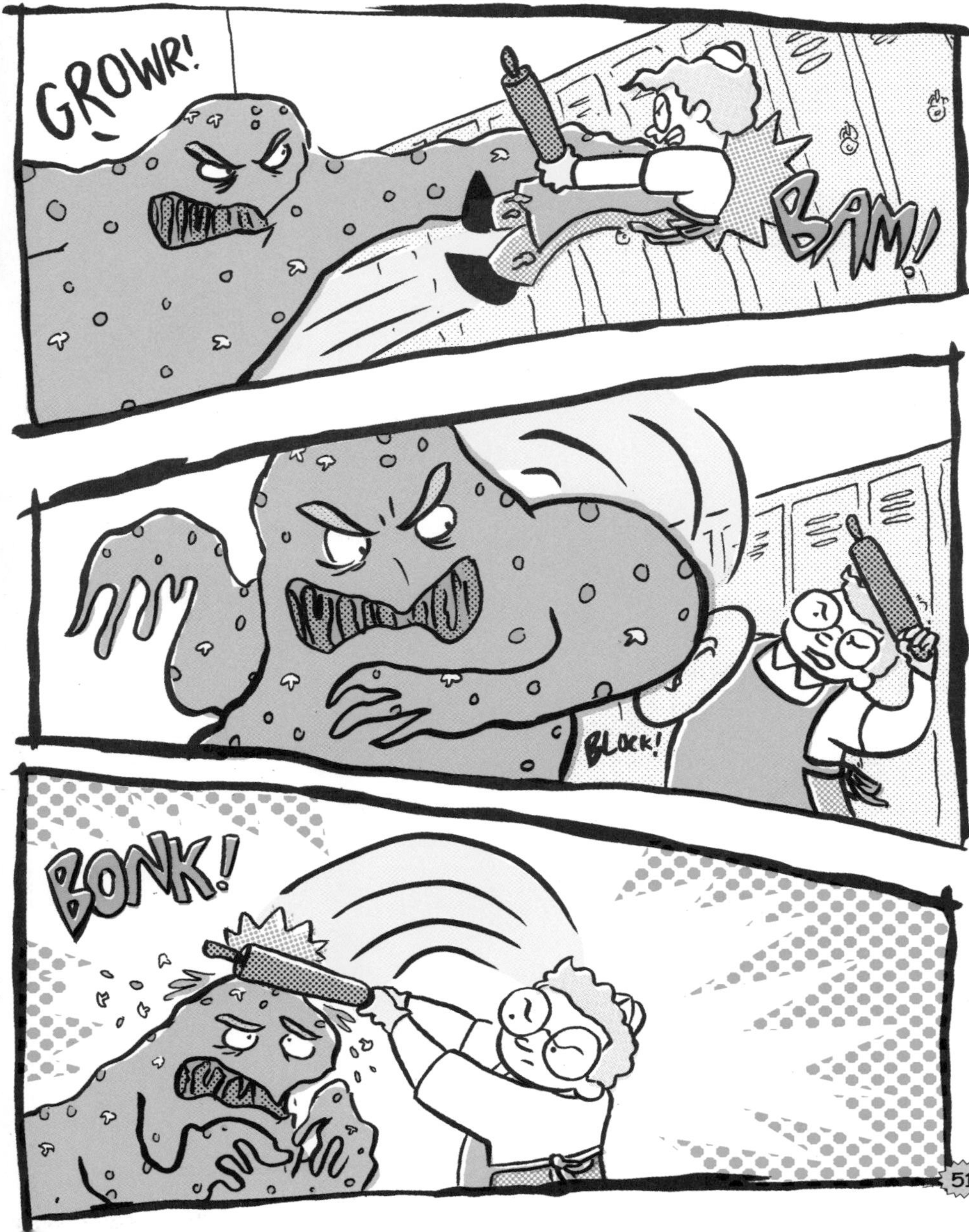
GROWR!
BAM!
BLOCK!
BONK!

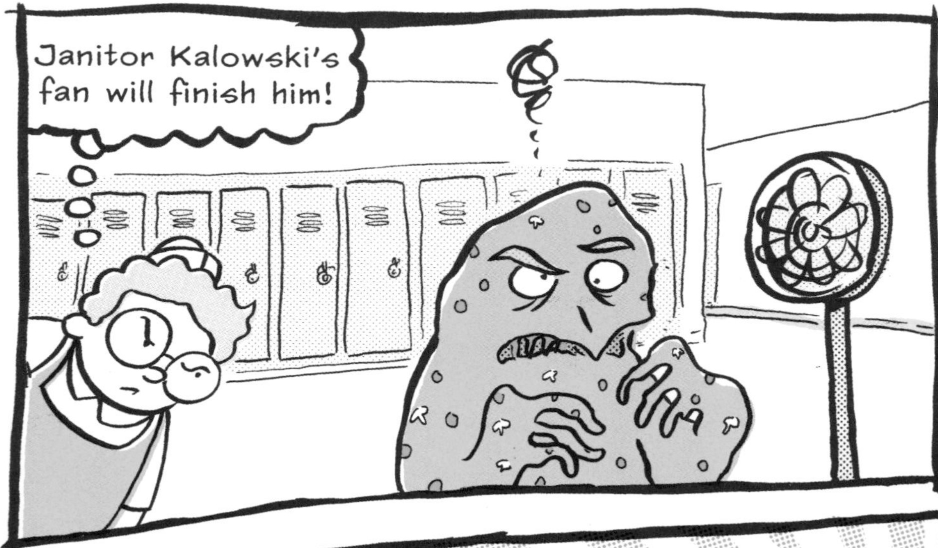
Janitor Kalowski's fan will finish him!

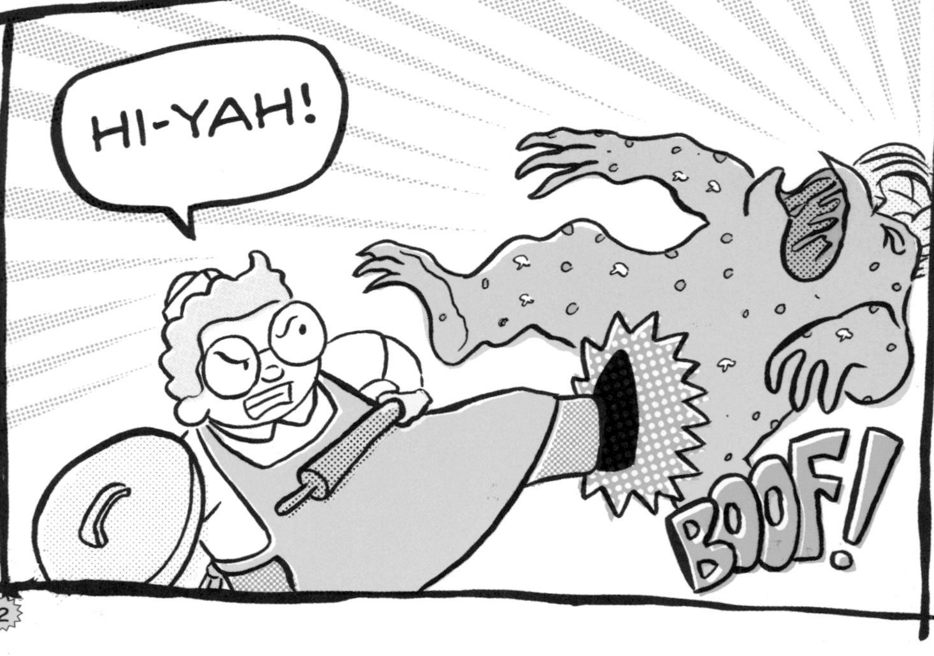
HI-YAH!
BOOF!

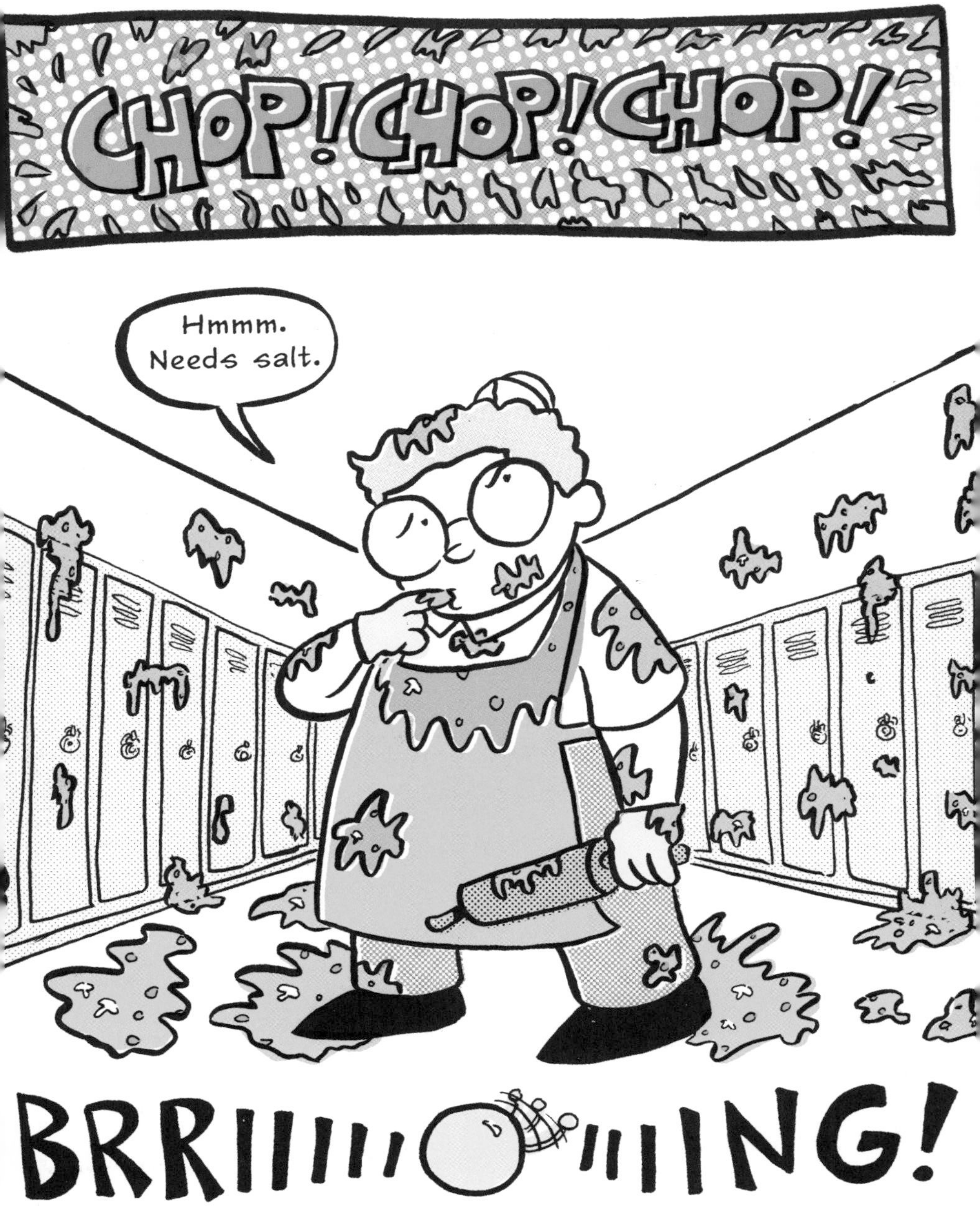
CHOP! CHOP! CHOP!
Hmmm. Needs salt.
BRRIIIIIIIIIIING!

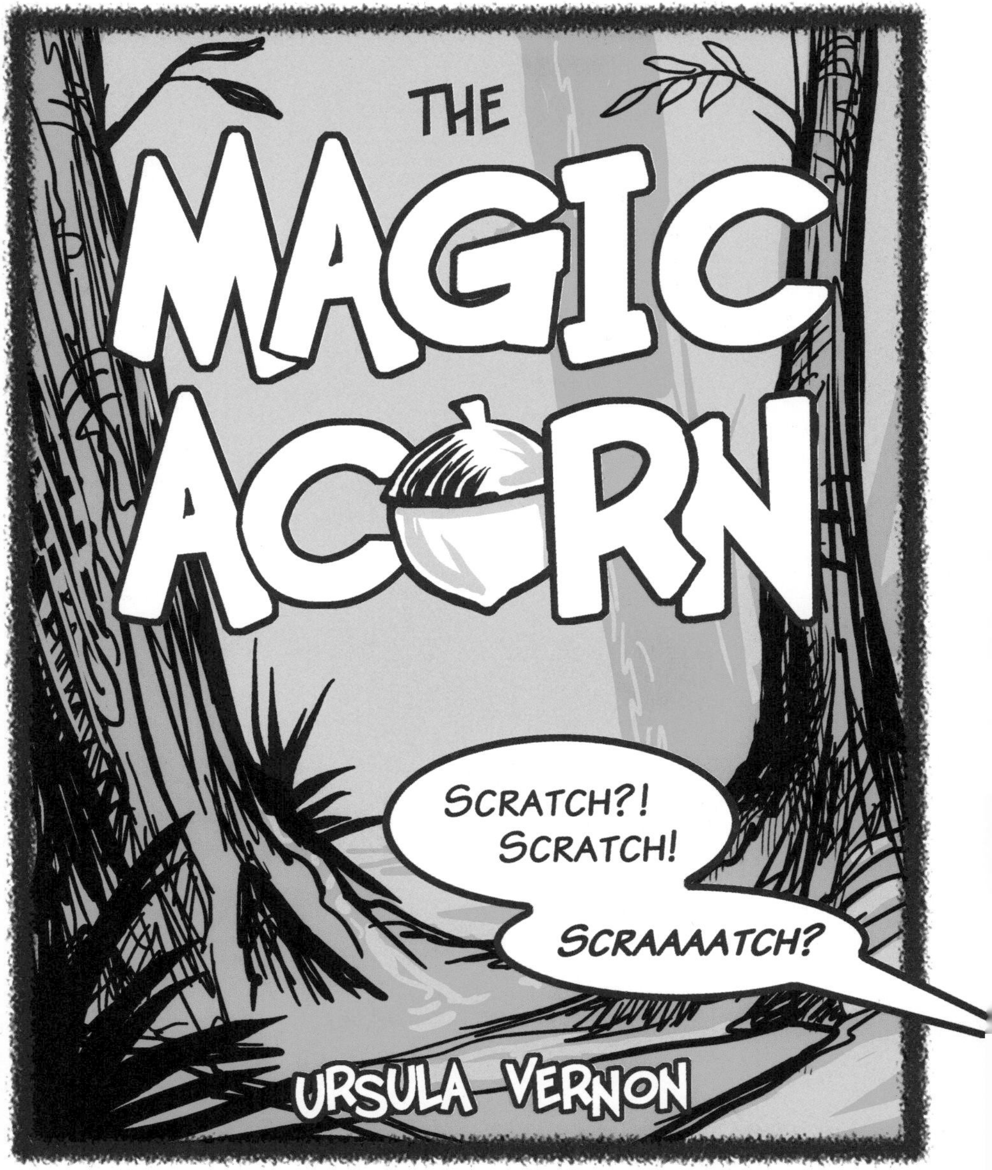
THE MAGIC ACORN
SCRATCH?! SCRATCH!
SCRAAAATCH?
URSULA VERNON

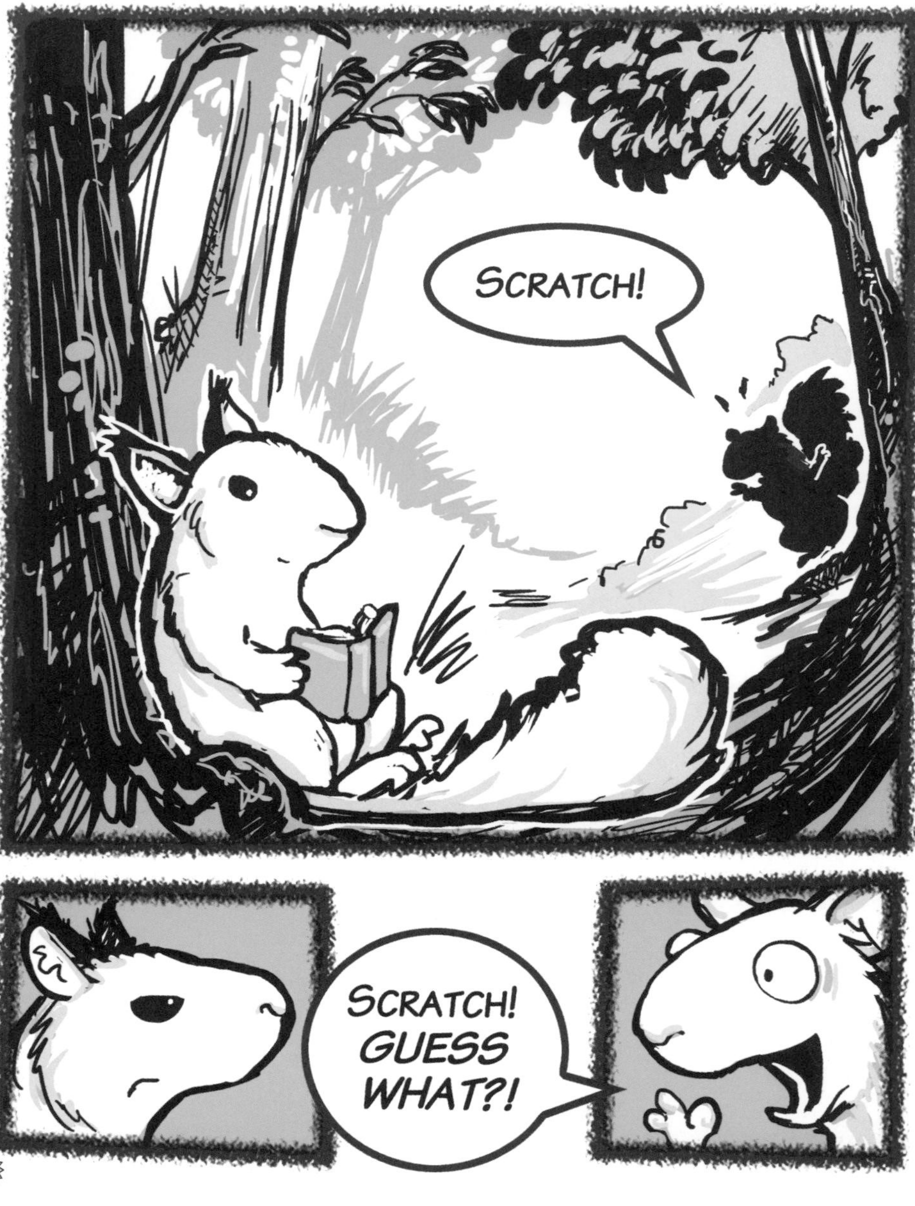
SCRATCH!
SCRATCH! GUESS WHAT?!

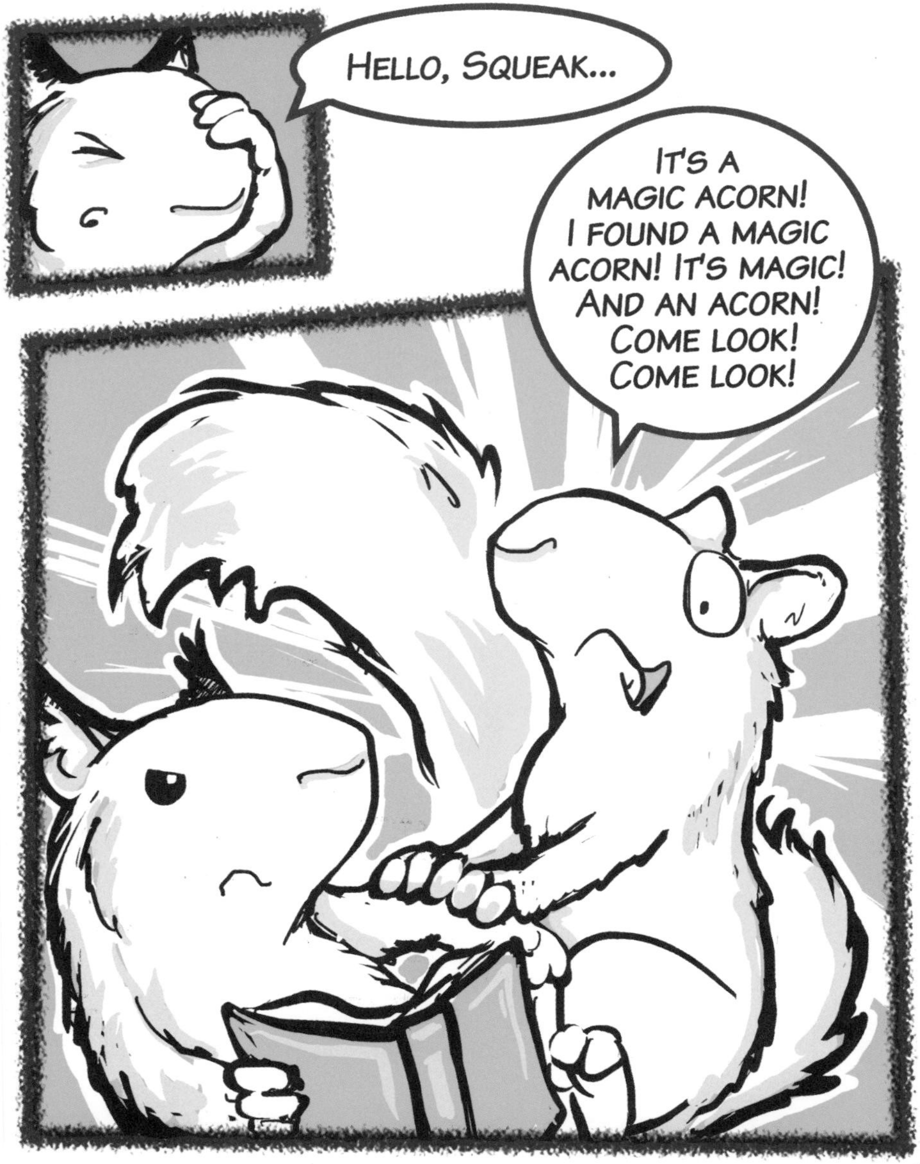
HELLO, SQUEAK...
IT'S A MAGIC ACORN! I FOUND A MAGIC ACORN! IT'S MAGIC! AND AN ACORN! COME LOOK! COME LOOK!

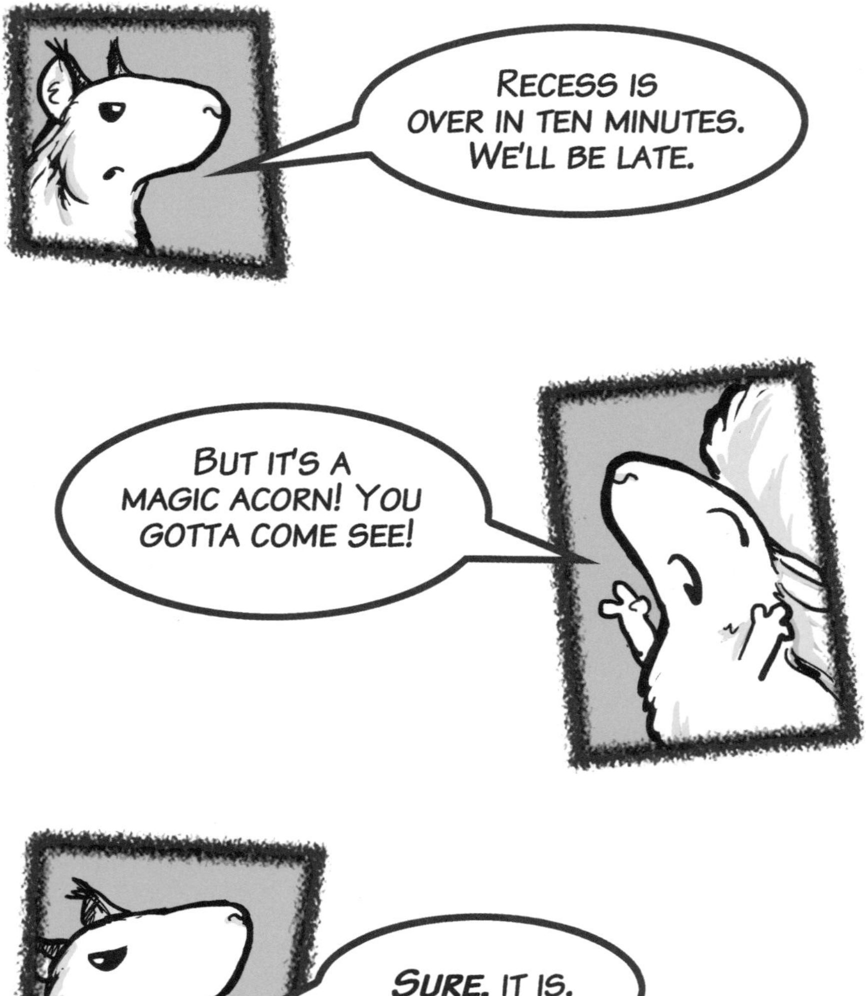
RECESS IS OVER IN TEN MINUTES. WE'LL BE LATE.
BUT IT'S A MAGIC ACORN! YOU GOTTA COME SEE!
SURE, IT IS.

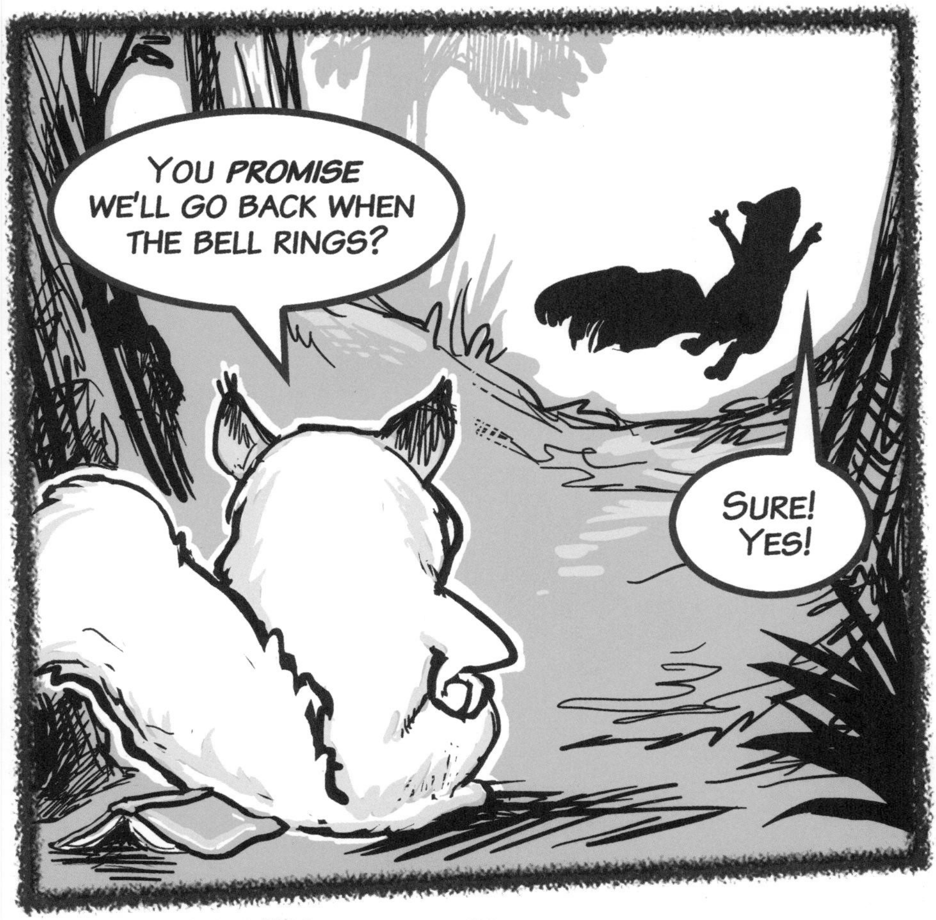
YOU *PROMISE* WE'LL GO BACK WHEN THE BELL RINGS?
SURE! YES!

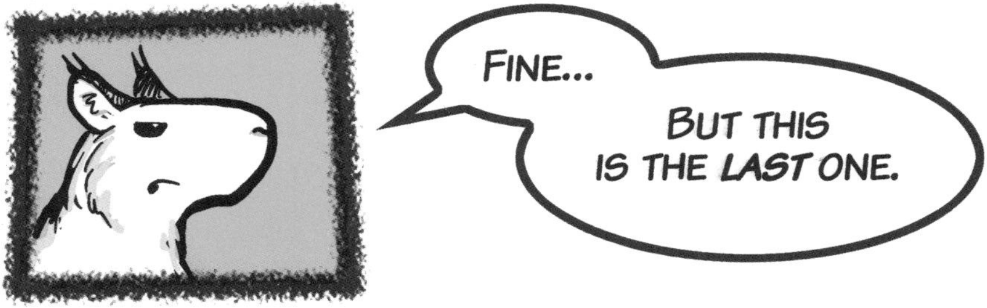
FINE...
BUT THIS IS THE *LAST* ONE.

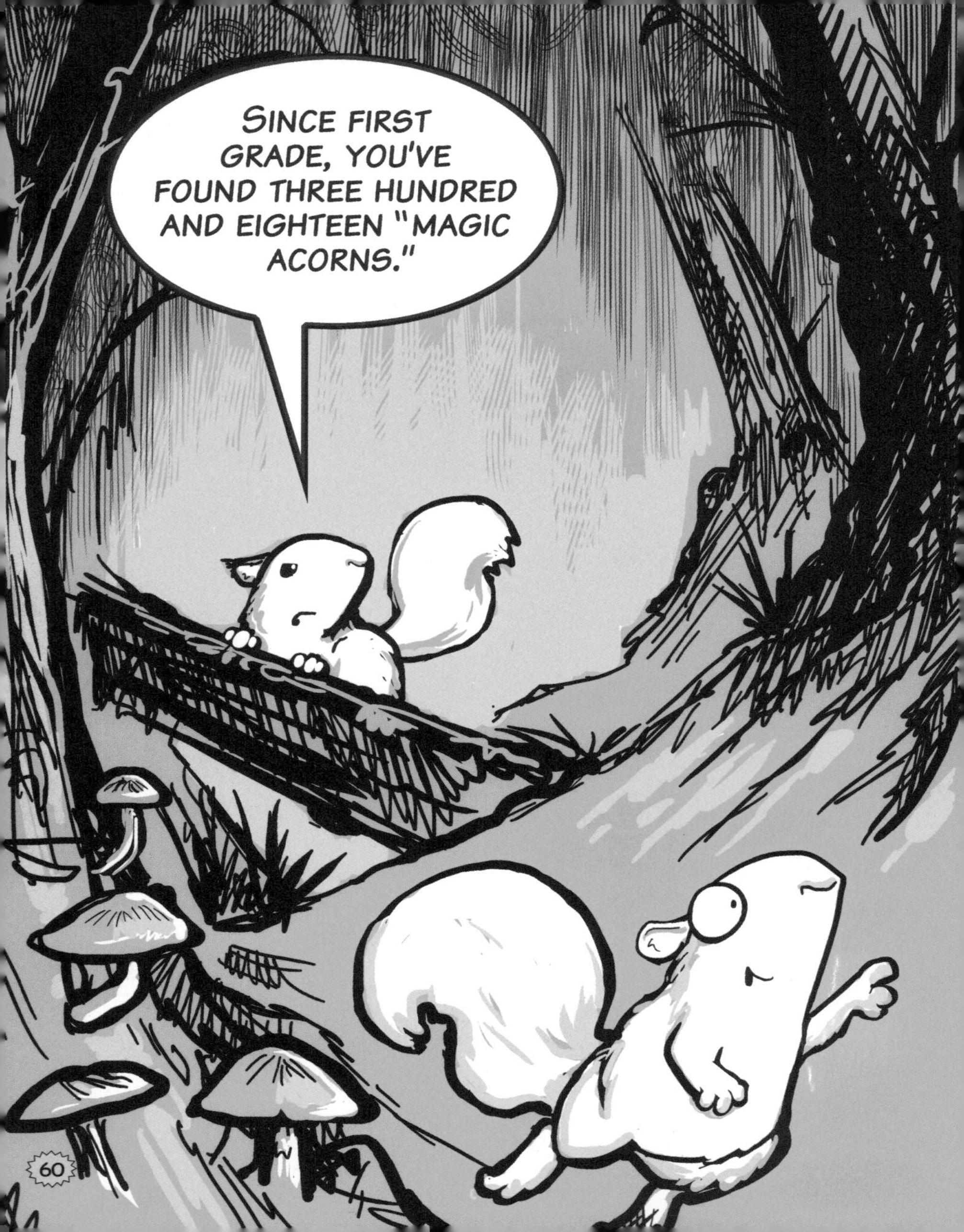
SINCE FIRST GRADE, YOU'VE FOUND THREE HUNDRED AND EIGHTEEN "MAGIC ACORNS."

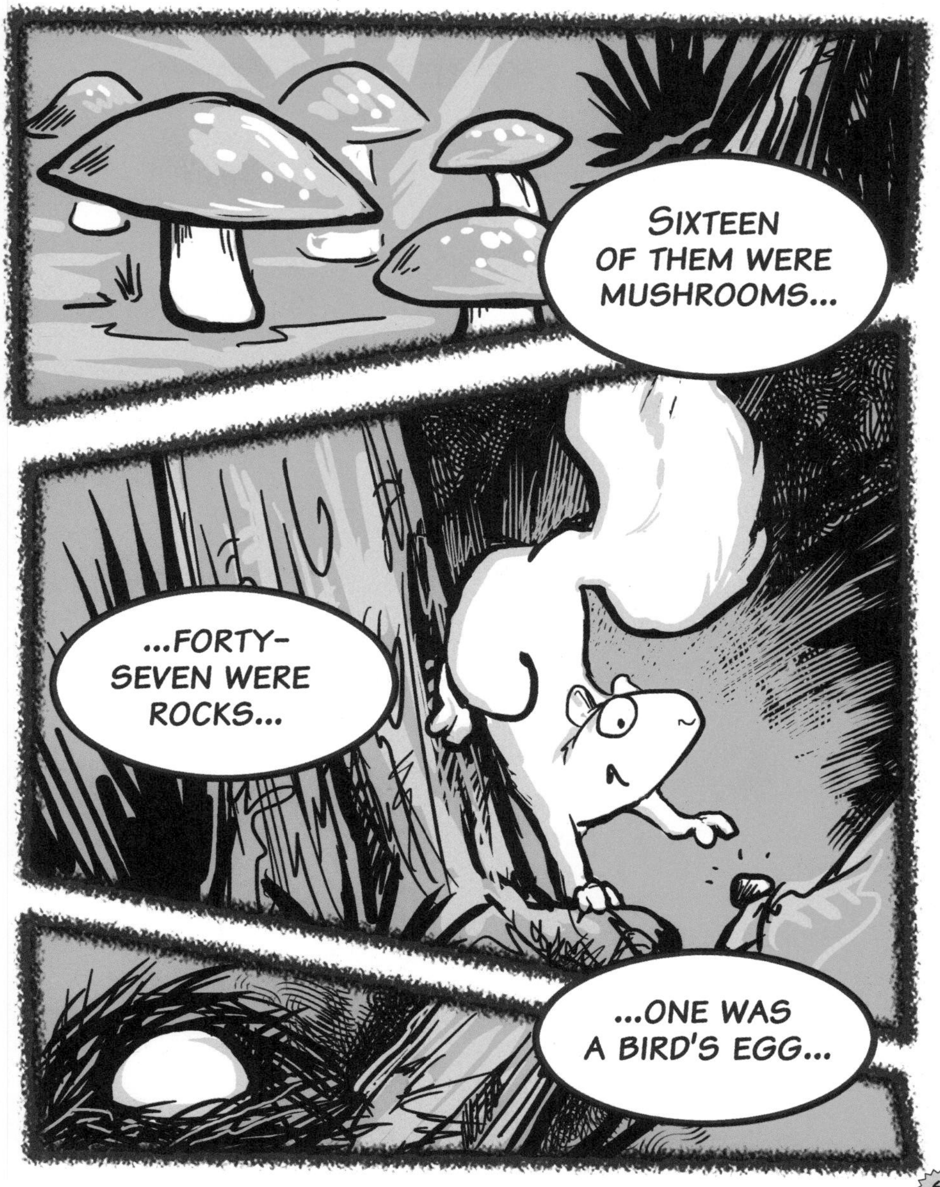
SIXTEEN OF THEM WERE MUSHROOMS...
...FORTY-SEVEN WERE ROCKS...
...ONE WAS A BIRD'S EGG...

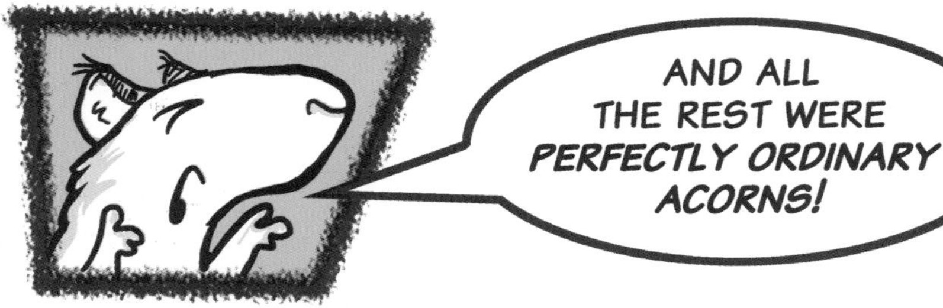
AND ALL THE REST WERE *PERFECTLY ORDINARY* ACORNS!

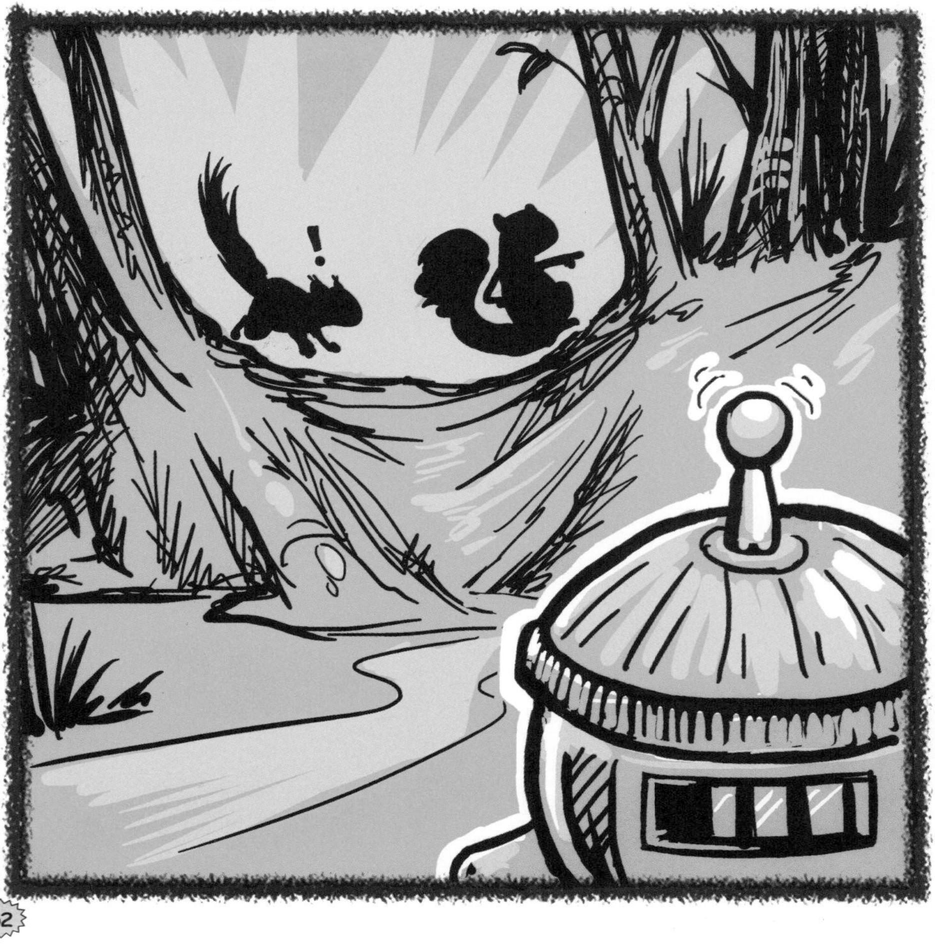
!

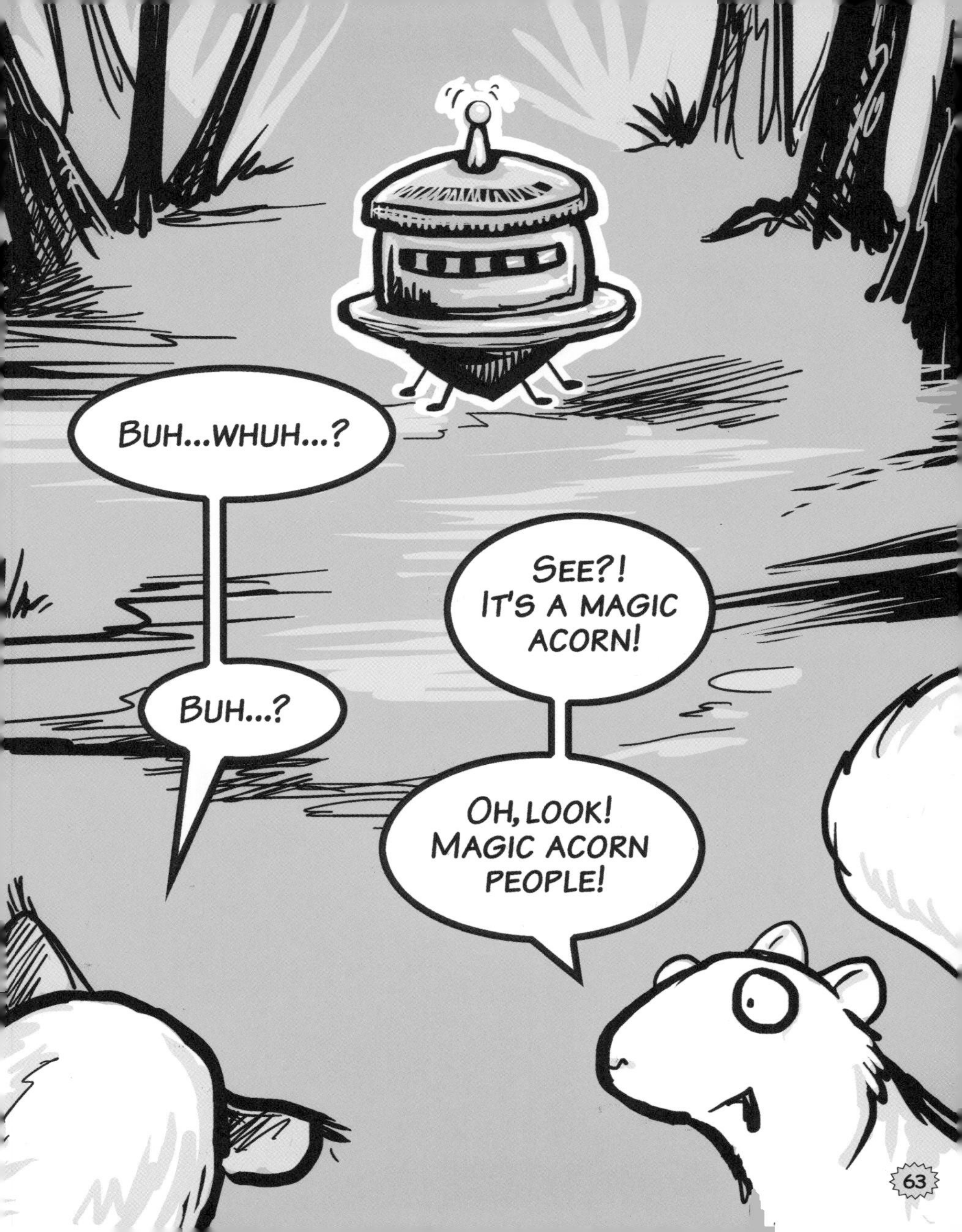
BUH...WHUH...?
BUH...?
SEE?! IT'S A MAGIC ACORN!
OH, LOOK! MAGIC ACORN PEOPLE!

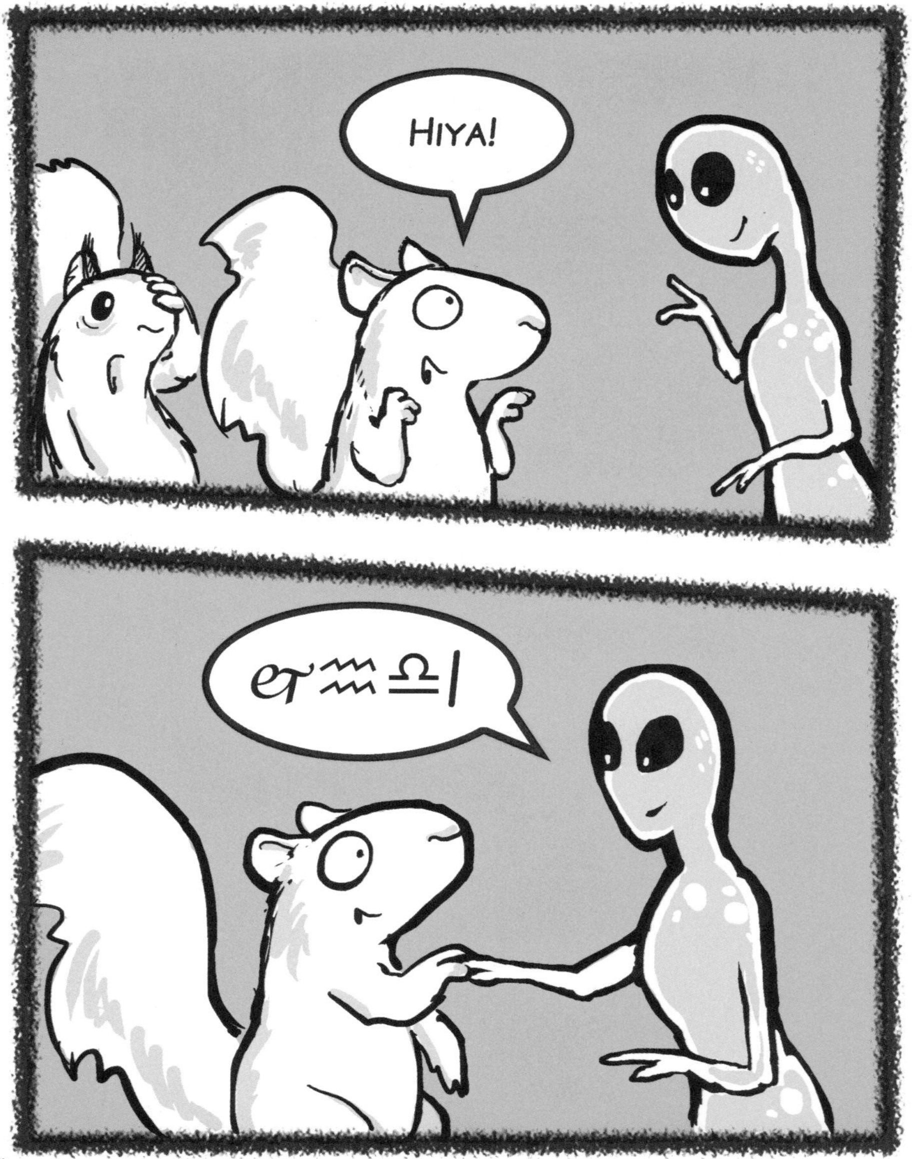
HIYA!

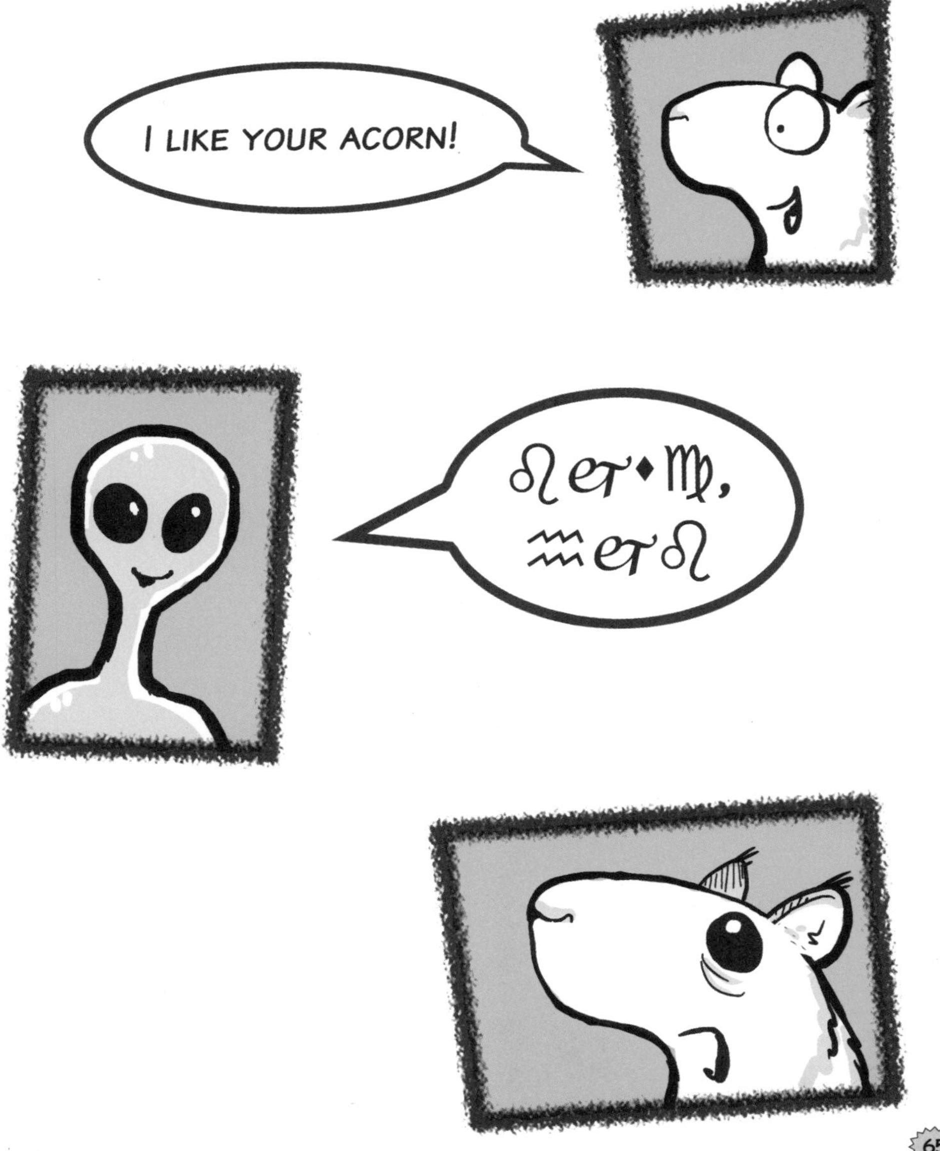
I LIKE YOUR ACORN!

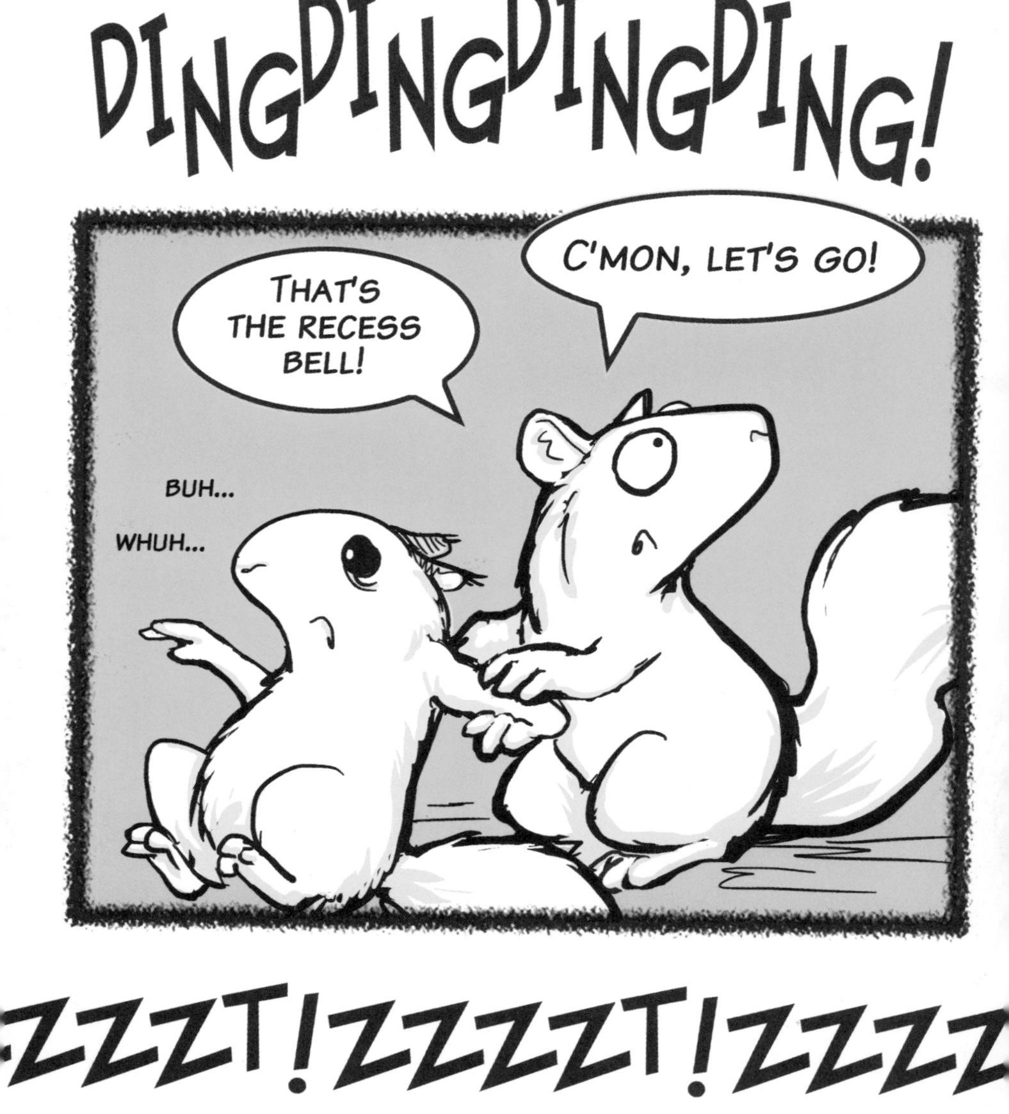
DINGDINGDINGDING!
THAT'S THE RECESS BELL!
C'MON, LET'S GO!
BUH...
WHUH...
ZZZT!ZZZZT!ZZZZ

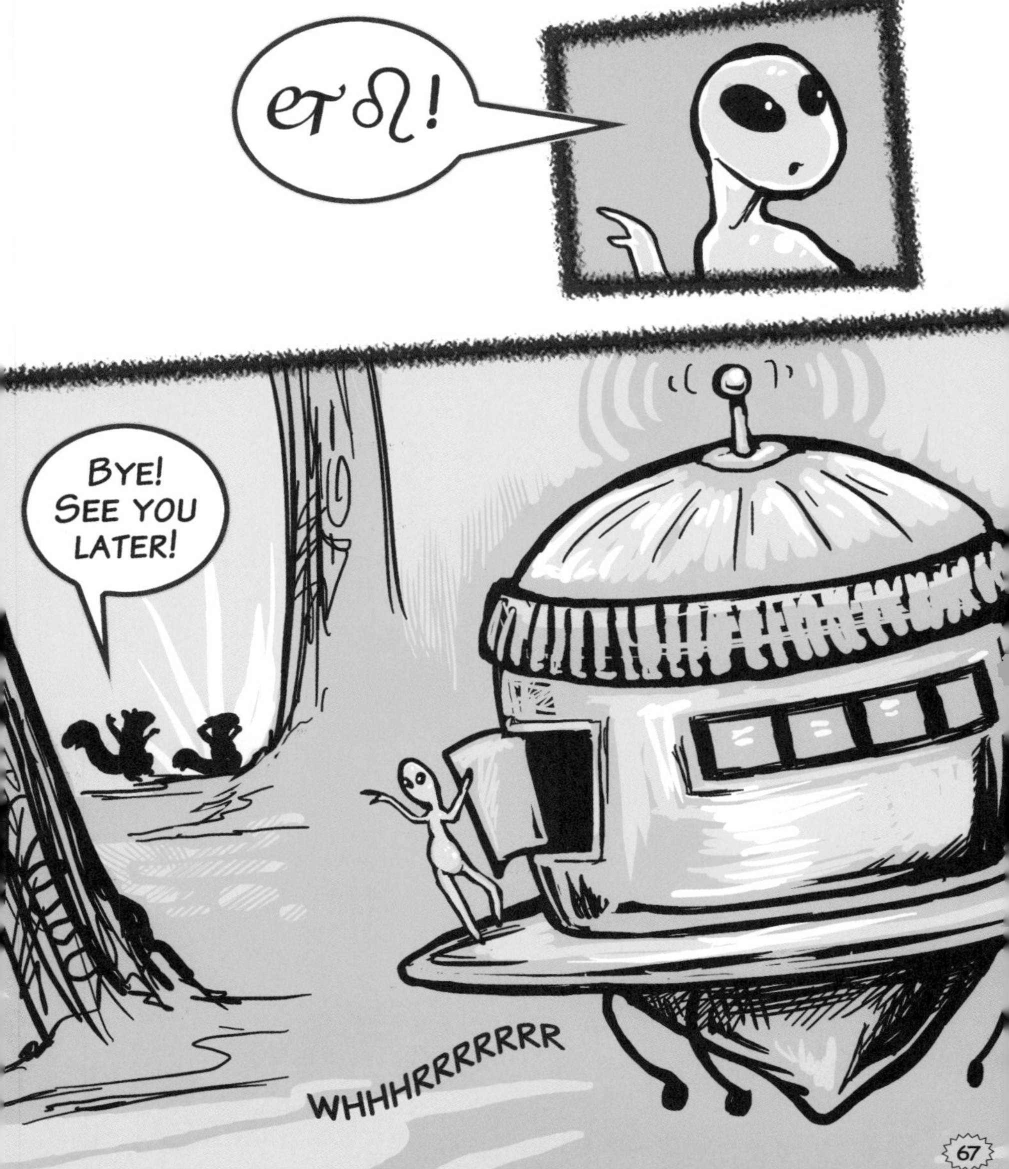
BYE! SEE YOU LATER!
WHHHRRRRRRR

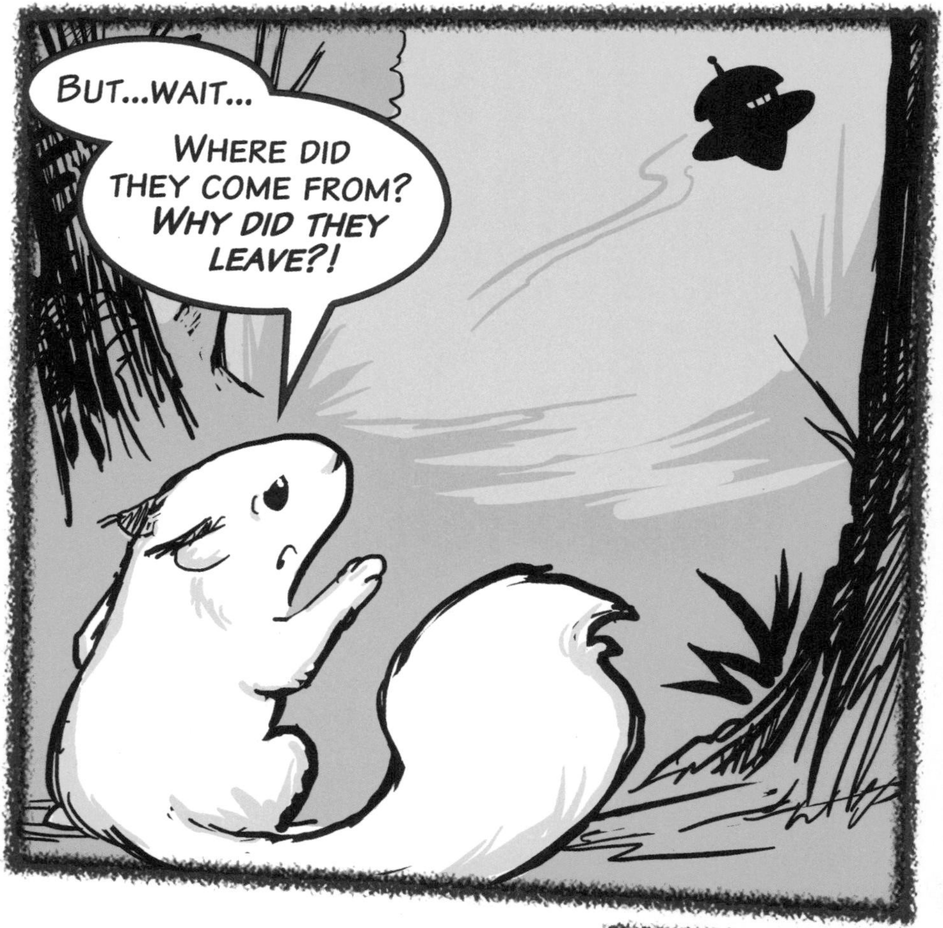
BUT...WAIT...
WHERE DID THEY COME FROM? WHY DID THEY LEAVE?!

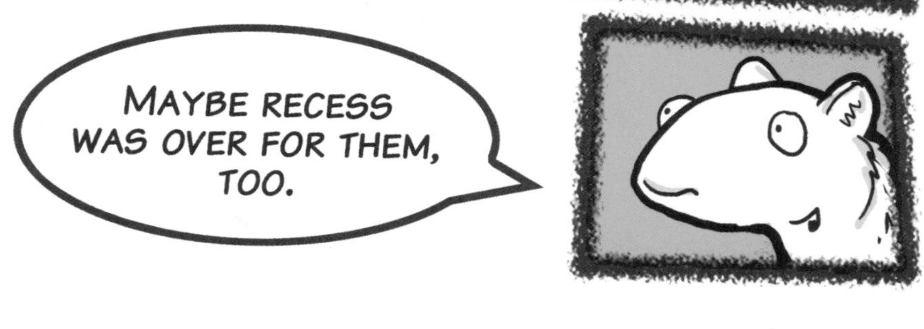
MAYBE RECESS WAS OVER FOR THEM, TOO.

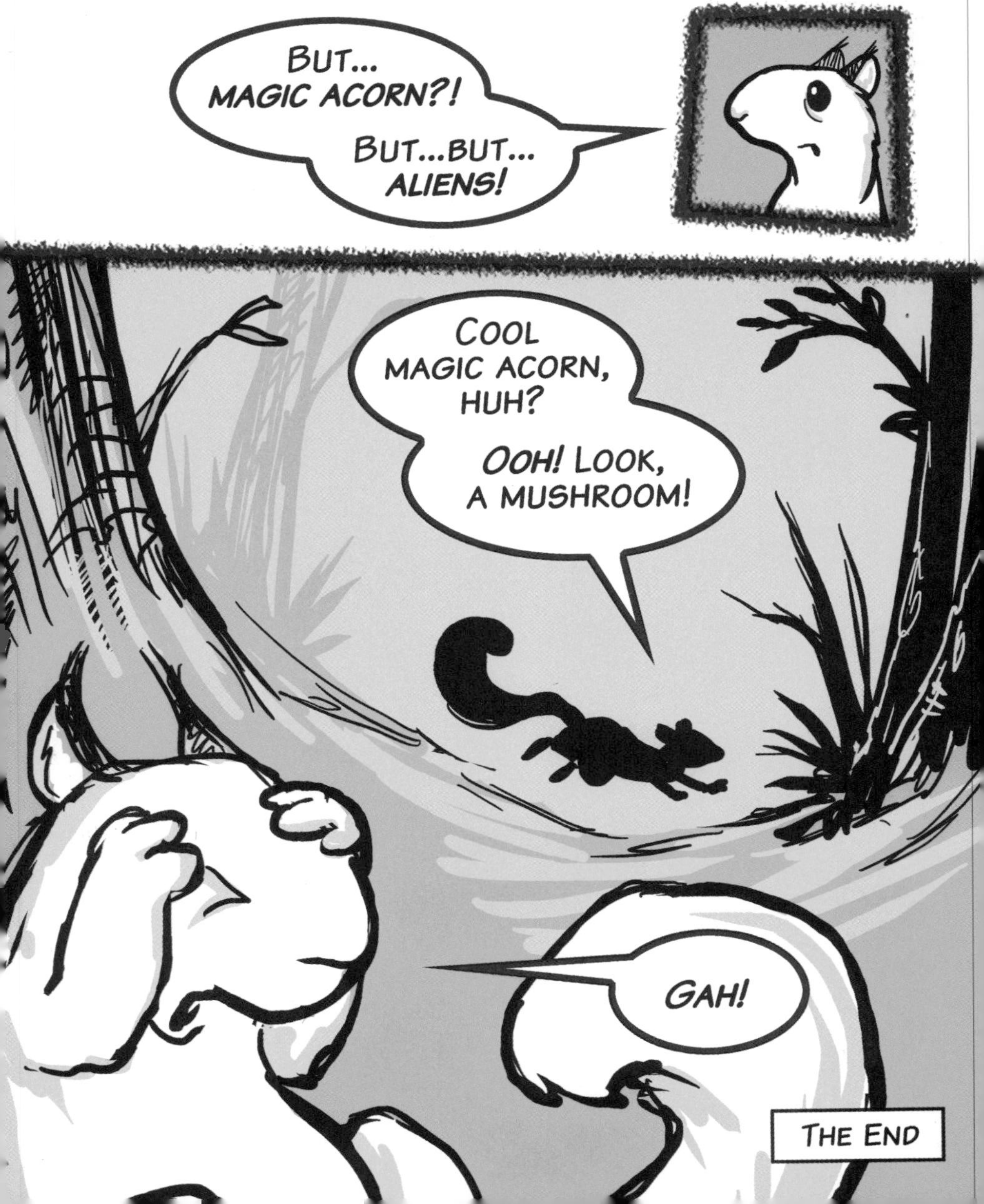

BUT...
MAGIC ACORN?!
BUT...BUT...
ALIENS!
COOL MAGIC ACORN, HUH?
OOH! LOOK, A MUSHROOM!
GAH!
THE END

BABYMOUSE

THE QUEST FOR RECESS

BY JENNIFER L. HOLM & MATTHEW HOLM

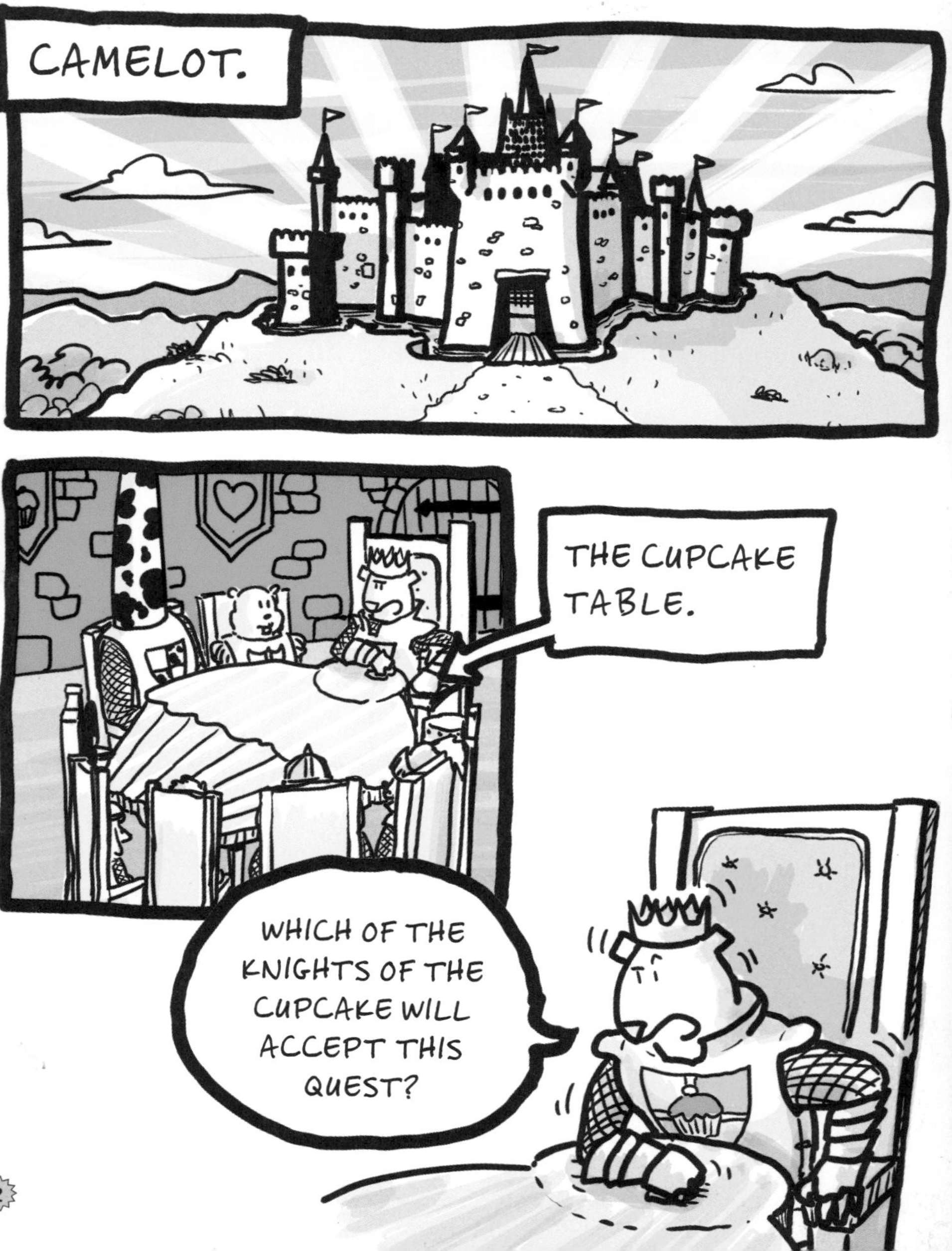
CAMELOT.
THE CUPCAKE TABLE.
WHICH OF THE KNIGHTS OF THE CUPCAKE WILL ACCEPT THIS QUEST?

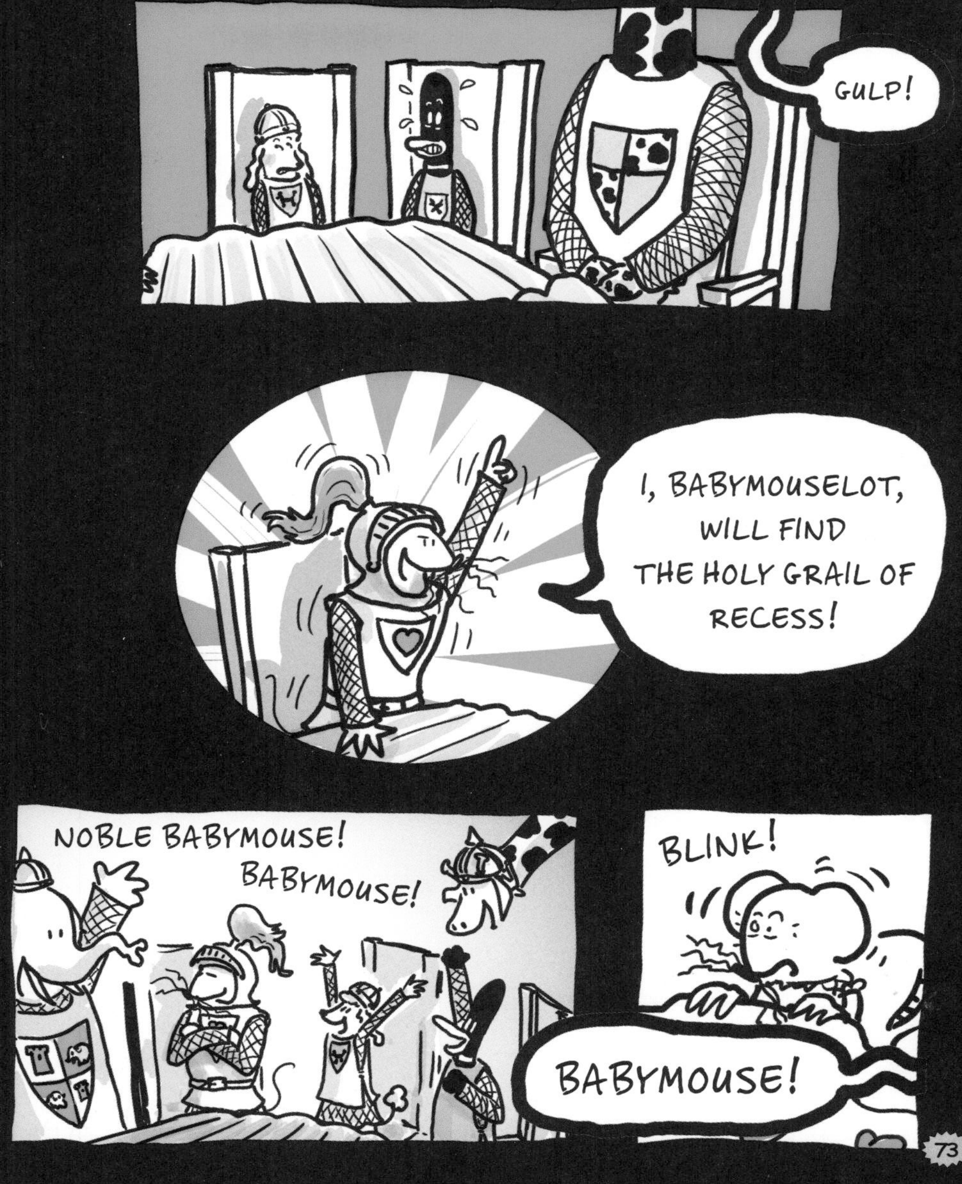
GULP!
I, BABYMOUSELOT, WILL FIND THE HOLY GRAIL OF RECESS!
NOBLE BABYMOUSE!
BABYMOUSE!
BLINK!
BABYMOUSE!

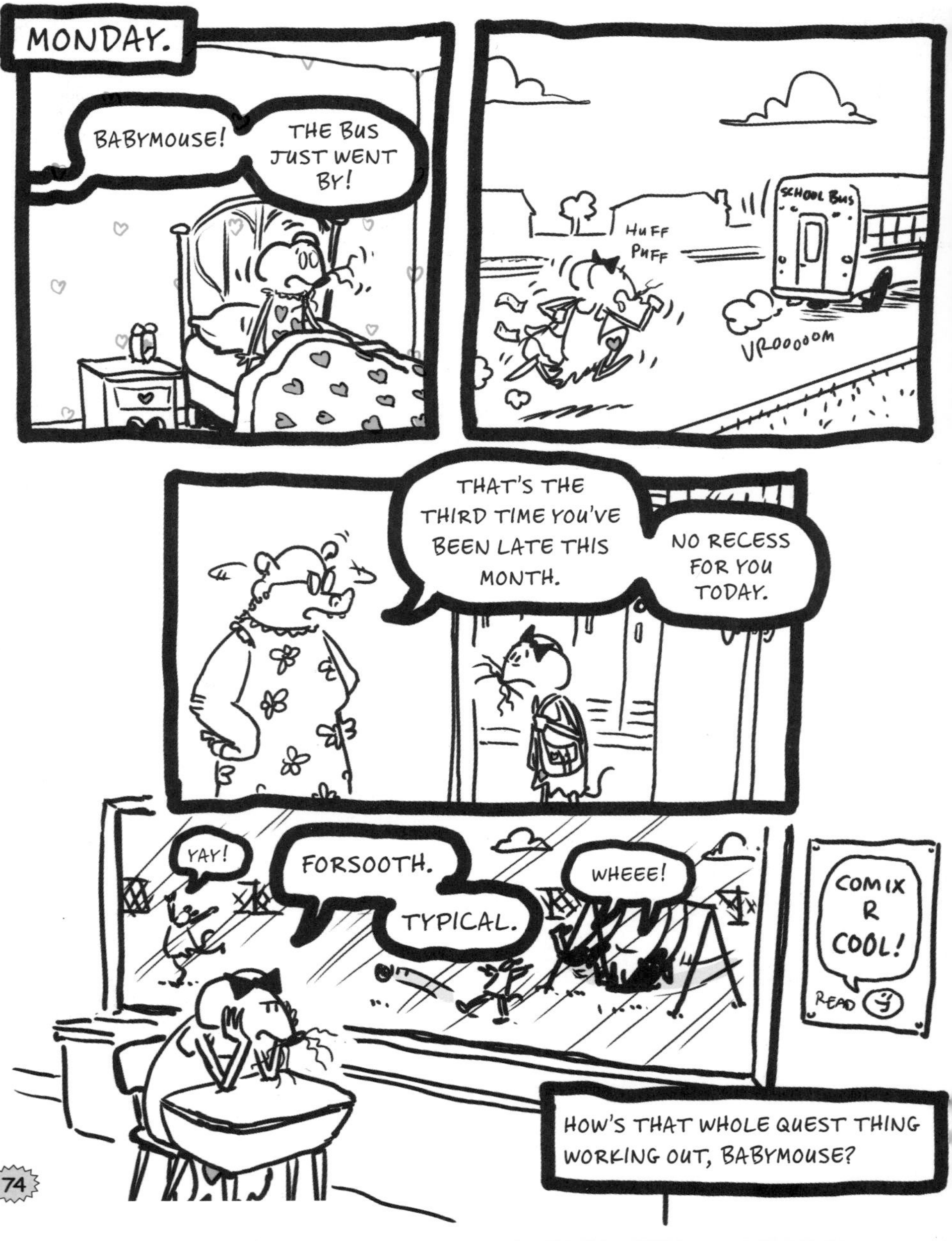
MONDAY.
BABYMOUSE!
THE BUS JUST WENT BY!
SCHOOL BUS
HUFF PUFF
VROOOOOOM
THAT'S THE THIRD TIME YOU'VE BEEN LATE THIS MONTH.
NO RECESS FOR YOU TODAY.
YAY!
FORSOOTH.
TYPICAL.
WHEEE!
COMIX R COOL!
READ
HOW'S THAT WHOLE QUEST THING WORKING OUT, BABYMOUSE?

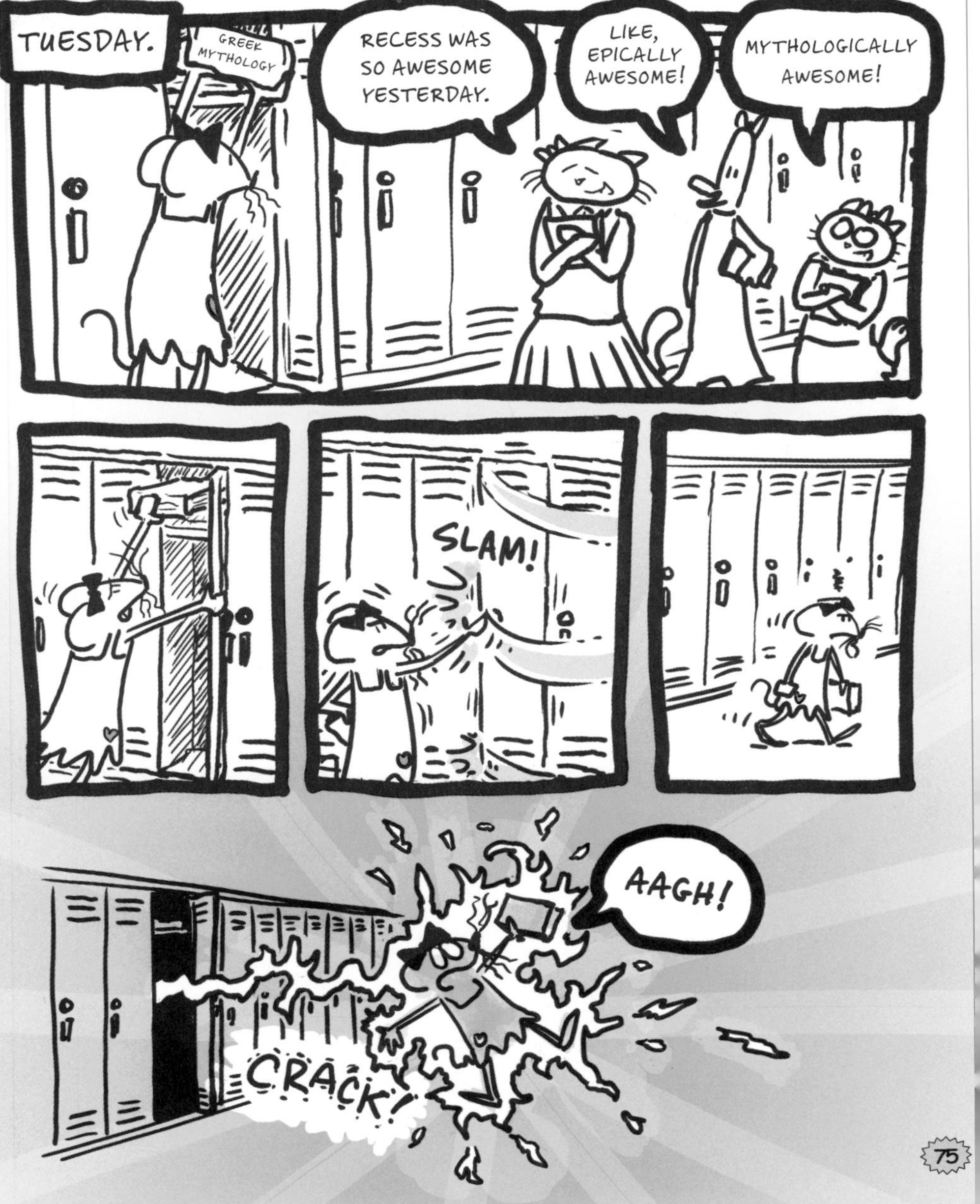
TUESDAY.
GREEK MYTHOLOGY
RECESS WAS SO AWESOME YESTERDAY.
LIKE, EPICALLY AWESOME!
MYTHOLOGICALLY AWESOME!
SLAM!
AAGH!
CRACK!

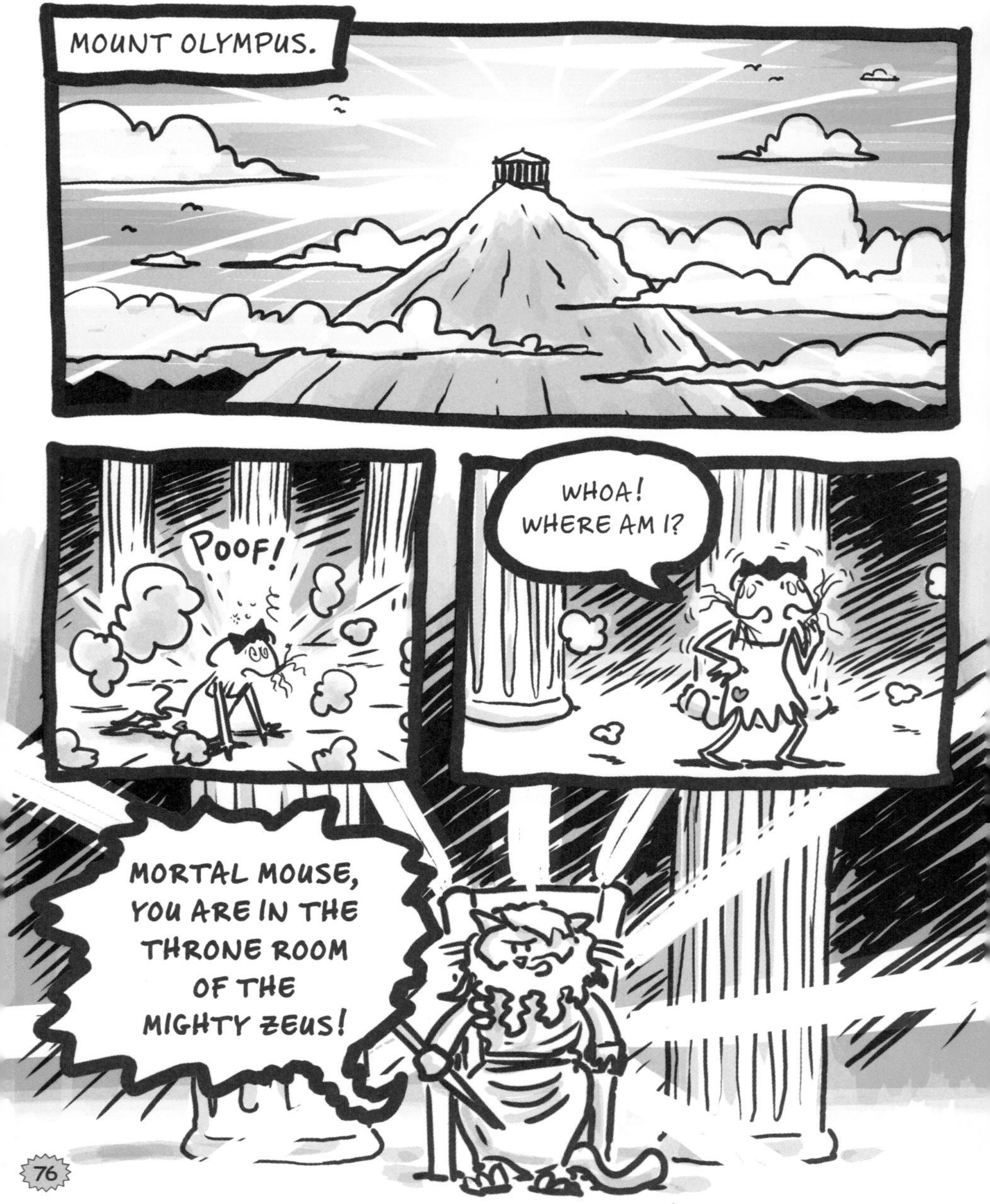
MOUNT OLYMPUS.
POOF!
WHOA! WHERE AM I?
MORTAL MOUSE, YOU ARE IN THE THRONE ROOM OF THE MIGHTY ZEUS!

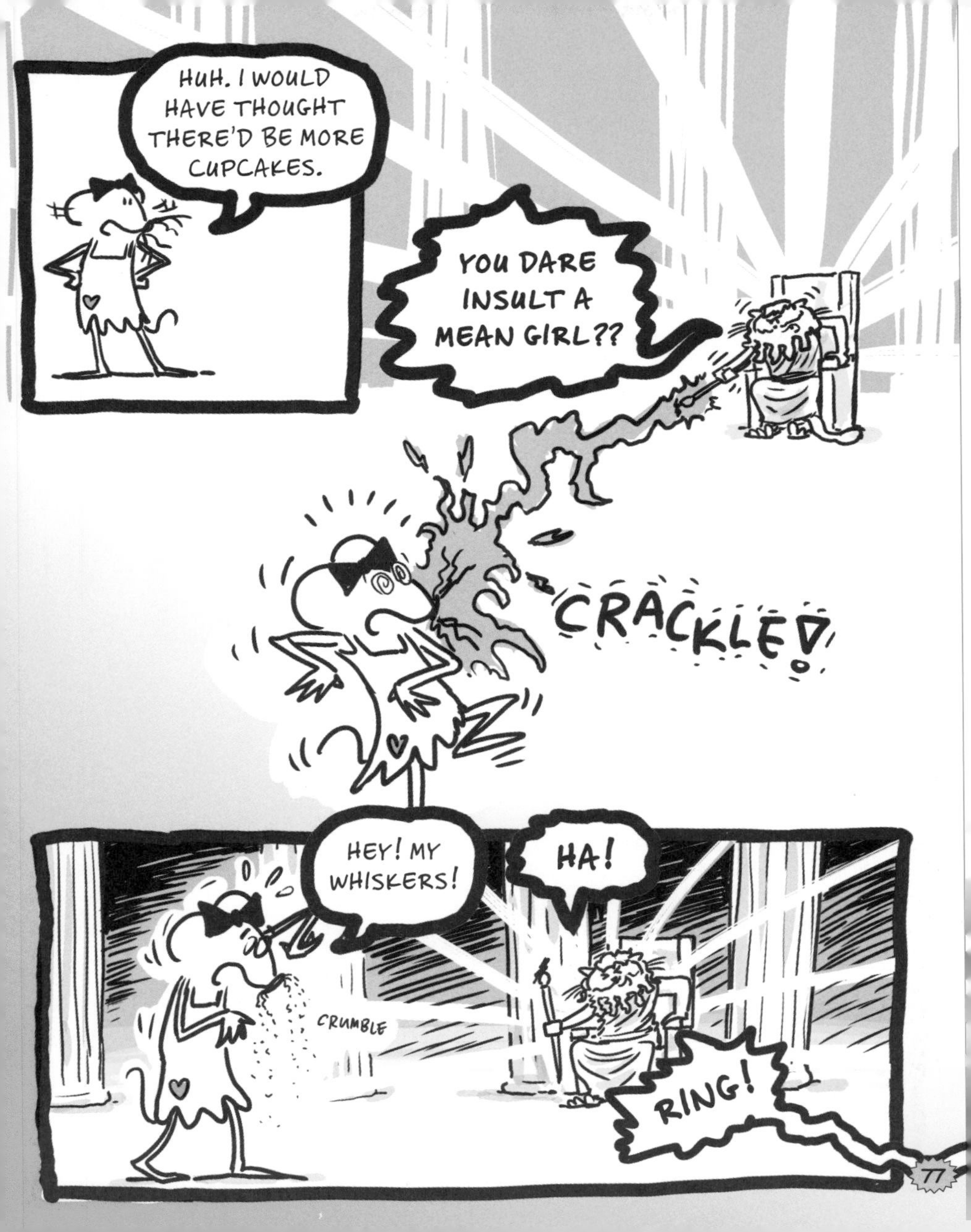

HUH. I WOULD HAVE THOUGHT THERE'D BE MORE CUPCAKES.
YOU DARE INSULT A MEAN GIRL??
CRACKLE!
HEY! MY WHISKERS!
HA!
CRUMBLE
RING!

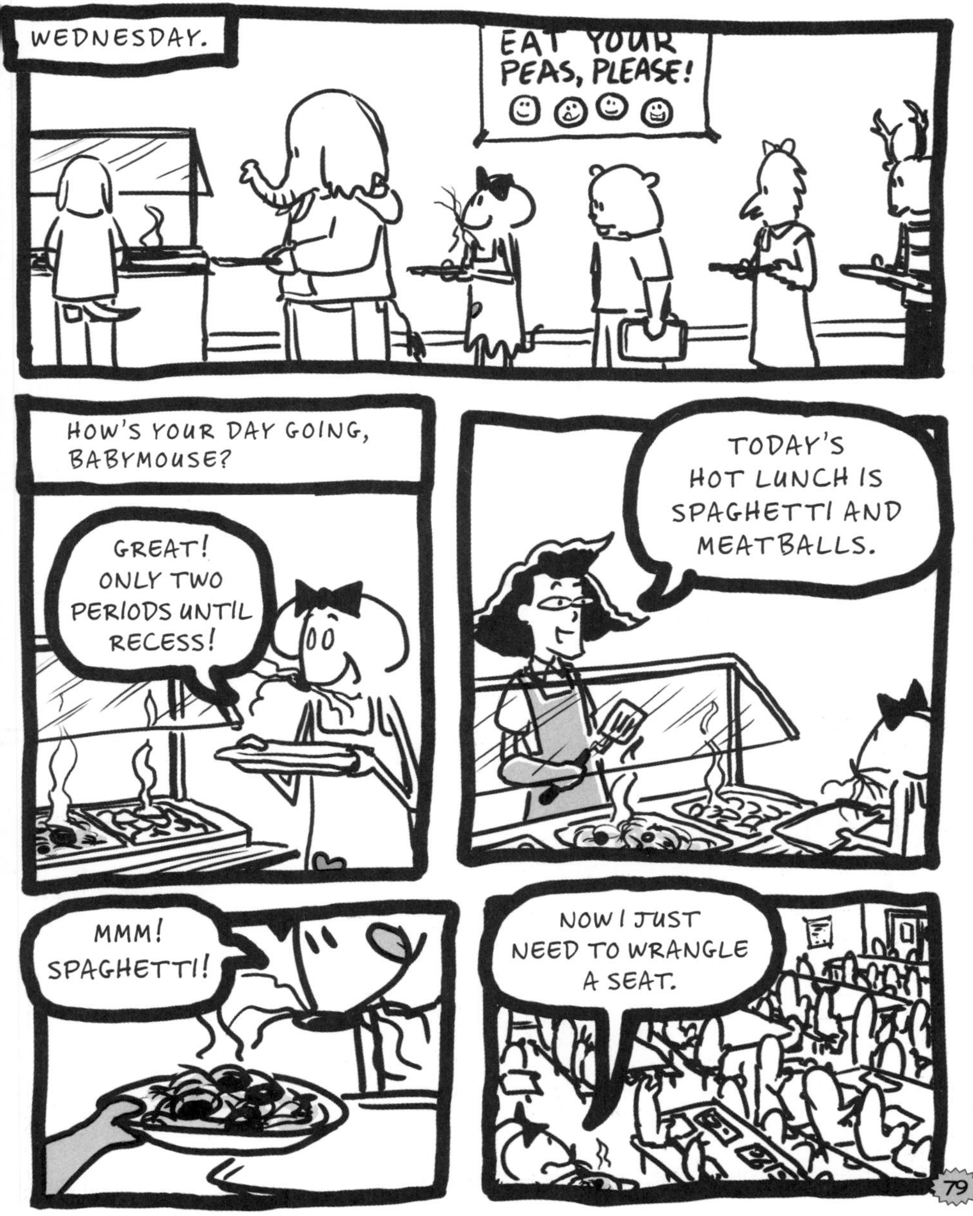
WEDNESDAY.
EAT YOUR PEAS, PLEASE!
HOW'S YOUR DAY GOING, BABYMOUSE?
GREAT! ONLY TWO PERIODS UNTIL RECESS!
TODAY'S HOT LUNCH IS SPAGHETTI AND MEATBALLS.
MMM! SPAGHETTI!
NOW I JUST NEED TO WRANGLE A SEAT.

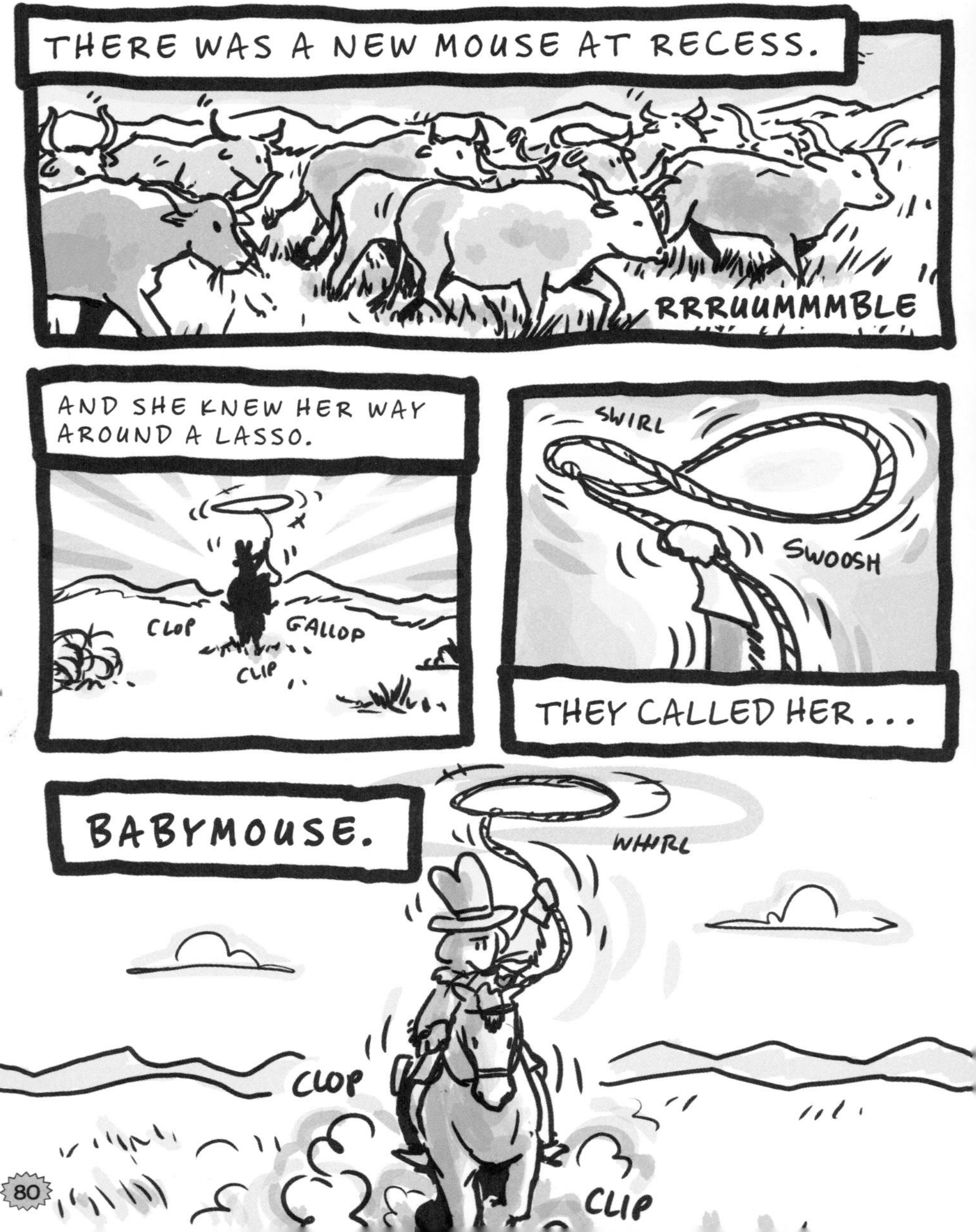
THERE WAS A NEW MOUSE AT RECESS.
RRRUUMMMMBLE
AND SHE KNEW HER WAY AROUND A LASSO.
CLOP
GALLOP
CLIP
SWIRL
SWOOSH
THEY CALLED HER . . .
BABYMOUSE.
WHIRL
CLOP
CLIP

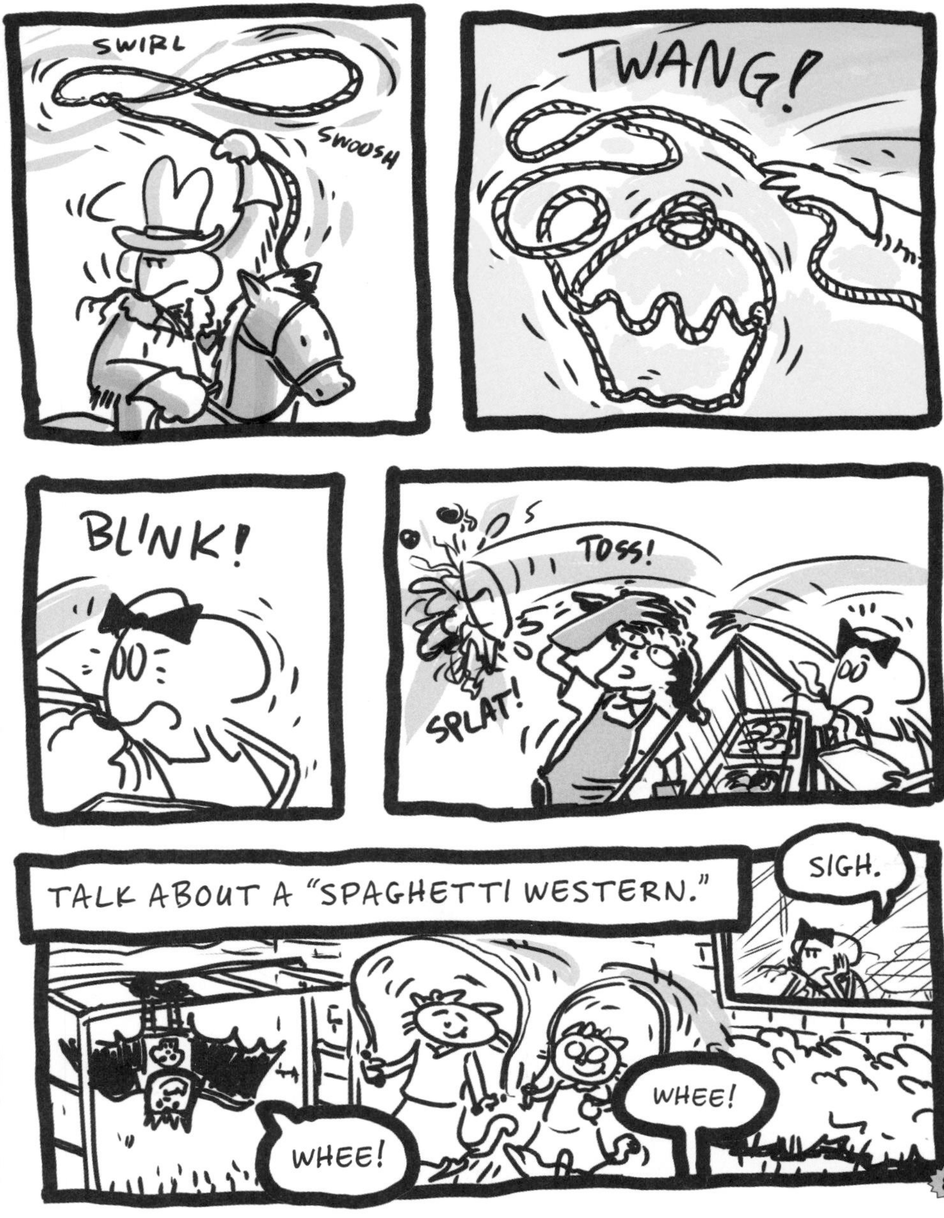
SWIRL
SWOOSH
TWANG!
BLINK!
TOSS!
SPLAT!
TALK ABOUT A "SPAGHETTI WESTERN."
SIGH.
WHEE!
WHEE!

THURSDAY. MATH.

MATH

$\frac{1}{2} + \frac{3}{7} =$

YOU HAVE TWENTY MINUTES TO FINISH YOUR WORK.

IN THE HISTORY OF CIVILIZATION ...

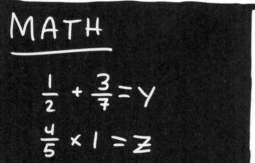

MATH

$$\frac{1}{2} + \frac{3}{7} = y$$

$$\frac{4}{5} \times 1 = z$$

SQUINT

MATH

MARCH MARCH

$$\frac{1}{2} + \frac{3}{7} = y$$

$$\frac{4}{5} \times 1 = z$$

?

MATH WAS A NEVER-ENDING BATTLE.

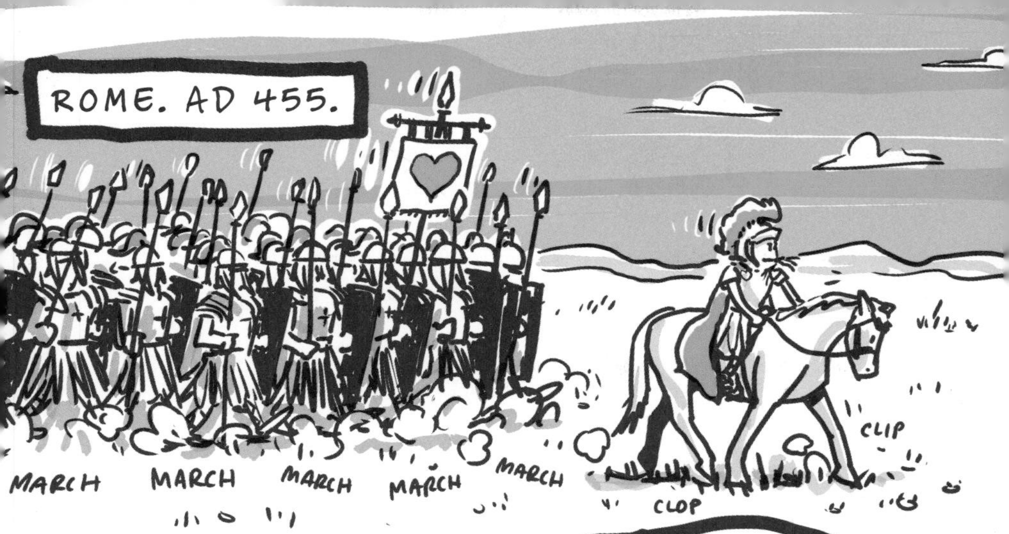
ROME. AD 455.
MARCH
MARCH
MARCH
MARCH
MARCH
CLIP
CLOP

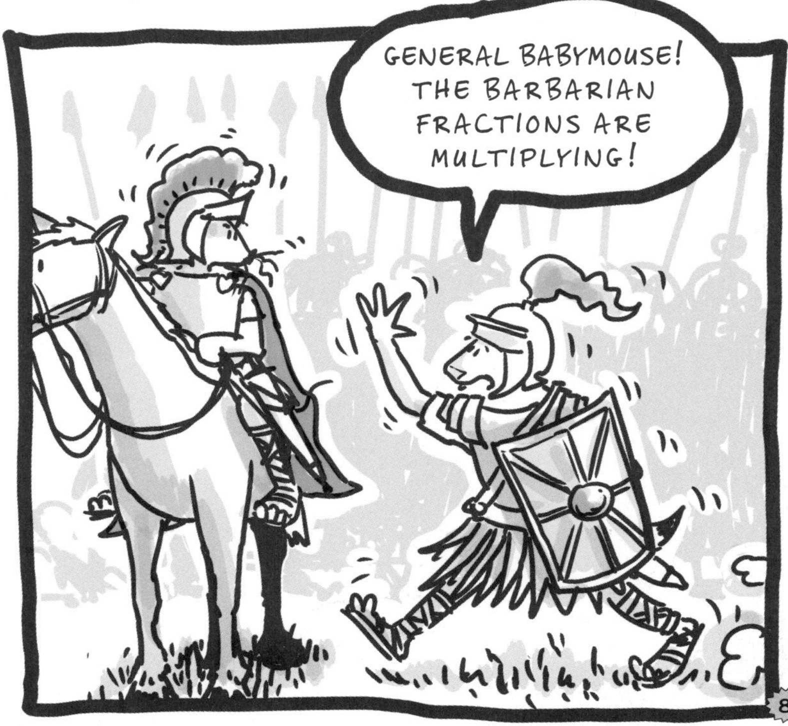
GENERAL BABYMOUSE! THE BARBARIAN FRACTIONS ARE MULTIPLYING!

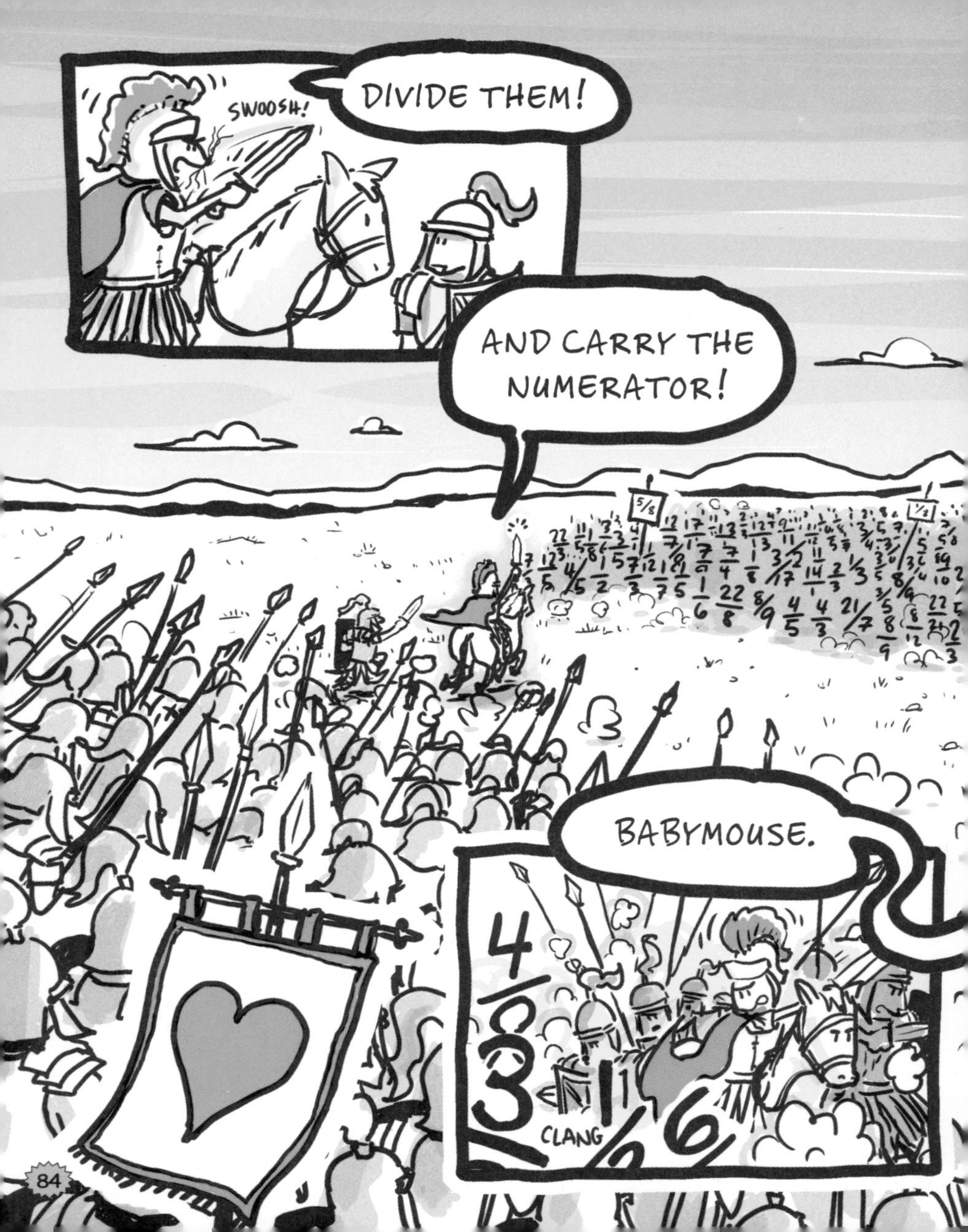
SWOOSH!
DIVIDE THEM!
AND CARRY THE NUMERATOR!
BABYMOUSE.
CLANG

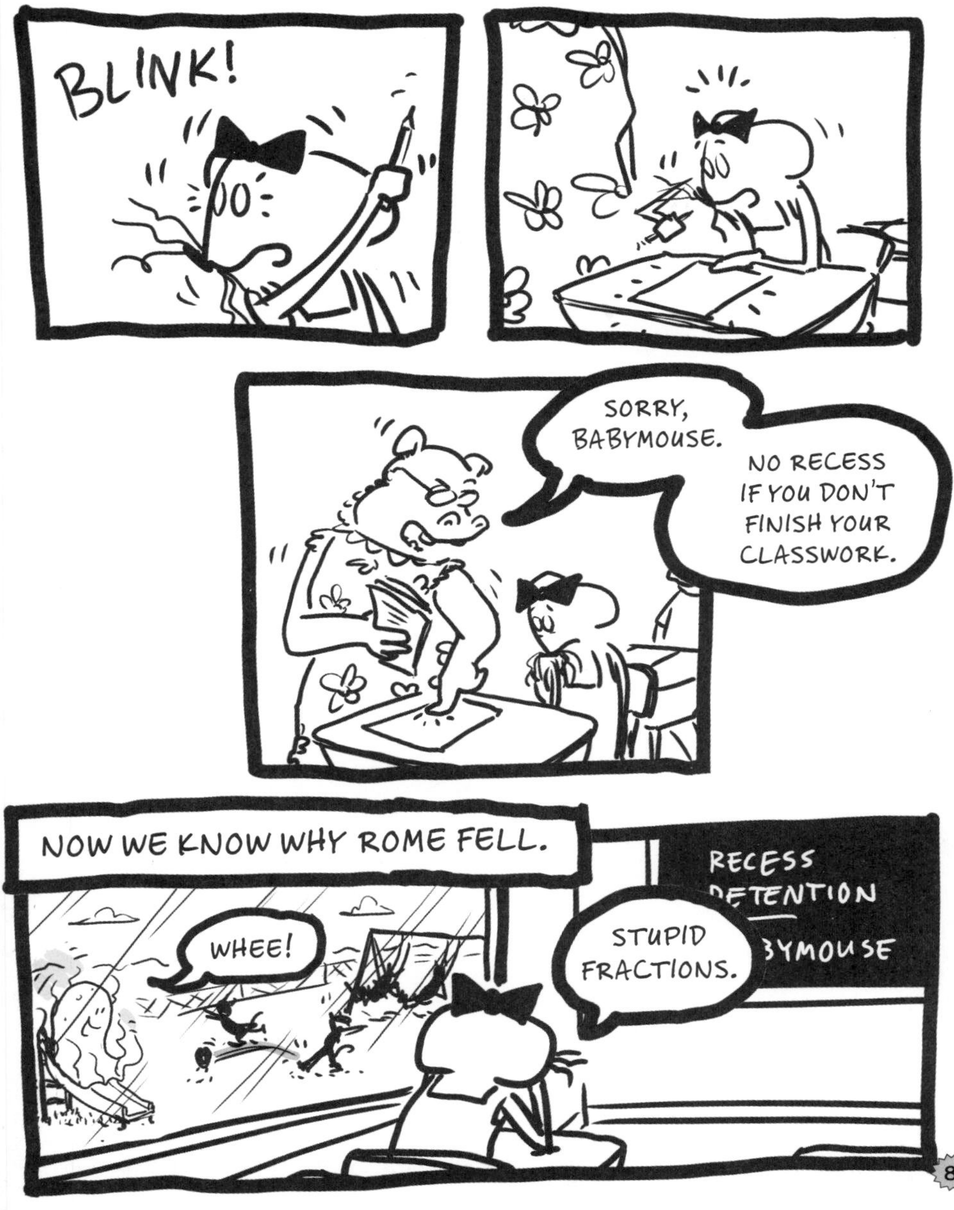
BLINK!
SORRY, BABYMOUSE.
NO RECESS IF YOU DON'T FINISH YOUR CLASSWORK.
NOW WE KNOW WHY ROME FELL.
RECESS DETENTION
BYMOUSE
WHEE!
STUPID FRACTIONS.

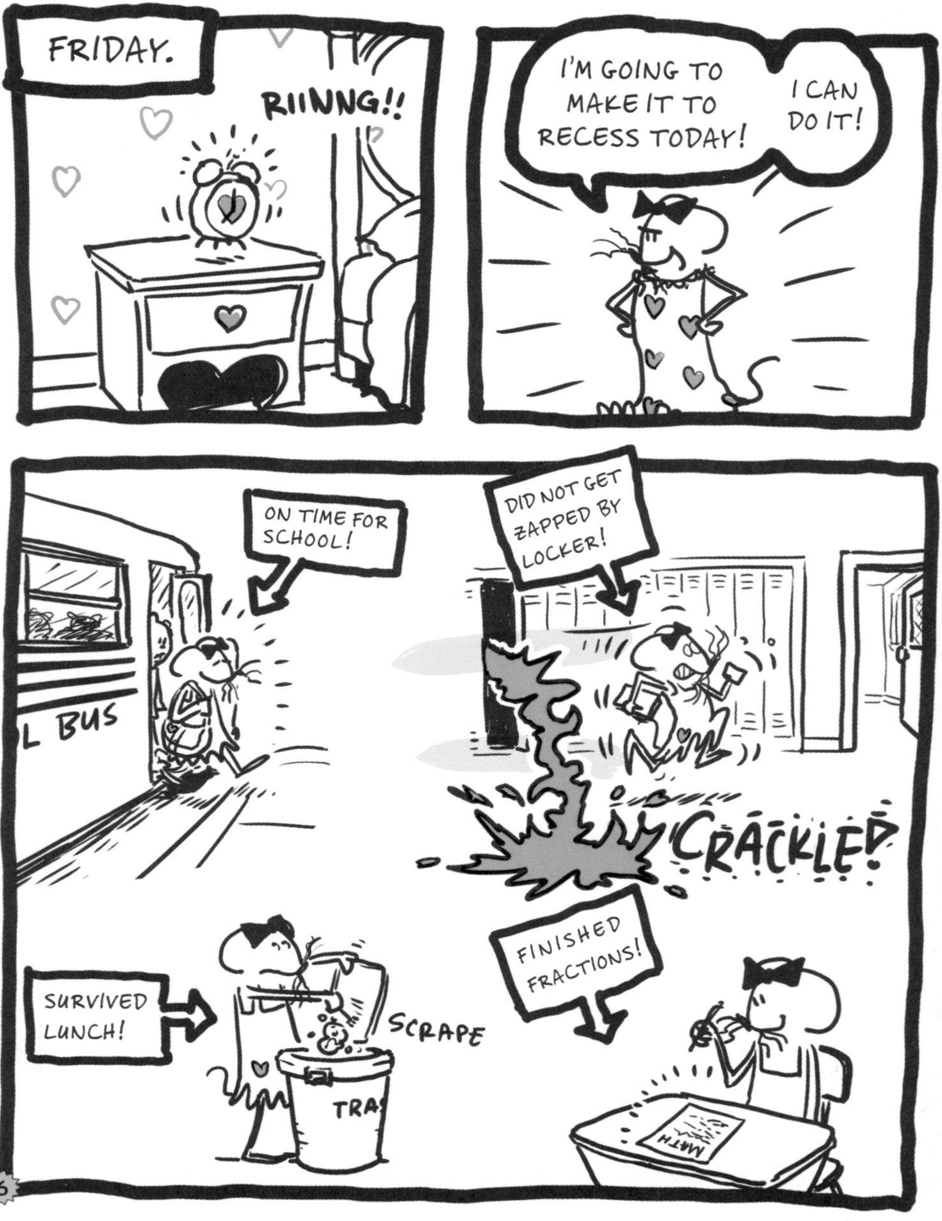
FRIDAY.
RIINNG!!
I'M GOING TO MAKE IT TO RECESS TODAY!
I CAN DO IT!
ON TIME FOR SCHOOL!
L BUS
DID NOT GET ZAPPED BY LOCKER!
CRACKLE!
SURVIVED LUNCH!
SCRAPE
TRA
FINISHED FRACTIONS!
MATH

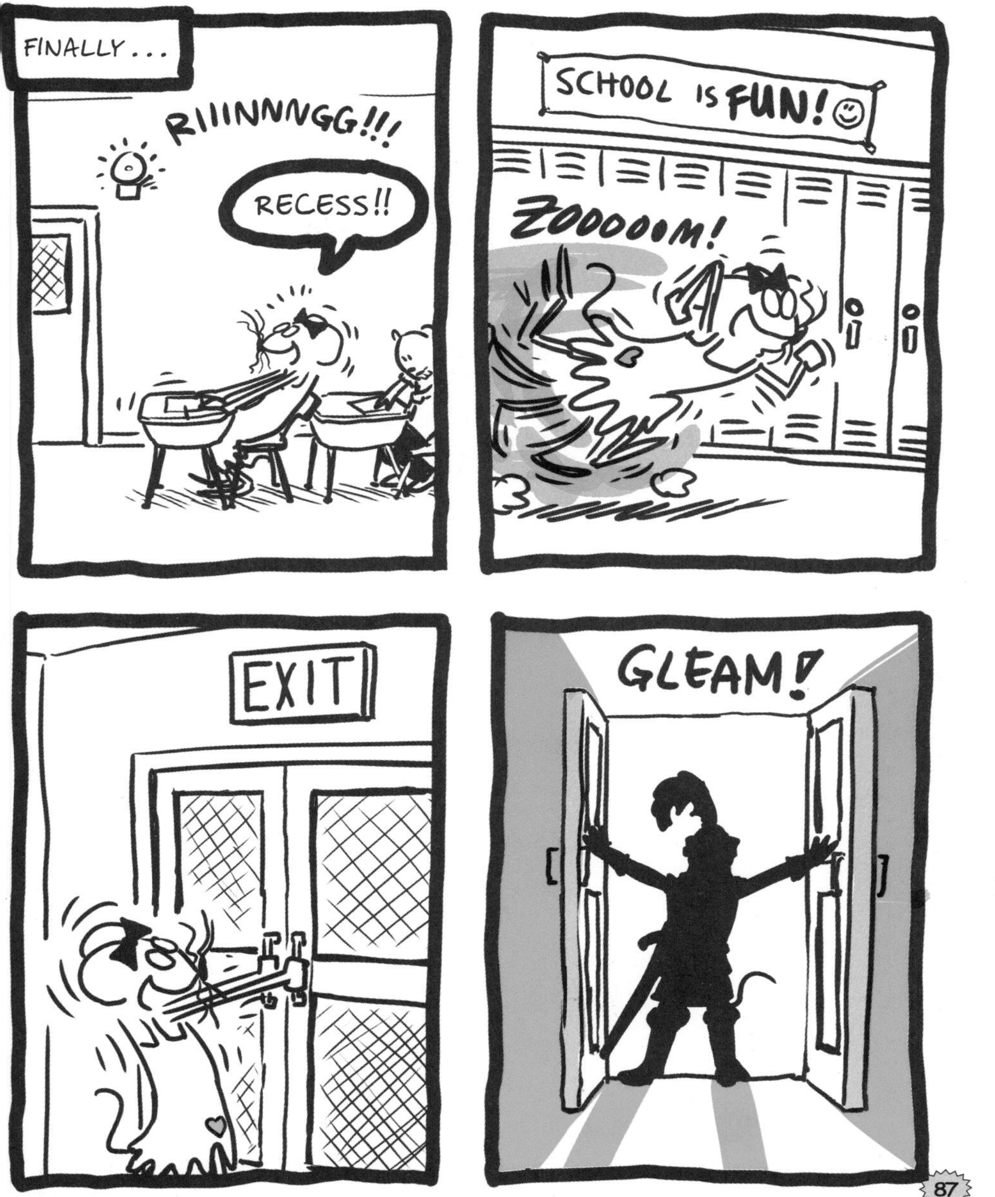
FINALLY . . .
RIIINNNGG!!!
RECESS!!
SCHOOL IS FUN!
ZOOOOOM!
EXIT
GLEAM!

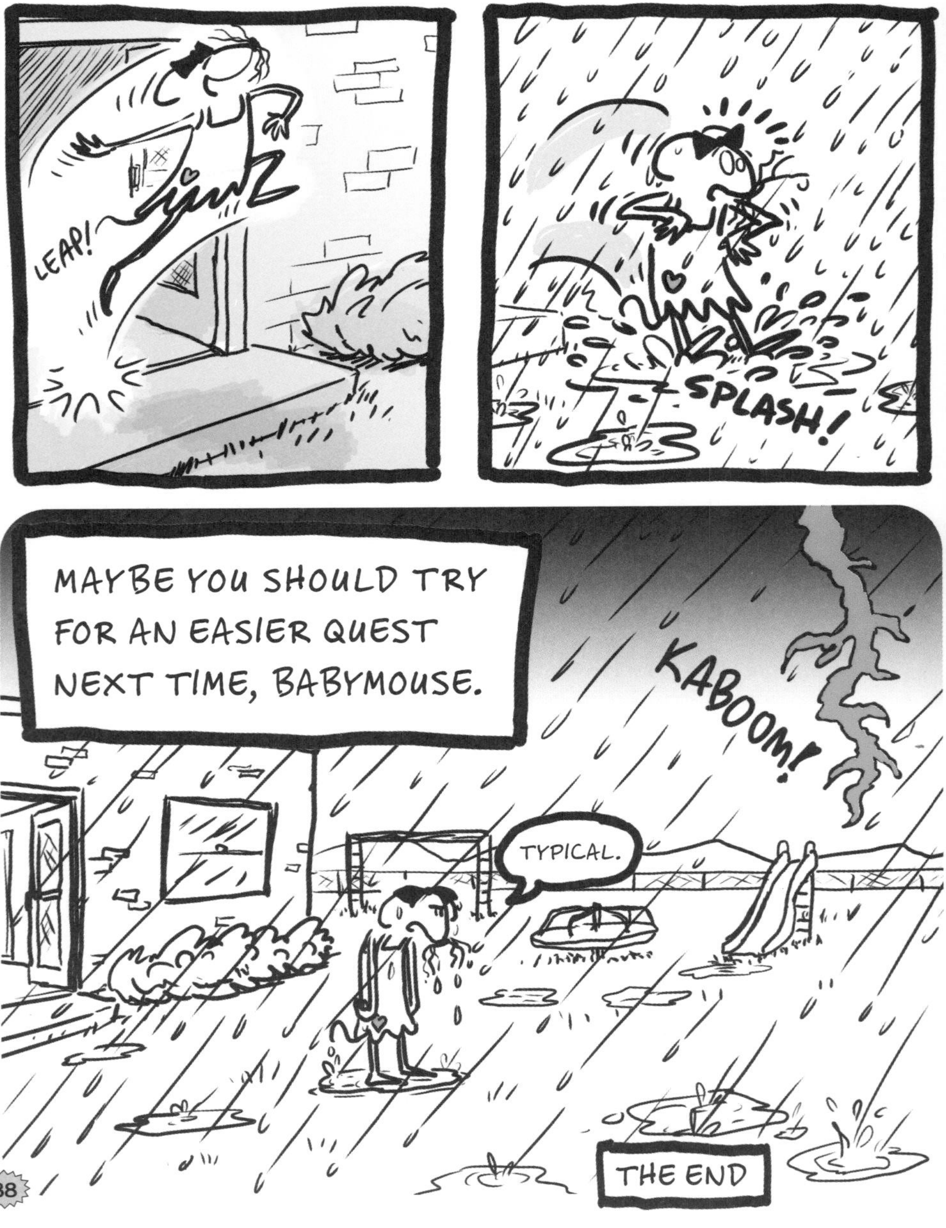
LEAP!
SPLASH!
MAYBE YOU SHOULD TRY FOR AN EASIER QUEST NEXT TIME, BABYMOUSE.
KABOOM!
TYPICAL.
THE END

Jiminy Sprinkles in "FREEZE TAG"

by Eric Wight

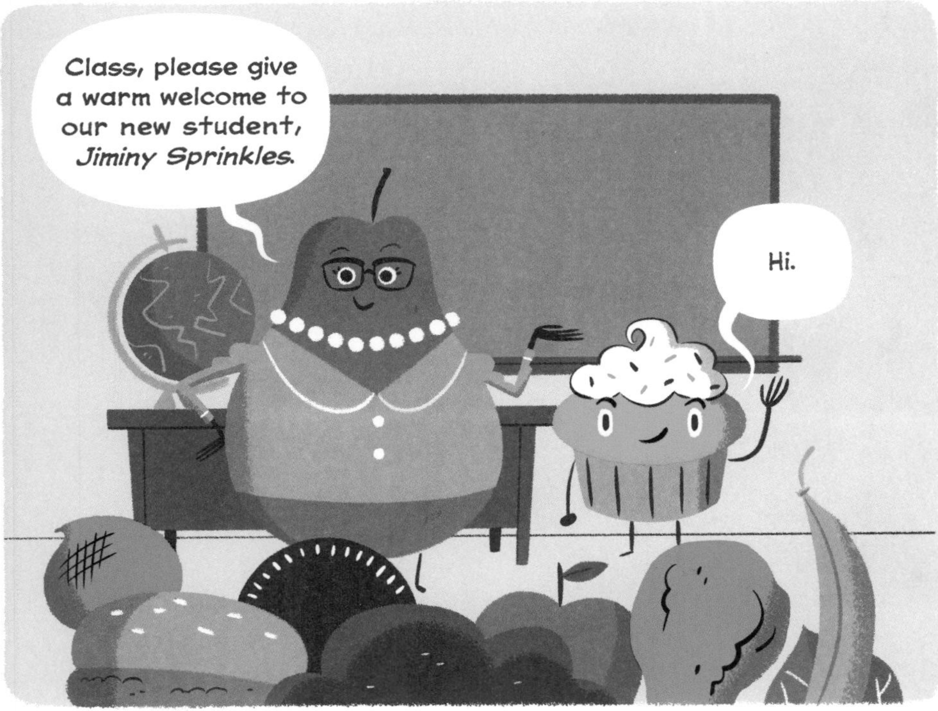
Class, please give a warm welcome to our new student, Jiminy Sprinkles.
Hi.

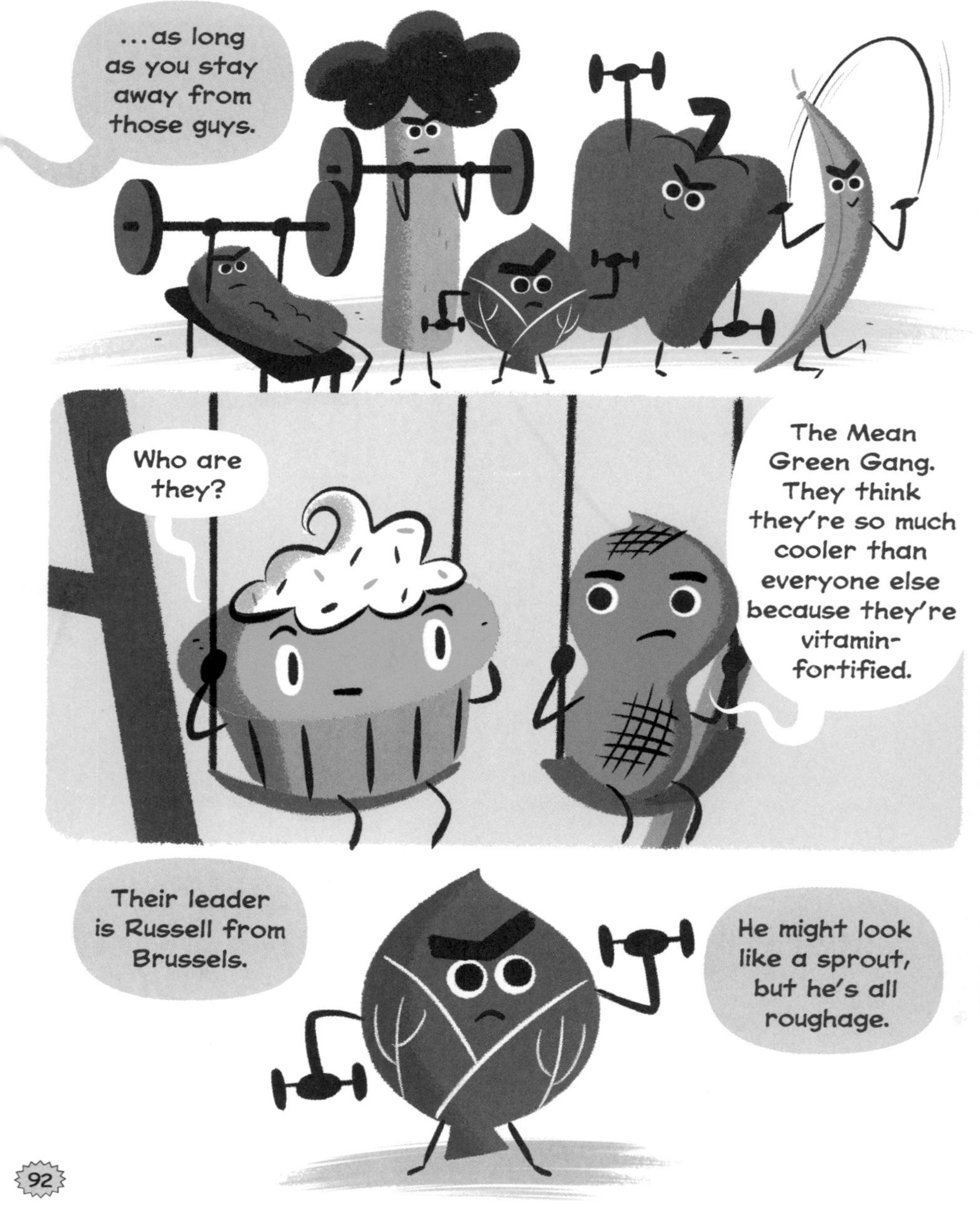
...as long as you stay away from those guys.
Who are they?
The Mean Green Gang. They think they're so much cooler than everyone else because they're vitamin-fortified.
Their leader is Russell from Brussels.
He might look like a sprout, but he's all roughage.

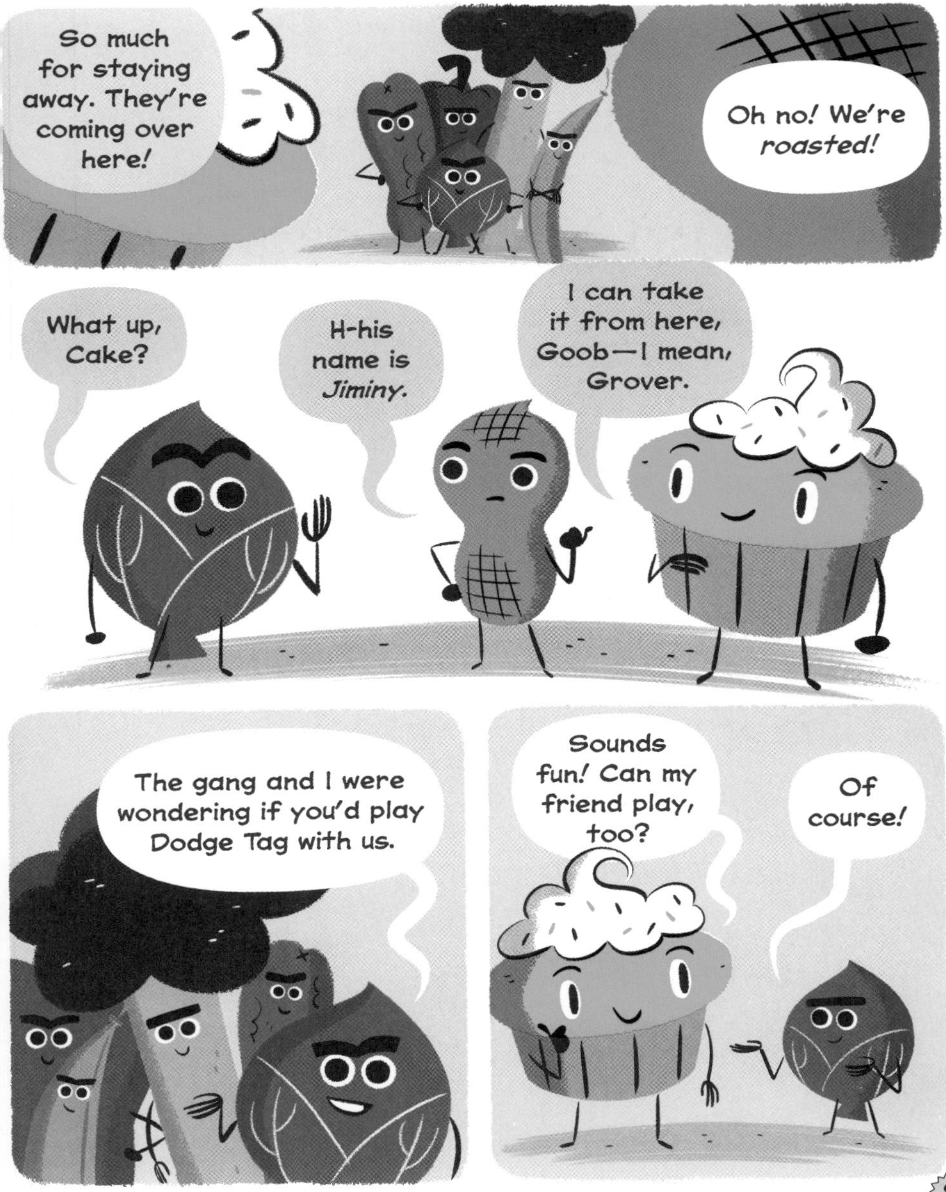
So much for staying away. They're coming over here!
Oh no! We're *roasted!*
What up, Cake?
H-his name is *Jiminy.*
I can take it from here, Goob—I mean, Grover.
The gang and I were wondering if you'd play Dodge Tag with us.
Sounds fun! Can my friend play, too?
Of course!

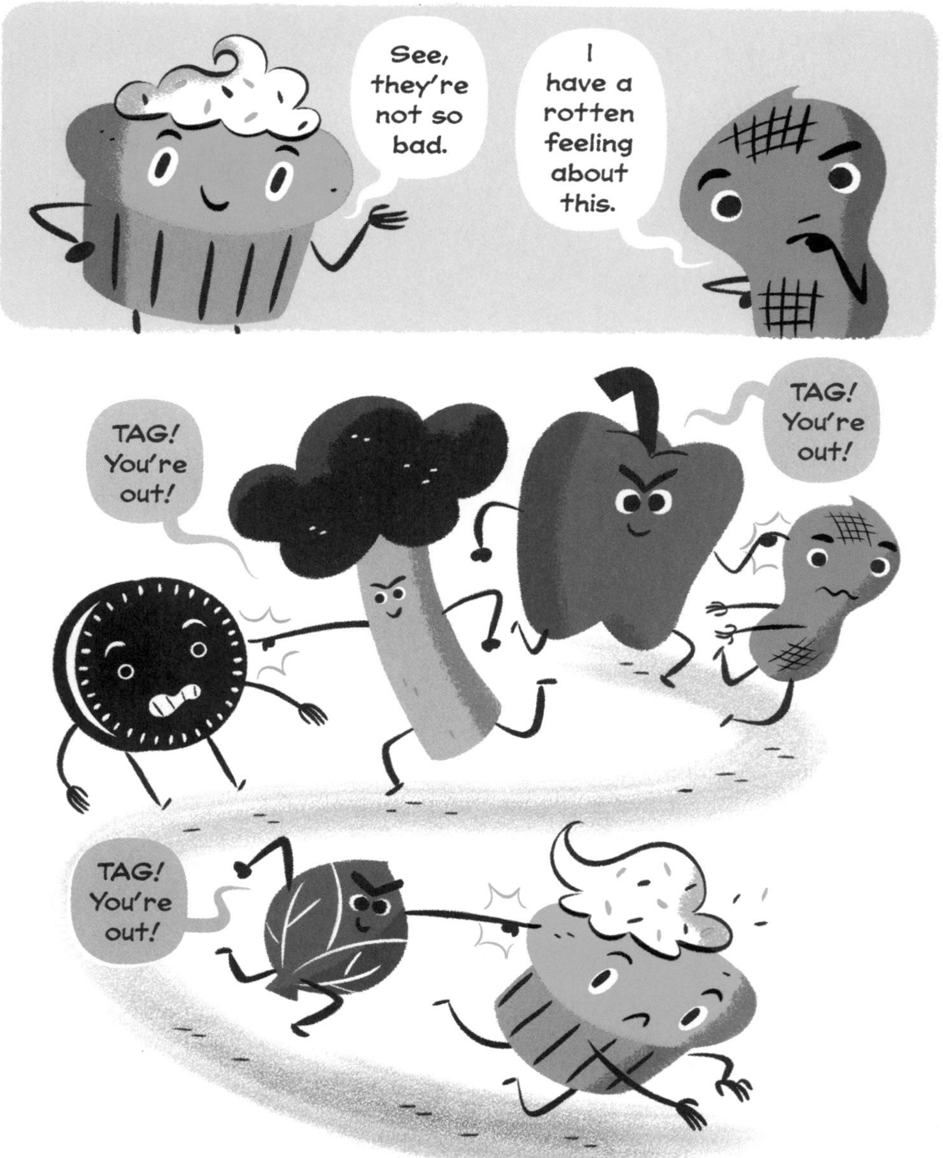
See, they're not so bad.
I have a rotten feeling about this.
TAG! You're out!
TAG! You're out!
TAG! You're out!

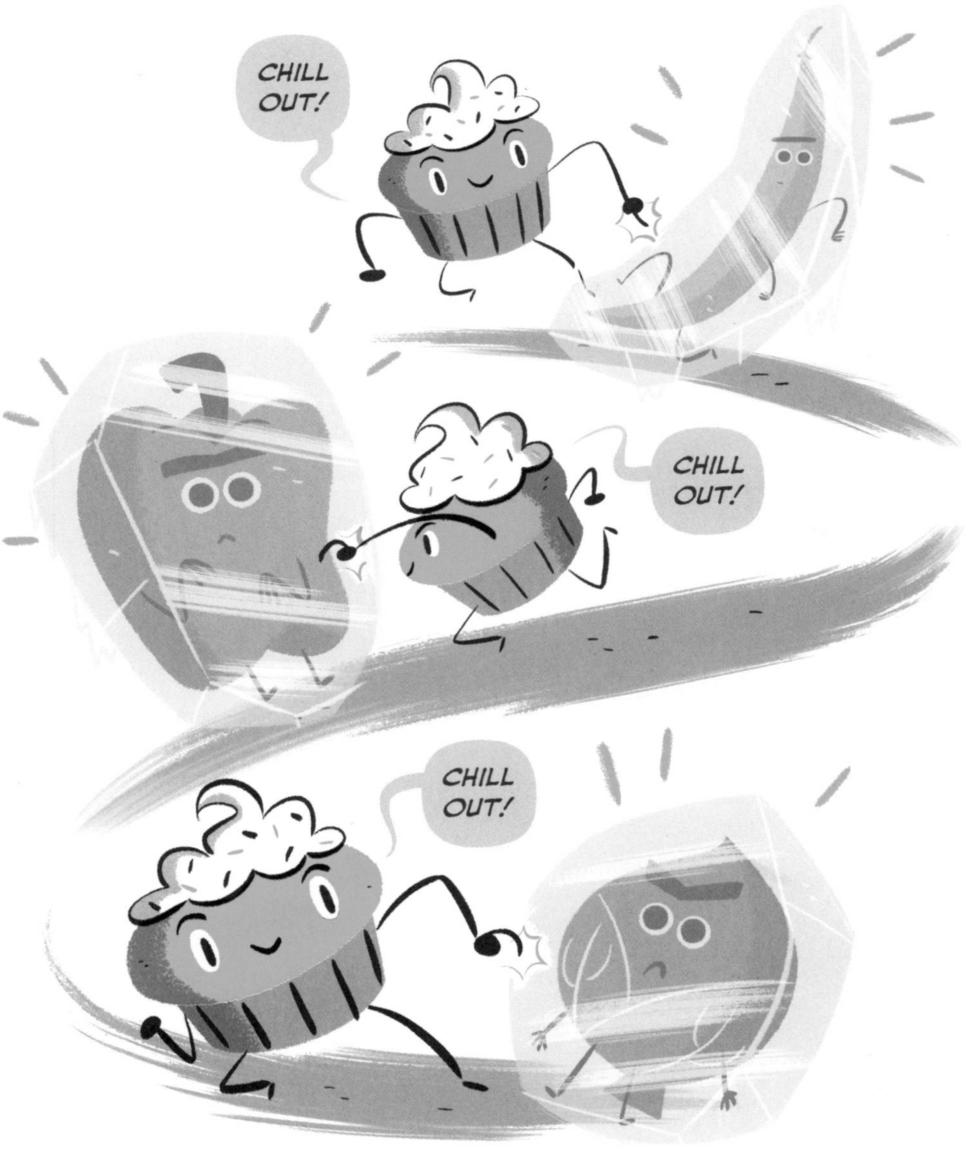
CHILL OUT!
CHILL OUT!
CHILL OUT!

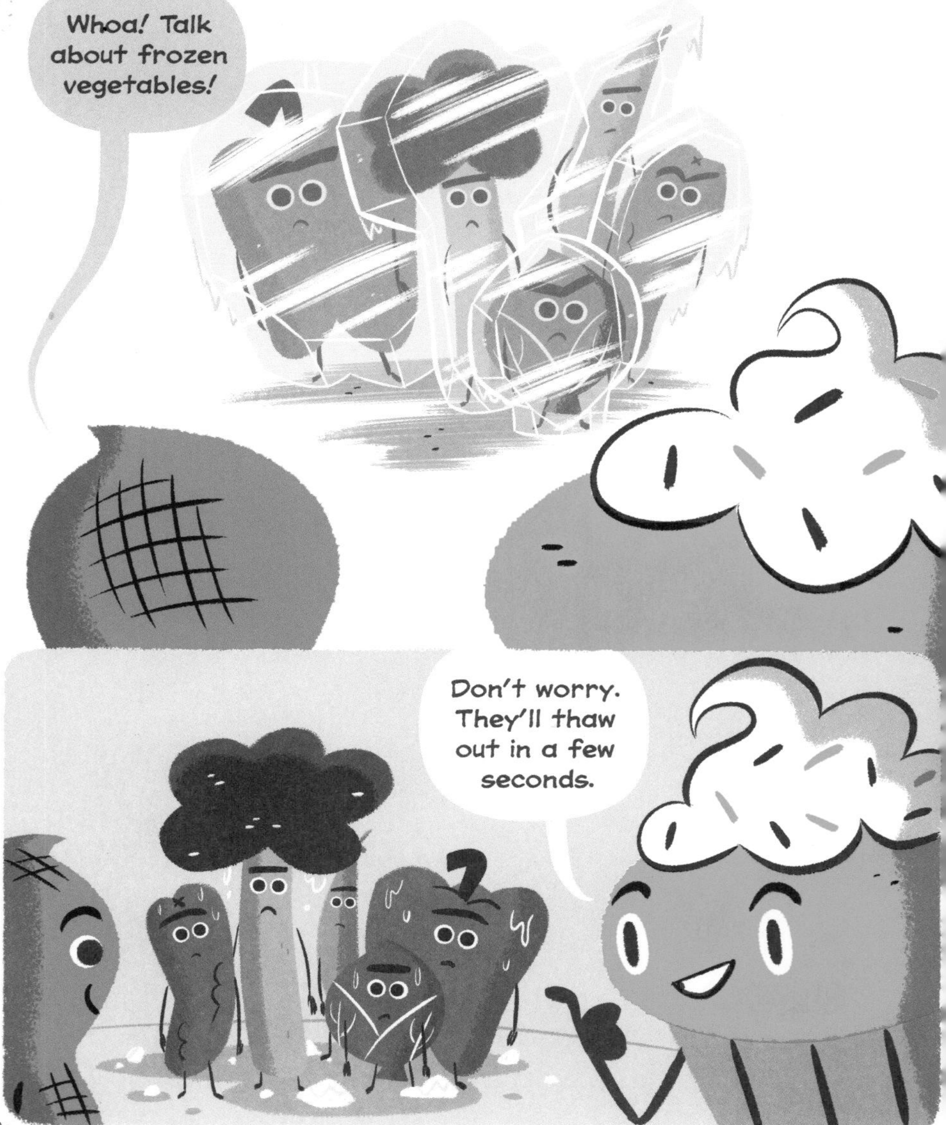
Whoa! Talk about frozen vegetables!
Don't worry. They'll thaw out in a few seconds.

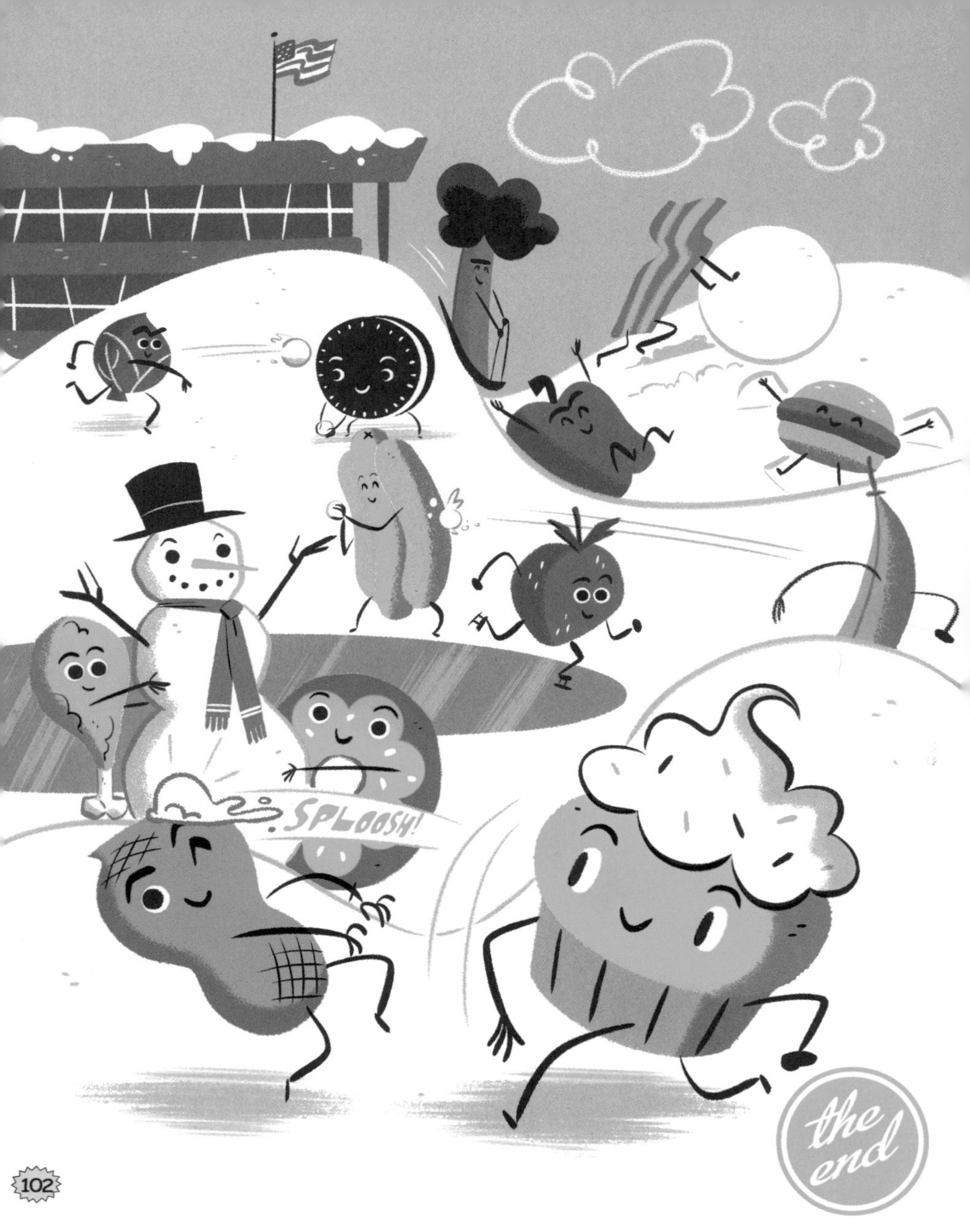
SPLOOSH!
the end

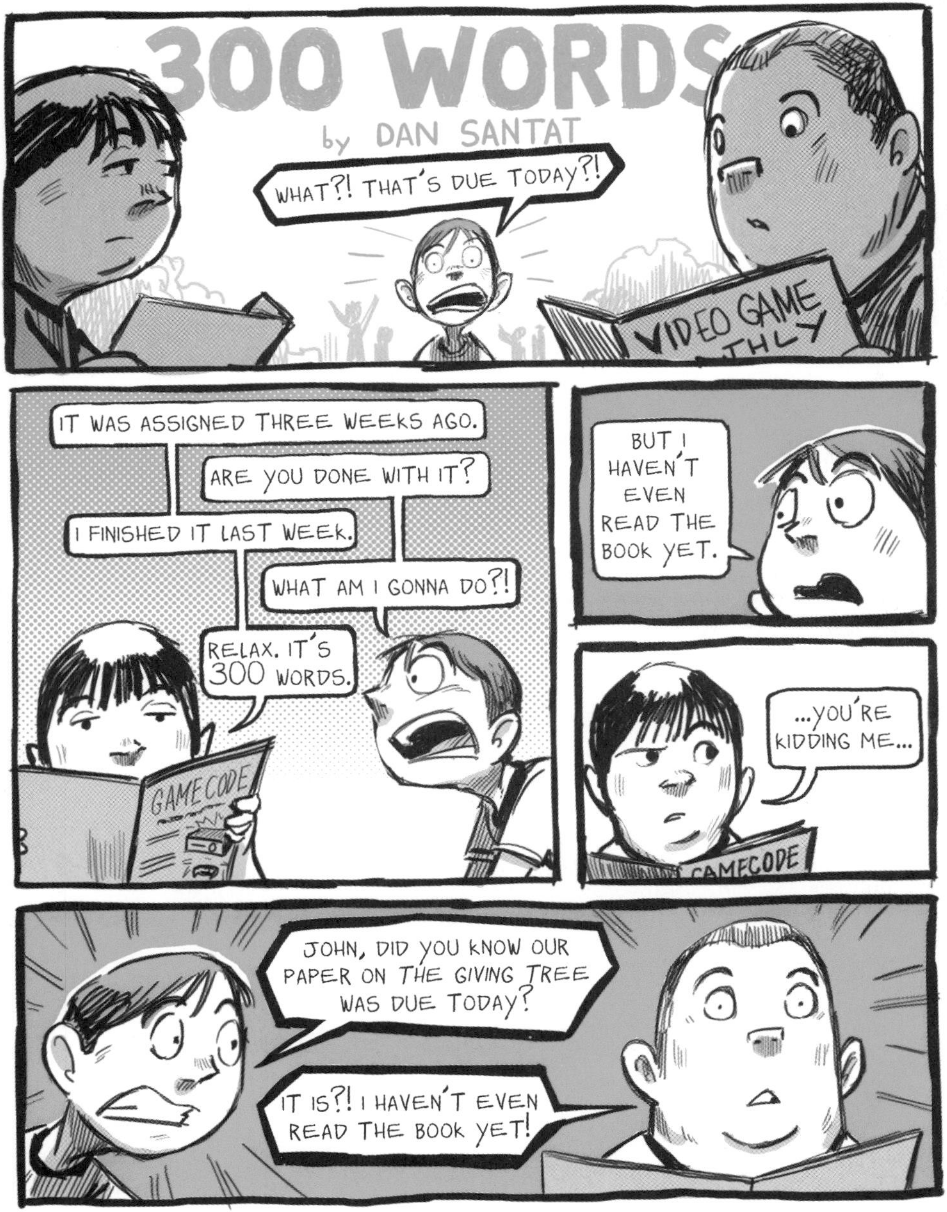
300 WORDS
by DAN SANTAT
WHAT?! THAT'S DUE TODAY?!
VIDEO GAME
IT WAS ASSIGNED THREE WEEKS AGO.
ARE YOU DONE WITH IT?
I FINISHED IT LAST WEEK.
WHAT AM I GONNA DO?!
RELAX. IT'S 300 WORDS.
GAMECODE
BUT I HAVEN'T EVEN READ THE BOOK YET.
...YOU'RE KIDDING ME...
GAMECODE
JOHN, DID YOU KNOW OUR PAPER ON *THE GIVING TREE* WAS DUE TODAY?
IT IS?! I HAVEN'T EVEN READ THE BOOK YET!

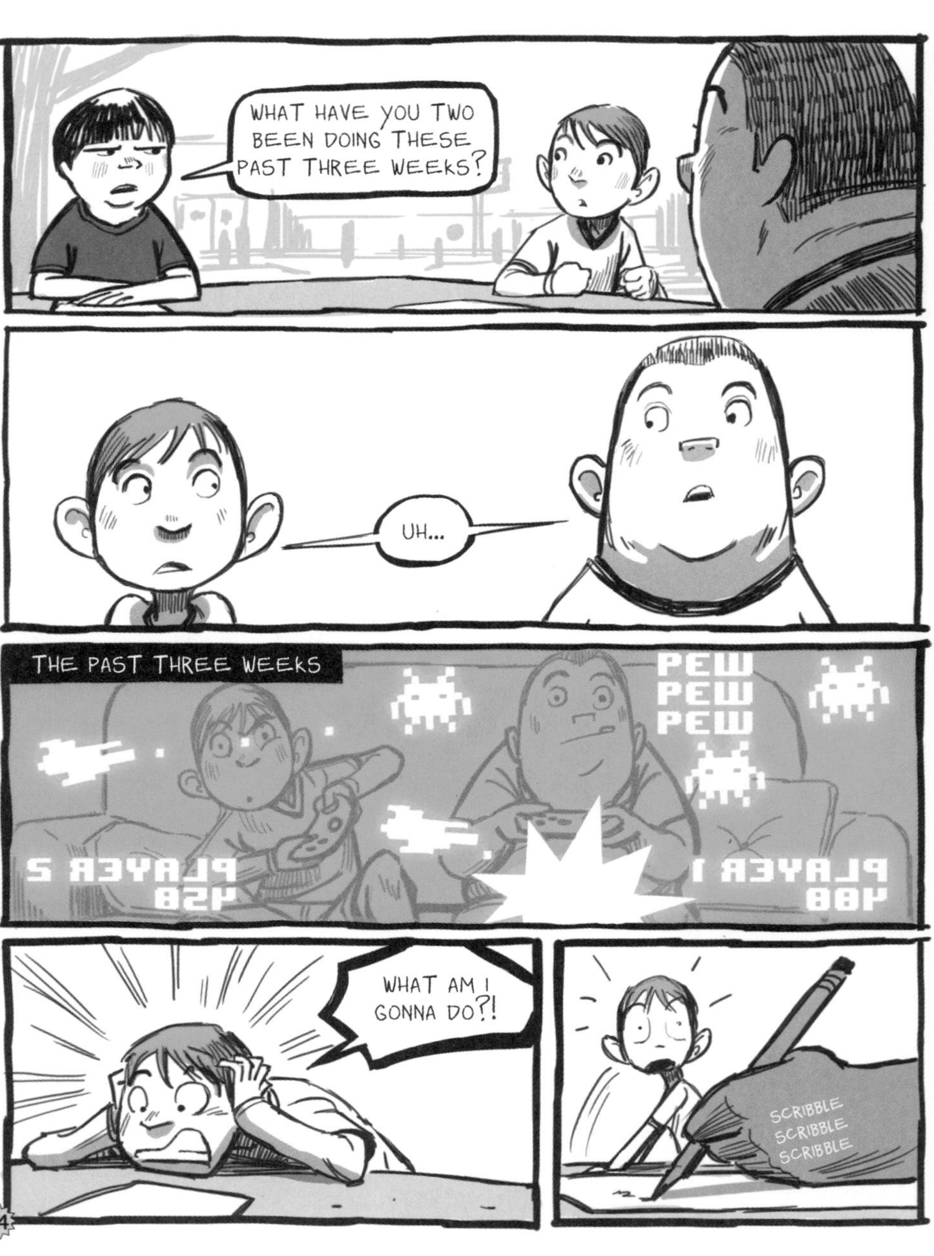
WHAT HAVE YOU TWO BEEN DOING THESE PAST THREE WEEKS?
UH...
THE PAST THREE WEEKS
PEW PEW PEW
WHAT AM I GONNA DO?!
SCRIBBLE SCRIBBLE SCRIBBLE

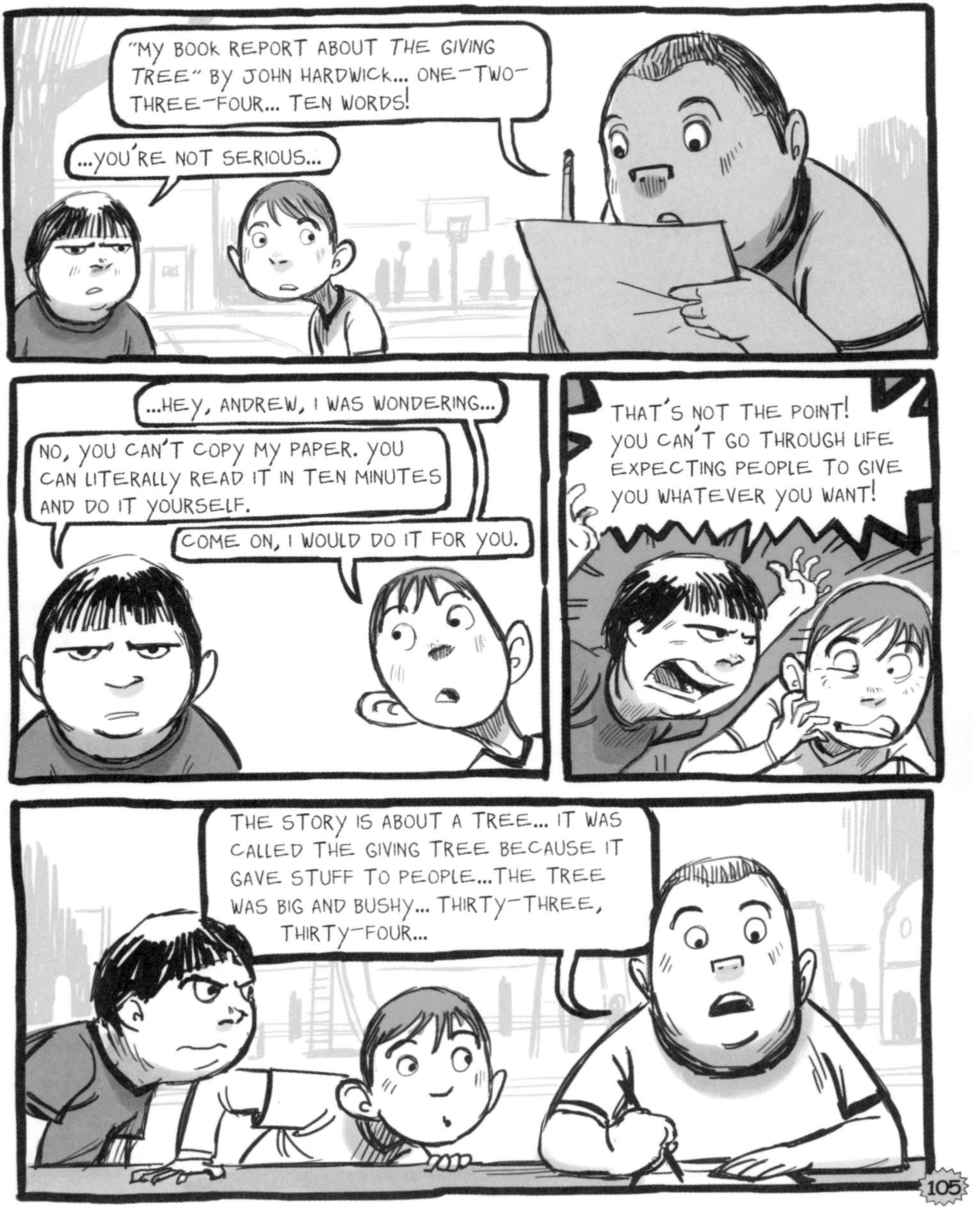
"MY BOOK REPORT ABOUT THE GIVING TREE" BY JOHN HARDWICK... ONE-TWO-THREE-FOUR... TEN WORDS!
...YOU'RE NOT SERIOUS...
...HEY, ANDREW, I WAS WONDERING...
NO, YOU CAN'T COPY MY PAPER. YOU CAN LITERALLY READ IT IN TEN MINUTES AND DO IT YOURSELF.
COME ON, I WOULD DO IT FOR YOU.
THAT'S NOT THE POINT! YOU CAN'T GO THROUGH LIFE EXPECTING PEOPLE TO GIVE YOU WHATEVER YOU WANT!
THE STORY IS ABOUT A TREE... IT WAS CALLED THE GIVING TREE BECAUSE IT GAVE STUFF TO PEOPLE...THE TREE WAS BIG AND BUSHY... THIRTY-THREE, THIRTY-FOUR...

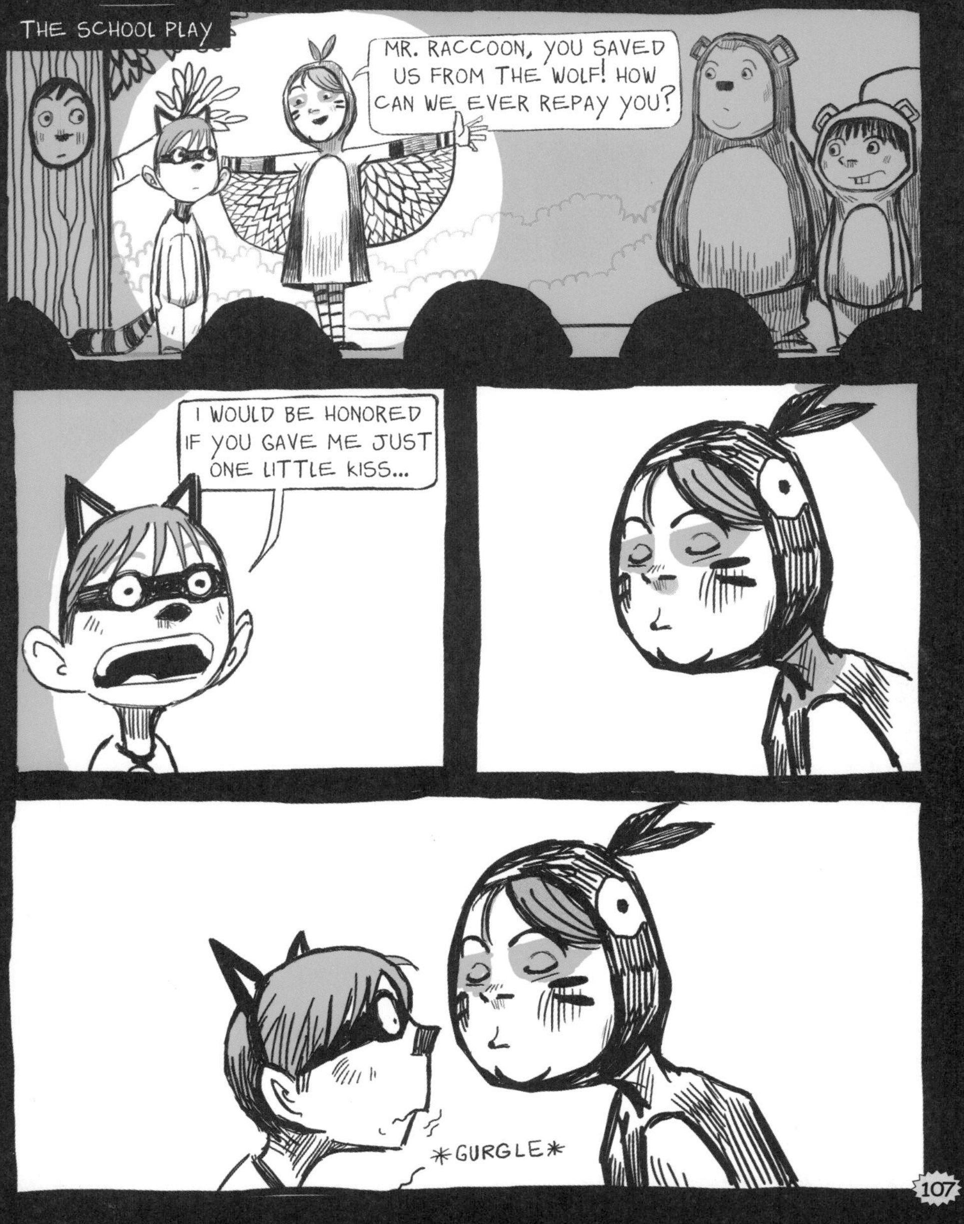
THE SCHOOL PLAY
MR. RACCOON, YOU SAVED US FROM THE WOLF! HOW CAN WE EVER REPAY YOU?
I WOULD BE HONORED IF YOU GAVE ME JUST ONE LITTLE KISS...
GURGLE

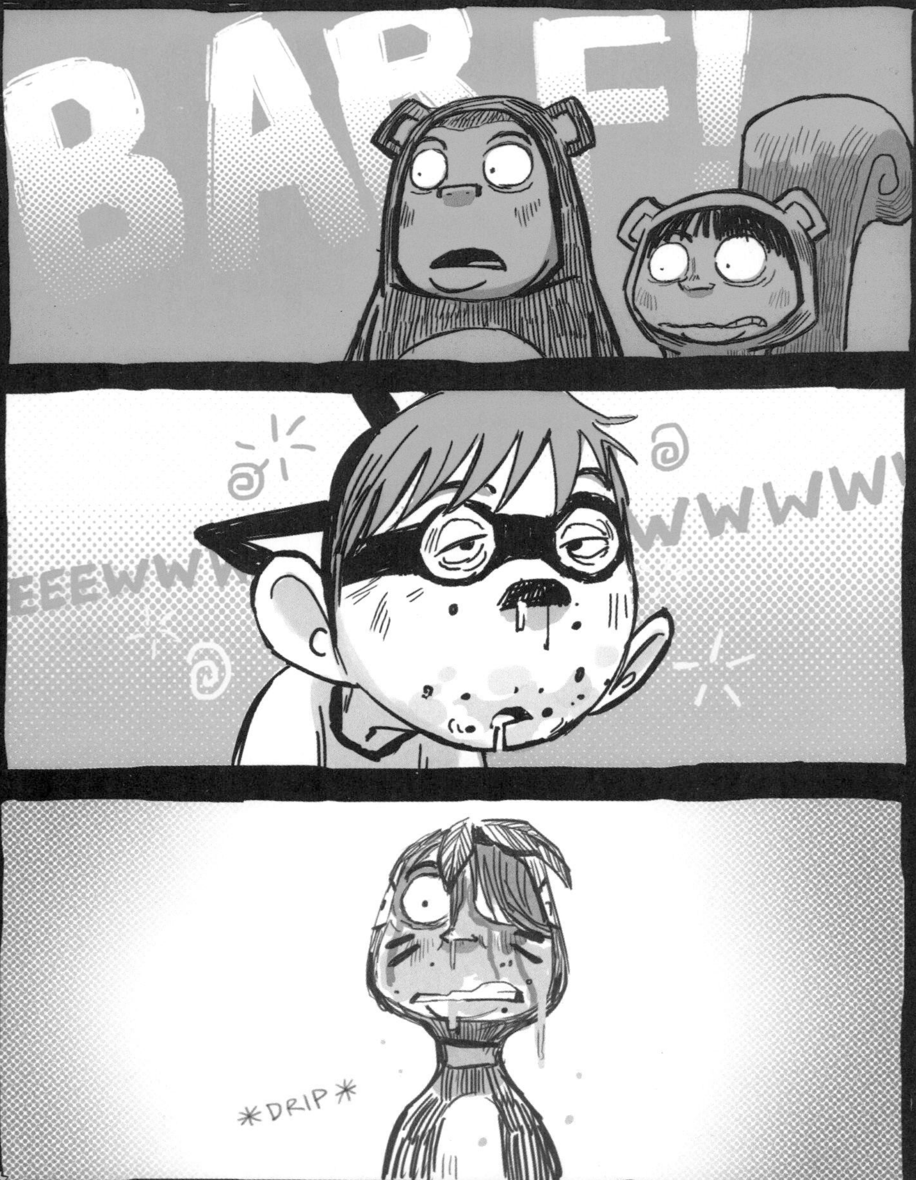
BARF!
EEEWWW
WWWWW
DRIP

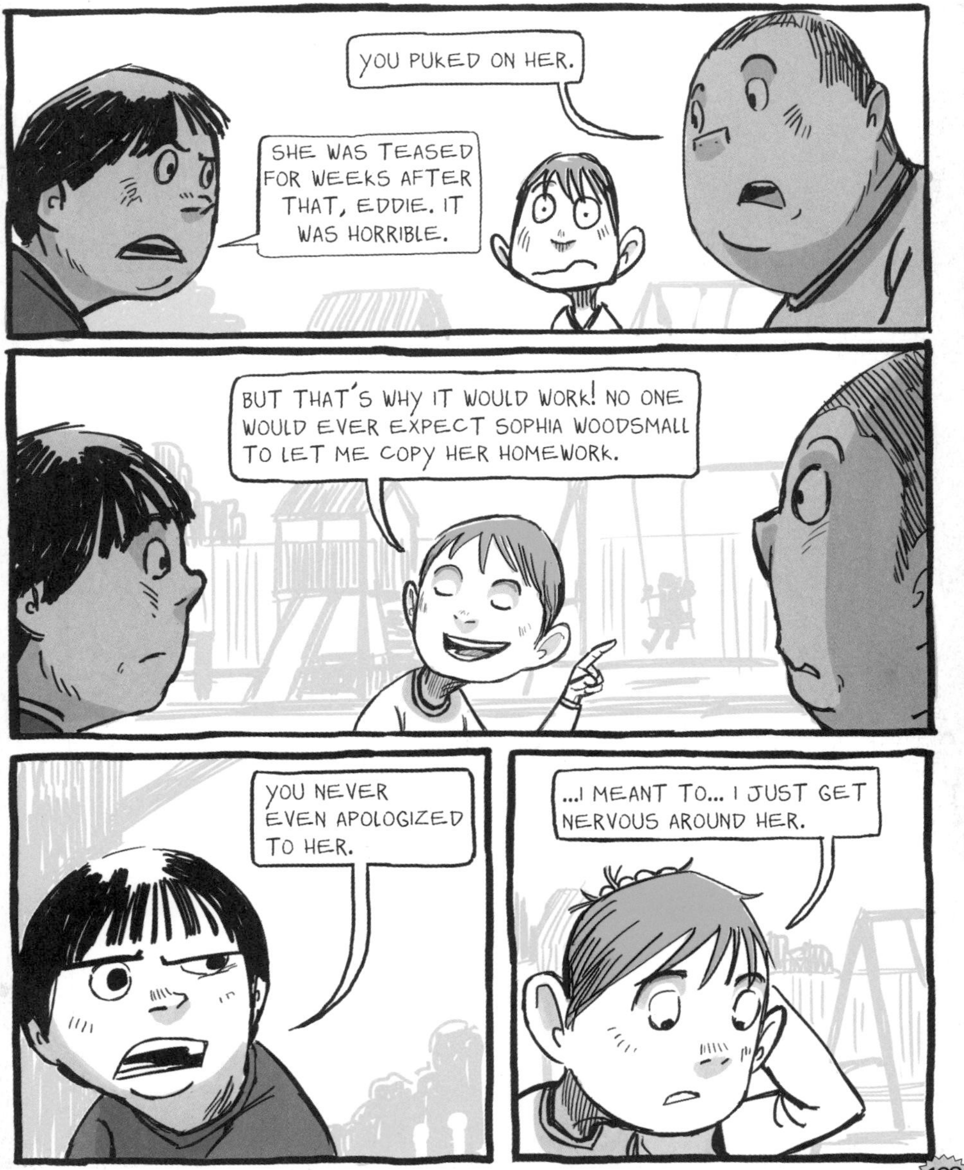
YOU PUKED ON HER.
SHE WAS TEASED FOR WEEKS AFTER THAT, EDDIE. IT WAS HORRIBLE.
BUT THAT'S WHY IT WOULD WORK! NO ONE WOULD EVER EXPECT SOPHIA WOODSMALL TO LET ME COPY HER HOMEWORK.
YOU NEVER EVEN APOLOGIZED TO HER.
...I MEANT TO... I JUST GET NERVOUS AROUND HER.

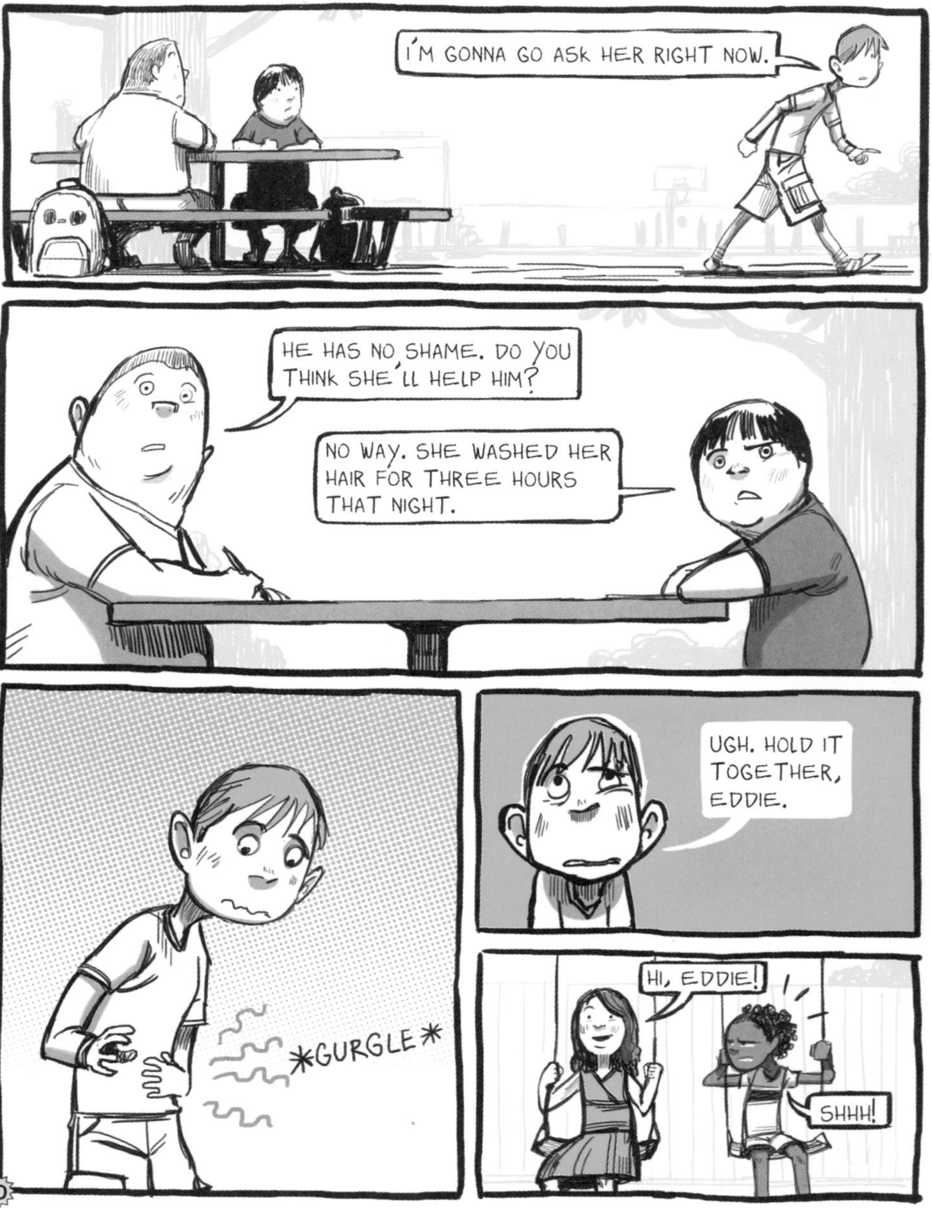
I'M GONNA GO ASK HER RIGHT NOW.
HE HAS NO SHAME. DO YOU THINK SHE'LL HELP HIM?
NO WAY. SHE WASHED HER HAIR FOR THREE HOURS THAT NIGHT.
GURGLE
UGH. HOLD IT TOGETHER, EDDIE.
HI, EDDIE!
SHHH!

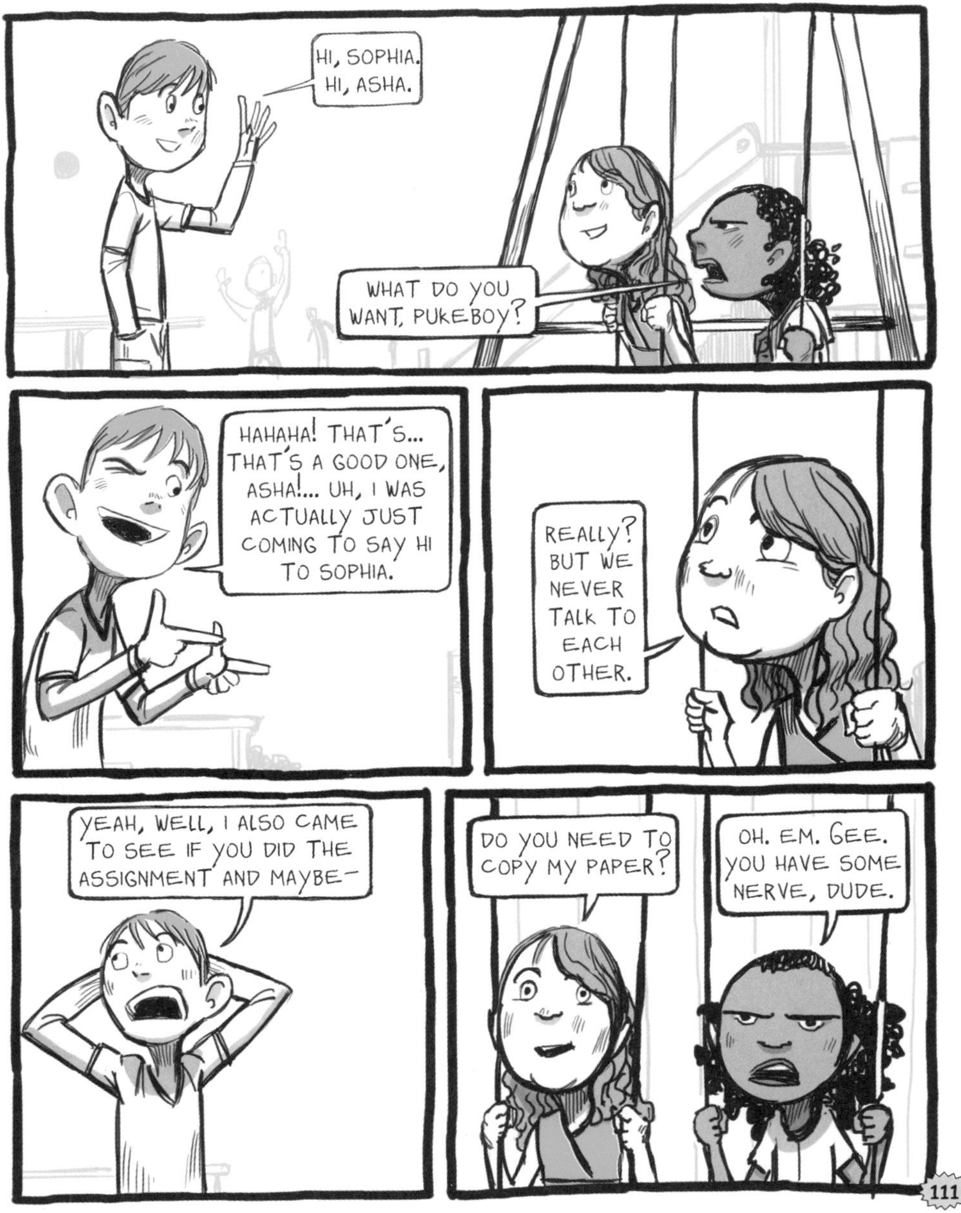
HI, SOPHIA.
HI, ASHA.
WHAT DO YOU WANT, PUKEBOY?
HAHAHA! THAT'S... THAT'S A GOOD ONE, ASHA!... UH, I WAS ACTUALLY JUST COMING TO SAY HI TO SOPHIA.
REALLY? BUT WE NEVER TALK TO EACH OTHER.
YEAH, WELL, I ALSO CAME TO SEE IF YOU DID THE ASSIGNMENT AND MAYBE—
DO YOU NEED TO COPY MY PAPER?
OH. EM. GEE. YOU HAVE SOME NERVE, DUDE.

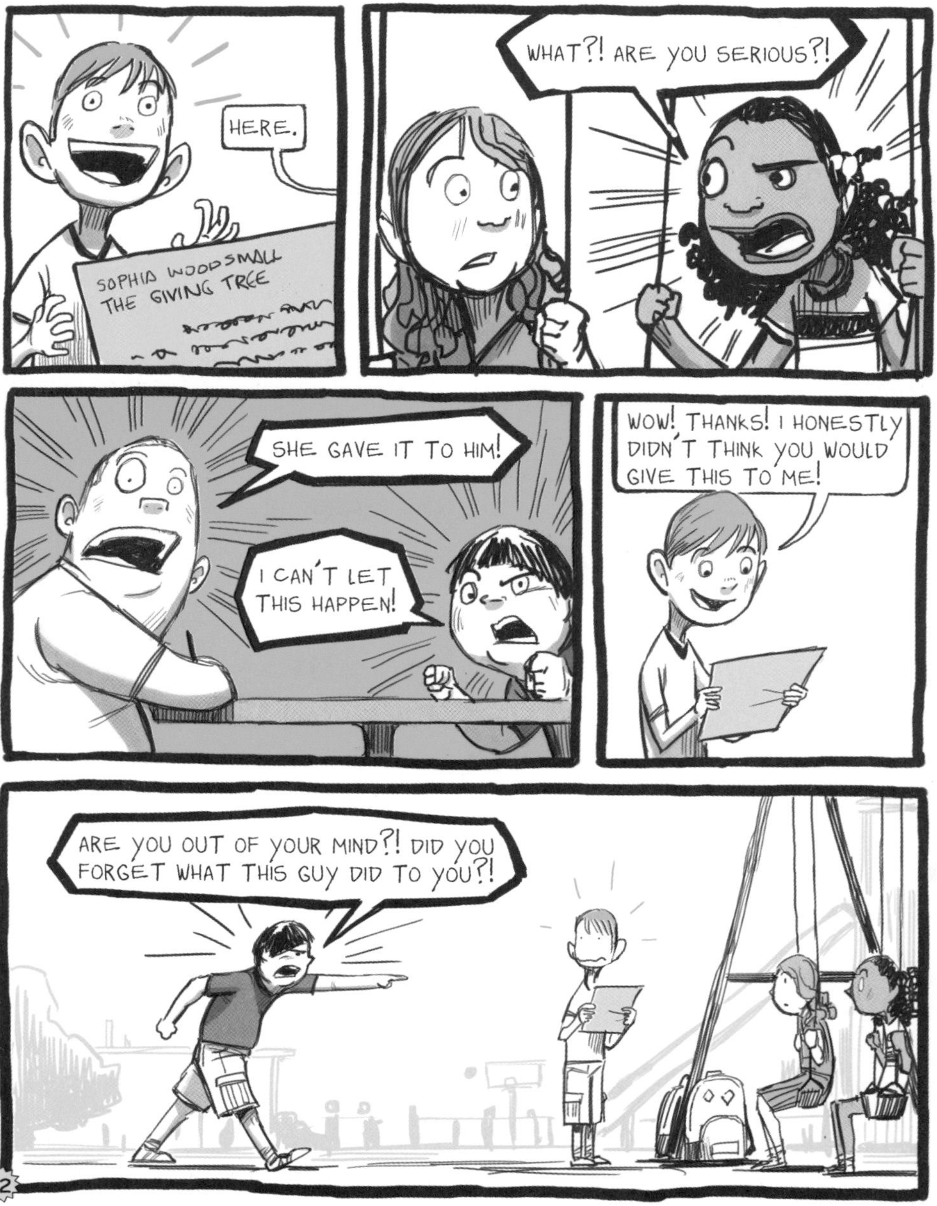
HERE.
SOPHIA WOODSMALL
THE GIVING TREE
WHAT?! ARE YOU SERIOUS?!
SHE GAVE IT TO HIM!
I CAN'T LET THIS HAPPEN!
WOW! THANKS! I HONESTLY DIDN'T THINK YOU WOULD GIVE THIS TO ME!
ARE YOU OUT OF YOUR MIND?! DID YOU FORGET WHAT THIS GUY DID TO YOU?!

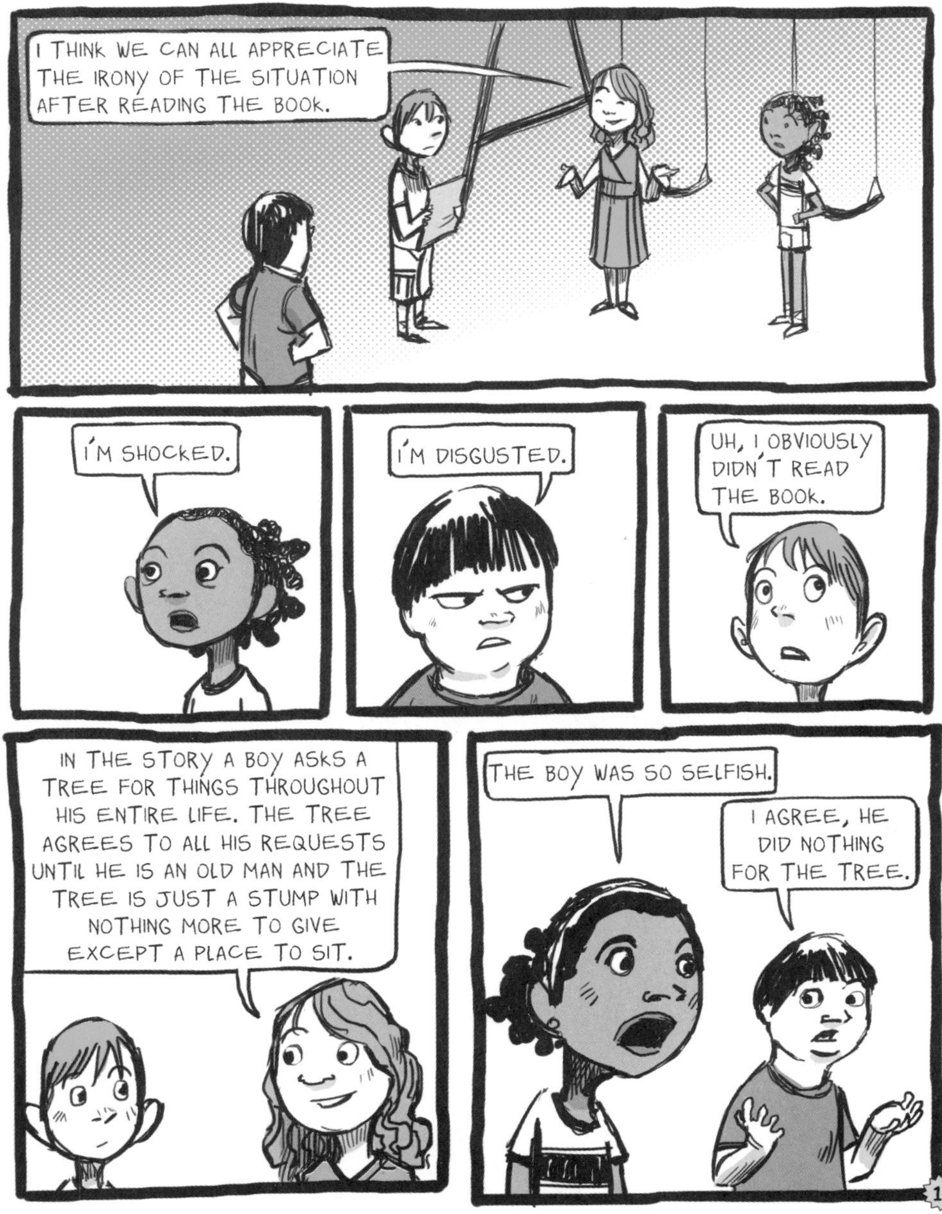
I THINK WE CAN ALL APPRECIATE THE IRONY OF THE SITUATION AFTER READING THE BOOK.
I'M SHOCKED.
I'M DISGUSTED.
UH, I OBVIOUSLY DIDN'T READ THE BOOK.
IN THE STORY A BOY ASKS A TREE FOR THINGS THROUGHOUT HIS ENTIRE LIFE. THE TREE AGREES TO ALL HIS REQUESTS UNTIL HE IS AN OLD MAN AND THE TREE IS JUST A STUMP WITH NOTHING MORE TO GIVE EXCEPT A PLACE TO SIT.
THE BOY WAS SO SELFISH.
I AGREE, HE DID NOTHING FOR THE TREE.

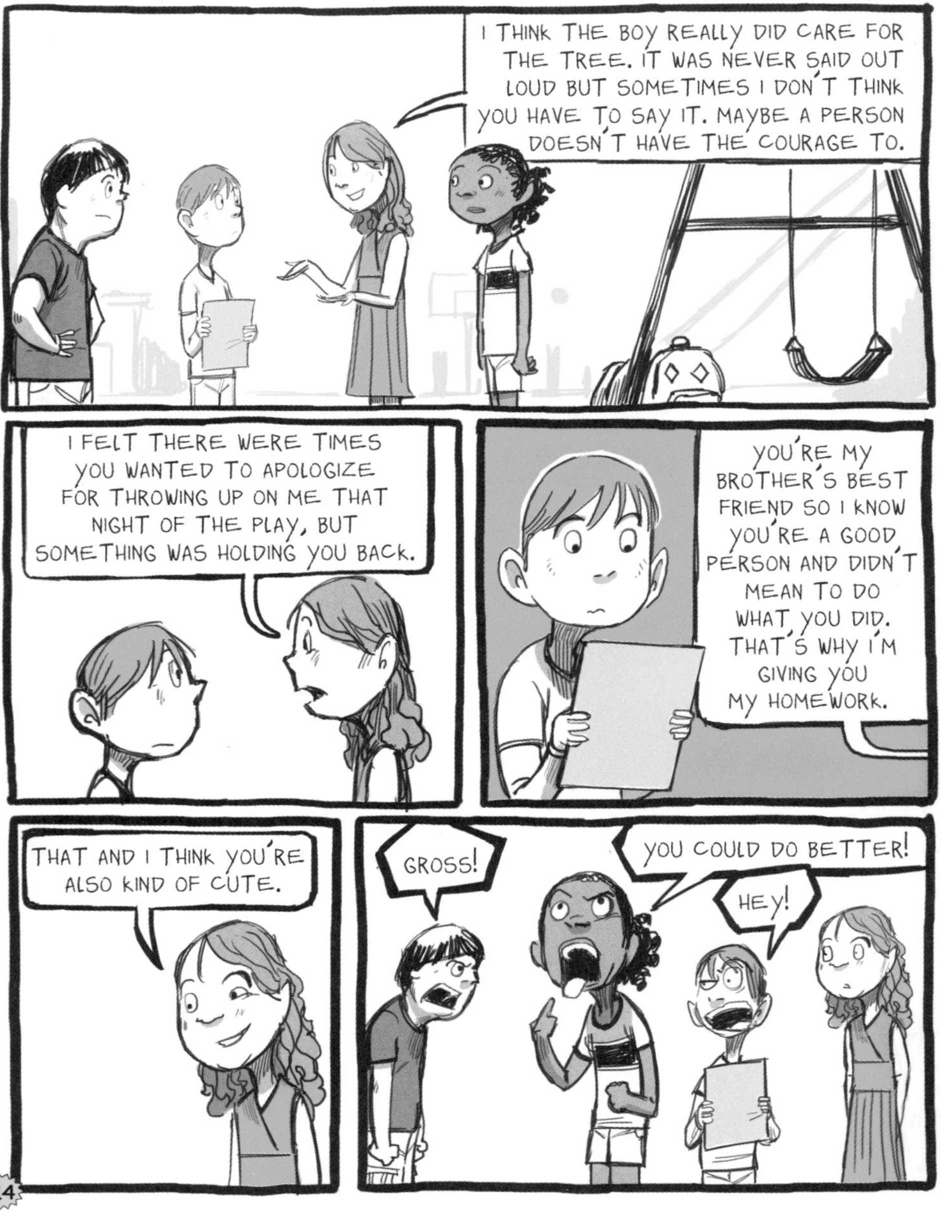
I THINK THE BOY REALLY DID CARE FOR THE TREE. IT WAS NEVER SAID OUT LOUD BUT SOMETIMES I DON'T THINK YOU HAVE TO SAY IT. MAYBE A PERSON DOESN'T HAVE THE COURAGE TO.
I FELT THERE WERE TIMES YOU WANTED TO APOLOGIZE FOR THROWING UP ON ME THAT NIGHT OF THE PLAY, BUT SOMETHING WAS HOLDING YOU BACK.
YOU'RE MY BROTHER'S BEST FRIEND SO I KNOW YOU'RE A GOOD PERSON AND DIDN'T MEAN TO DO WHAT YOU DID. THAT'S WHY I'M GIVING YOU MY HOMEWORK.
THAT AND I THINK YOU'RE ALSO KIND OF CUTE.
GROSS!
YOU COULD DO BETTER!
HEY!

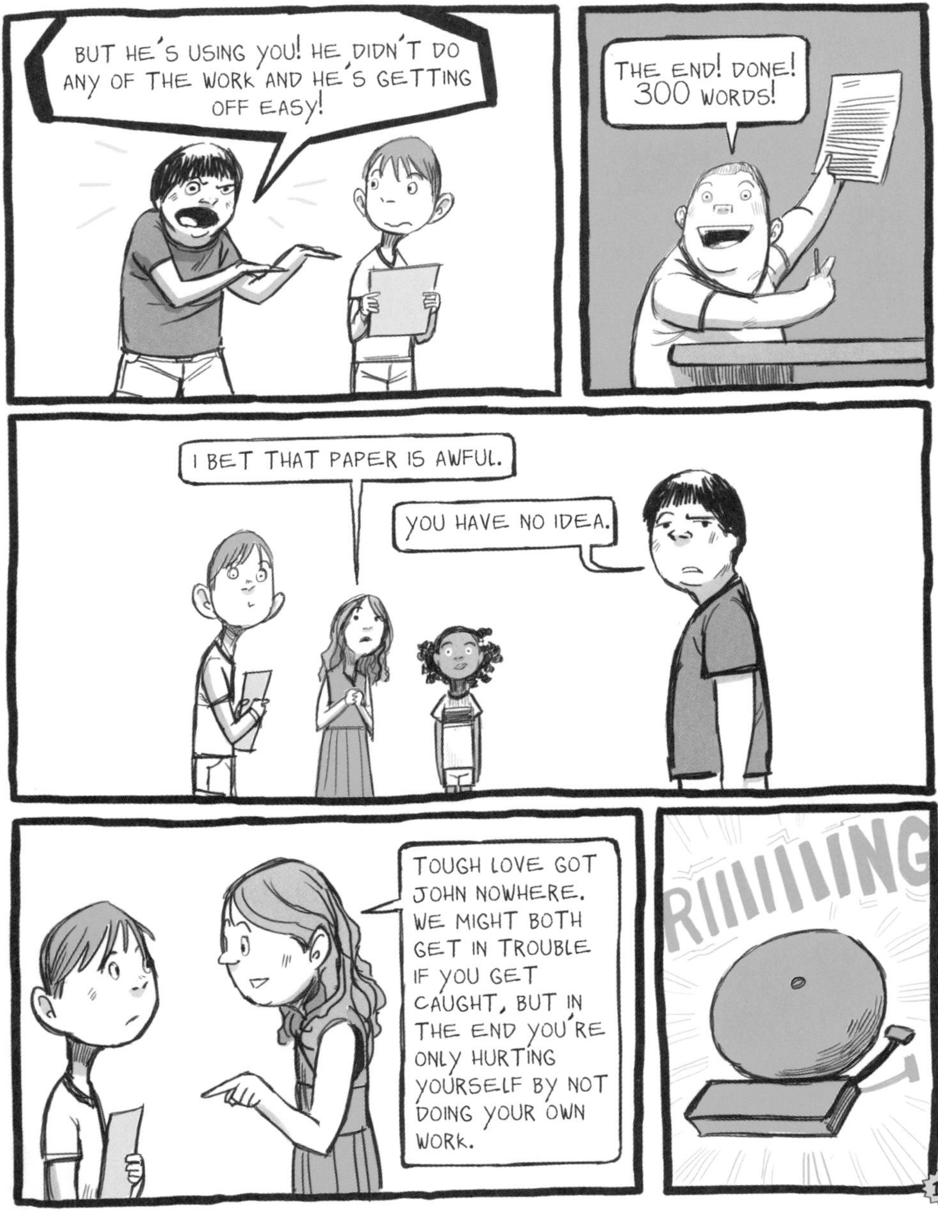

BUT HE'S USING YOU! HE DIDN'T DO ANY OF THE WORK AND HE'S GETTING OFF EASY!
THE END! DONE! 300 WORDS!
I BET THAT PAPER IS AWFUL.
YOU HAVE NO IDEA.
TOUGH LOVE GOT JOHN NOWHERE. WE MIGHT BOTH GET IN TROUBLE IF YOU GET CAUGHT, BUT IN THE END YOU'RE ONLY HURTING YOURSELF BY NOT DOING YOUR OWN WORK.
RIIIIIING

I THINK SHE MADE A HUGE MISTAKE.

I AM TOTALLY ASHAMED OF MY SISTER RIGHT NOW.

HOLD ON TO IT. YOU CAN GIVE IT BACK TO ME LATER IN CLASS.

HERE. I DON'T NEED IT. IT'S JUST A STUPID GRADE ANYWAY.

I'M SORRY I THREW UP ON YOU. I SHOULD HAVE SAID SOMETHING BEFORE, BUT I GET NERVOUS AROUND YOU, AND... WELL...

...I THINK YOU'RE CUTE TOO...

END

FOR SOPHIA AND ANDREW WOODS MALL

117

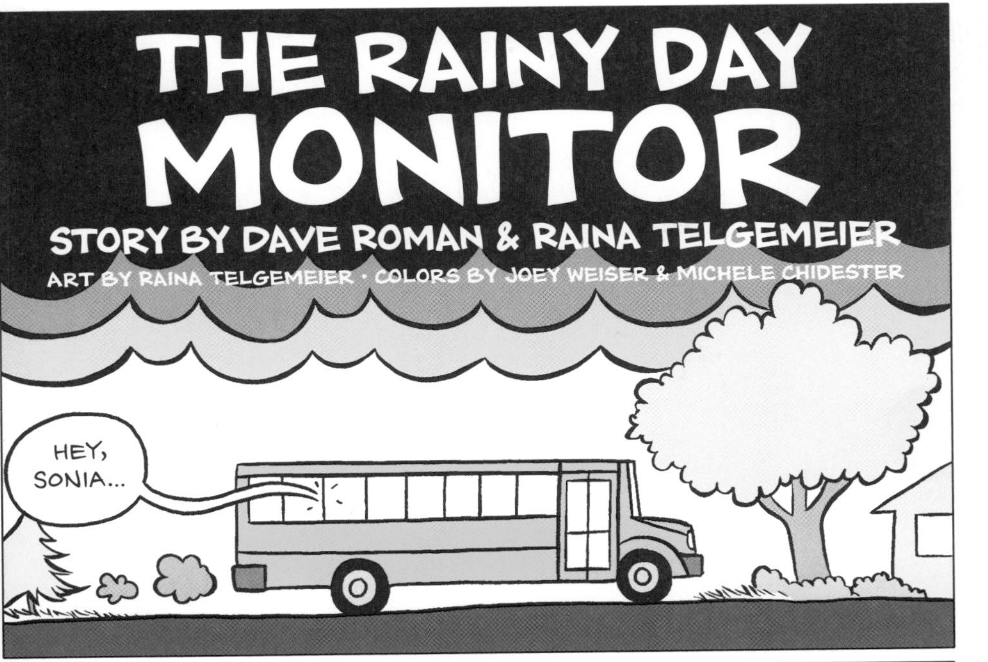
THE RAINY DAY MONITOR
STORY BY DAVE ROMAN & RAINA TELGEMEIER
ART BY RAINA TELGEMEIER · COLORS BY JOEY WEISER & MICHELE CHIDESTER
HEY, SONIA...

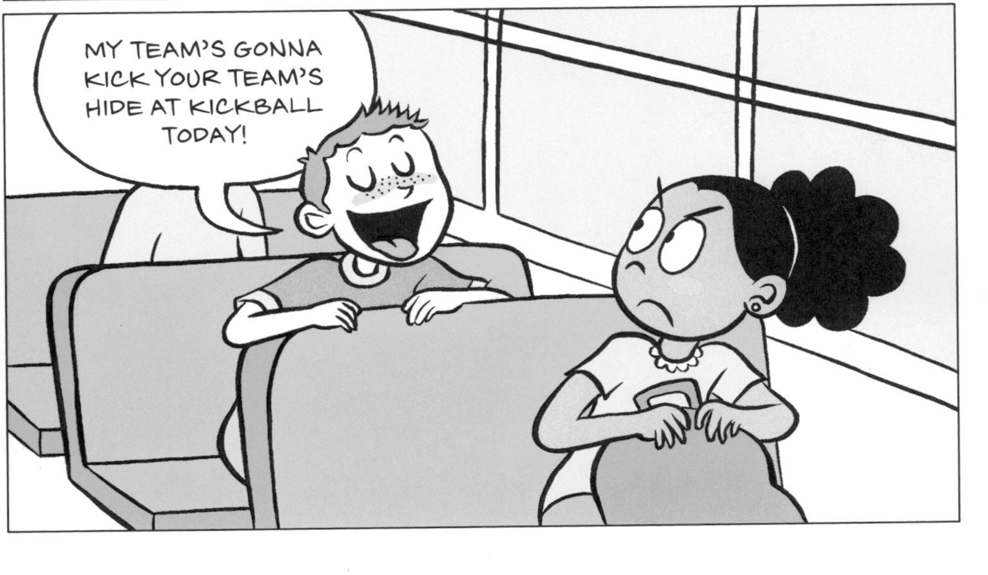
MY TEAM'S GONNA KICK YOUR TEAM'S HIDE AT KICKBALL TODAY!

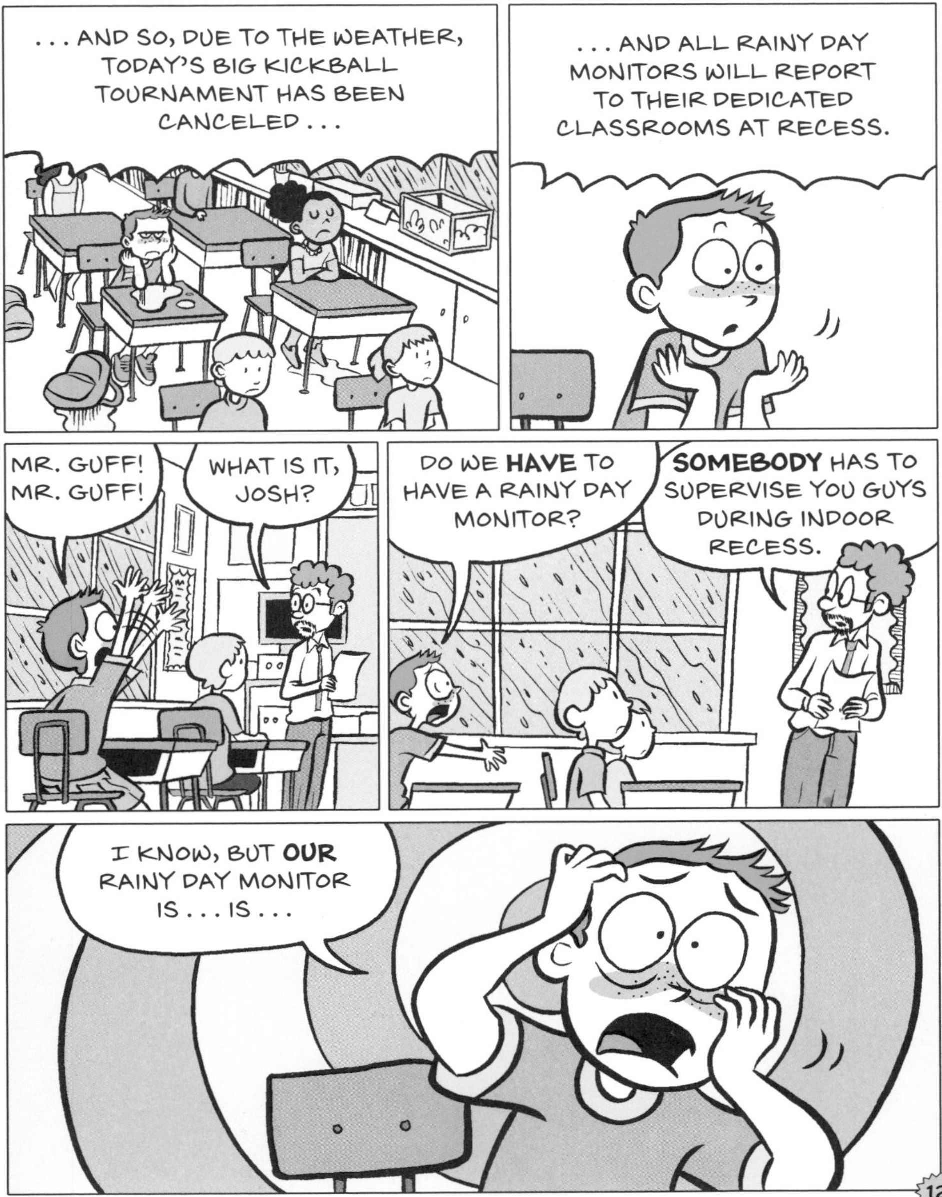
. . . AND SO, DUE TO THE WEATHER, TODAY'S BIG KICKBALL TOURNAMENT HAS BEEN CANCELED . . .
. . . AND ALL RAINY DAY MONITORS WILL REPORT TO THEIR DEDICATED CLASSROOMS AT RECESS.
MR. GUFF! MR. GUFF!
WHAT IS IT, JOSH?
DO WE **HAVE** TO HAVE A RAINY DAY MONITOR?
SOMEBODY HAS TO SUPERVISE YOU GUYS DURING INDOOR RECESS.
I KNOW, BUT **OUR** RAINY DAY MONITOR IS . . . IS . . .

BORING BECCA!

Fifth grader

Totally boring

ALL RIGHT, YOU KIDS. EVERYBODY JUST FIND SOMETHING **QUIET** TO DO FOR FORTY-FIVE MINUTES, OKAY?

CAN WE READ?

YES, YOU CAN READ.

CAN WE SET UP A GIANT OBSTACLE COURSE?

UH, **NO.** HOW ABOUT A CARD GAME?

THUNK

BOOOOOOOOOOOOOOOOOOOOOOOOOOORING.

NOW, CHOOSE YOUR TEAMS.

...

I WANT JORGE ON MY TEAM. HE'S THE BEST KICKER IN SECOND GRADE.

THAT'S WHO YOU'D CHOOSE? THIS IS **IMAGINARY**! YOU CAN CHOOSE **ANYBODY**!

ANYBODY?!

OKAY, THEN I CHOOSE...

JJ Gutierrez!

The best soccer player in the universe!

Strength +2
Dexterity +4
Charisma +6

I ALSO CHOOSE...

The President!

Charisma +8
Intelligence +9
Constitution +3

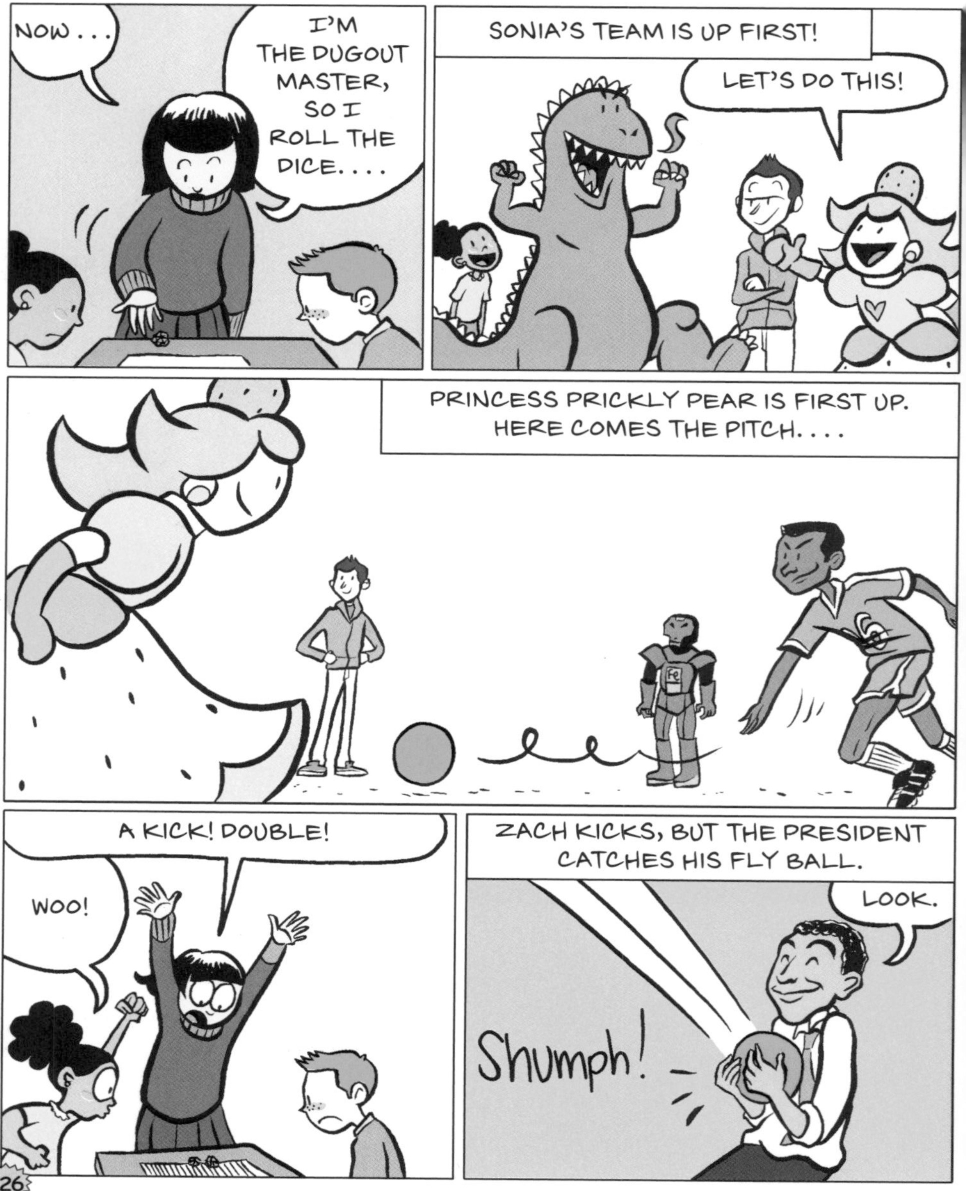
NOW . . .
I'M THE DUGOUT MASTER, SO I ROLL THE DICE. . . .
SONIA'S TEAM IS UP FIRST!
LET'S DO THIS!
PRINCESS PRICKLY PEAR IS FIRST UP. HERE COMES THE PITCH. . . .
A KICK! DOUBLE!
WOO!
ZACH KICKS, BUT THE PRESIDENT CATCHES HIS FLY BALL.
LOOK.
Shumph!

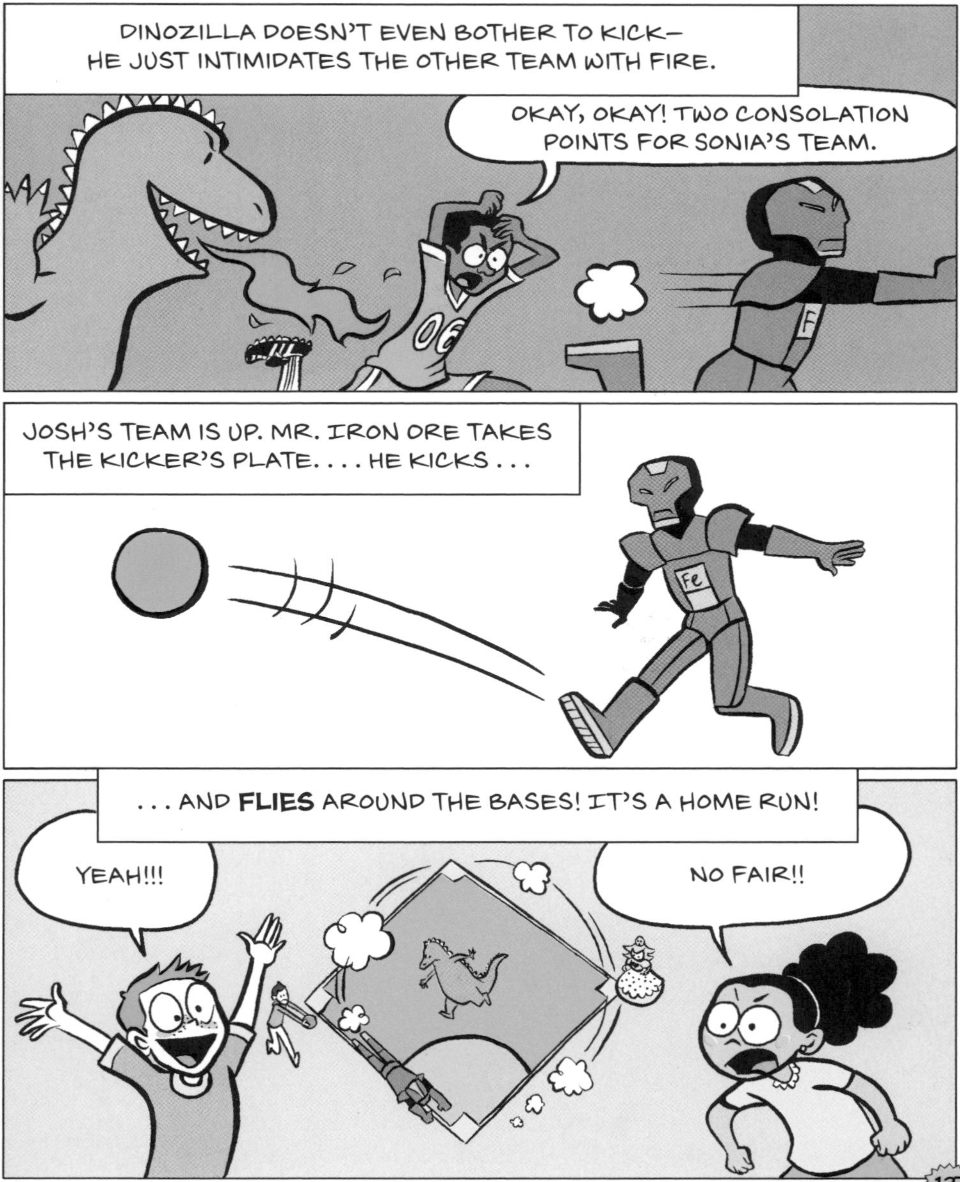
DINOZILLA DOESN'T EVEN BOTHER TO KICK—
HE JUST INTIMIDATES THE OTHER TEAM WITH FIRE.
OKAY, OKAY! TWO CONSOLATION POINTS FOR SONIA'S TEAM.
06
F
JOSH'S TEAM IS UP. MR. IRON ORE TAKES THE KICKER'S PLATE. . . . HE KICKS . . .
Fe
. . . AND **FLIES** AROUND THE BASES! IT'S A HOME RUN!
YEAH!!!
NO FAIR!!

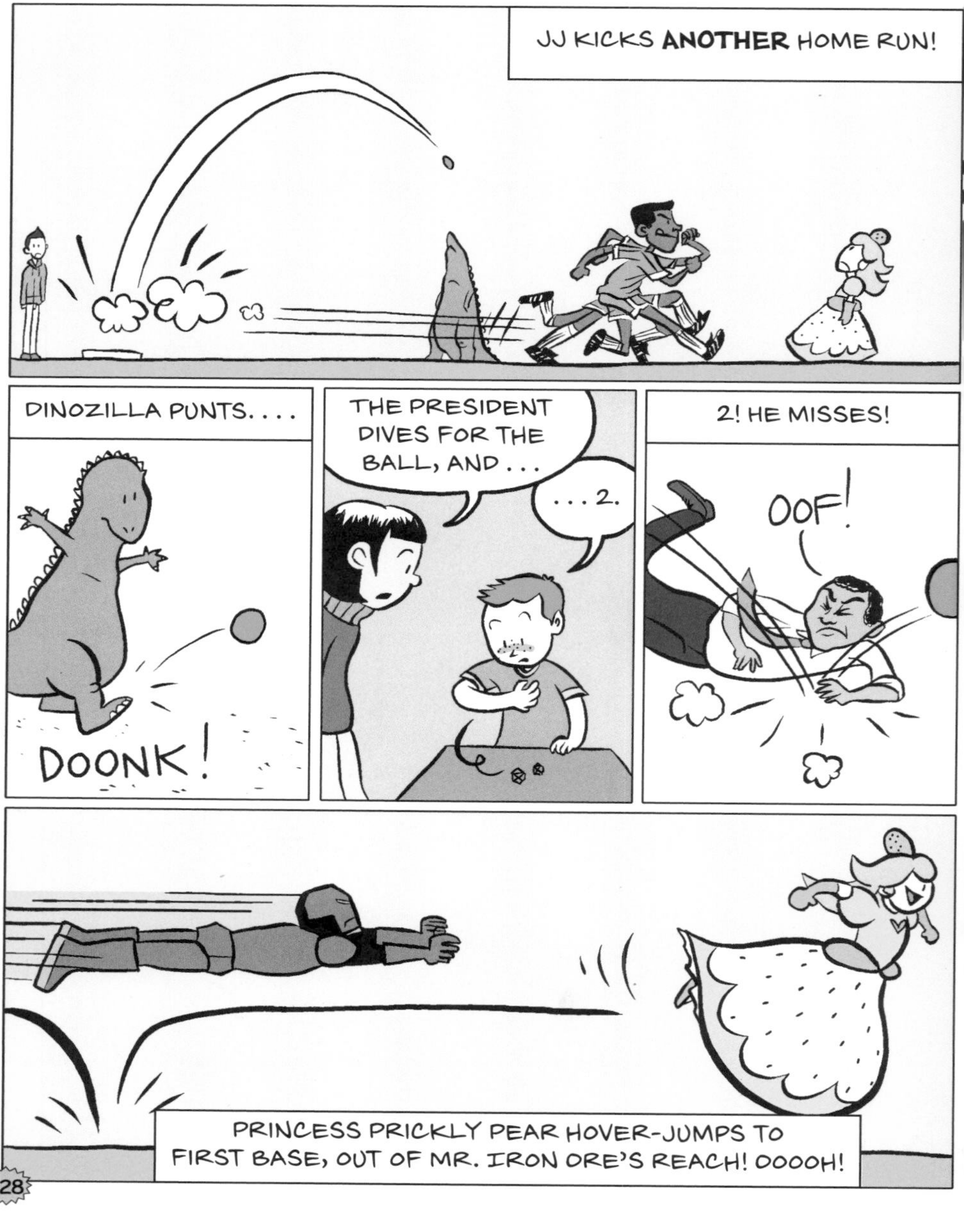
JJ KICKS **ANOTHER** HOME RUN!
DINOZILLA PUNTS. . . .
DOONK!
THE PRESIDENT DIVES FOR THE BALL, AND . . .
. . . 2.
2! HE MISSES!
OOF!
PRINCESS PRICKLY PEAR HOVER-JUMPS TO FIRST BASE, OUT OF MR. IRON ORE'S REACH! OOOOH!

131

THE END

DRAWING FUN!

Hey, Squish! Want to learn how to draw Betty in twelve easy steps?

Sounds great! I've always wanted to draw my own comics!

"Next, draw her hat and her perm."

"Draw two circles for her glasses."

1.

Two circles...

2.

Whoa! Slow down!

"Now draw her face!"

"And then the rest of her body!"

3.

What? How do I do that?

12.

What happened to step FOUR?!?!

This tutorial is terrible! Look at my drawing!

Sorry! I ran out of room. These pages are small!

★ ★ ★ ★ ABOUT THE

JENNIFER L. HOLM & MATTHEW HOLM

are the brother-sister team behind two graphic novel series, Babymouse and Squish. They grew up reading lots of comics, and they turned out just fine. (babymouse.com)

JARRETT J. KROSOCZKA

is the author and illustrator of the Lunch Lady graphic novel series, which chronicles the adventures of a spatula-wielding crime fighter. He has been reading and drawing comics since he was a kid, and he turned out all right, too. (studiojjk.com)

DAV PILKEY

is the author of the phenomenally popular Captain Underpants series. He spent most of his childhood making comics very much like the one in this book. He used to get in big trouble for it at school. Now it's his job. (pilkey.com)

AUTHORS ★ ★ ★ ★

DAN SANTAT

spends most of his time writing and illustrating comics and picture books for children. When he's not doing either of those things, he is most likely playing video games or eating. (dantat.com)

RAINA TELGEMEIER & DAVE ROMAN

are married and live under a pile of comic pages. Raina is the creator of *Smile.* Dave is the creator of the Astronaut Academy series. (goraina.com and yaytime.com)

URSULA VERNON

writes the comic series Dragonbreath. She still has not learned to tie her shoes correctly. (ursulavernon.com)

ERIC WIGHT

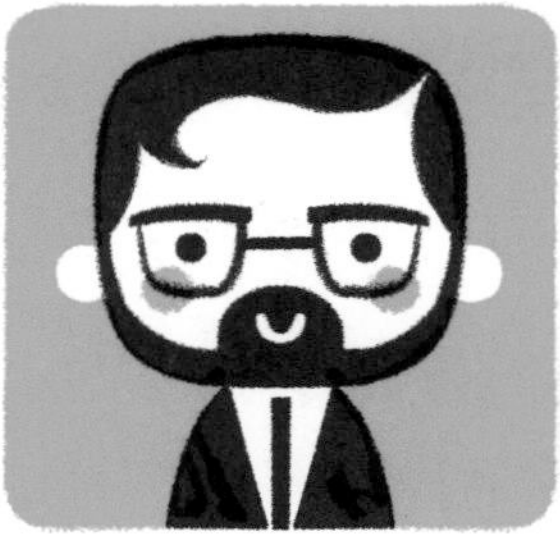

is the author and illustrator of the Frankie Pickle series. He ate A LOT of cupcakes to get inspiration for his new character, Jiminy Sprinkles. (about.me/ericwight)

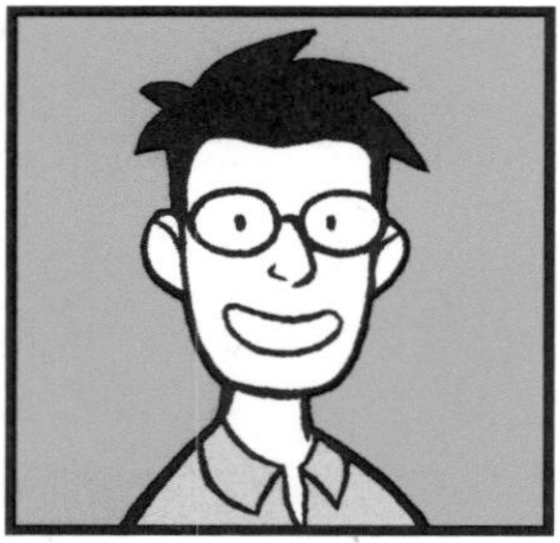

GENE LUEN YANG

began drawing comics in the fifth grade. He hasn't stopped. He's a two-time National Book Award finalist and author-illustrator of the Printz Award–winning graphic novel *American Born Chinese*. (geneyang.com)

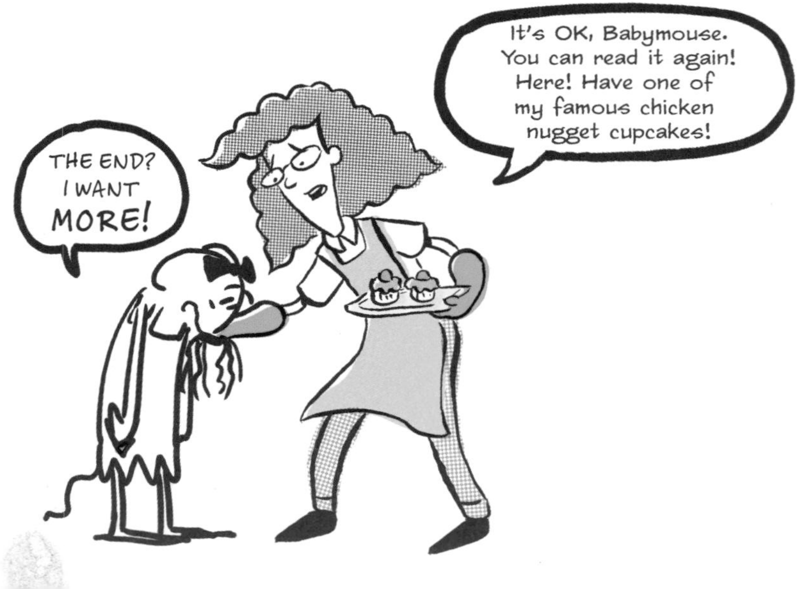
THE END? I WANT MORE!
It's OK, Babymouse. You can read it again! Here! Have one of my famous chicken nugget cupcakes!

LUNCH LADY

Serving justice! And serving lunch!

Jarrett J. Krosoczka
LUNCH LADY

© 2013 Jarrett J. Krosoczka